SACRIFICING SAPPHIRE

A Sapphire Dubois Mystery

MIA THOMPSON

DIVERSIONBOOKS

Also by Mia Thompson

Sapphire Dubois Mysteries
Stalking Sapphire
Silencing Sapphire
Sentencing Sapphire

Diversion Books
A Division of Diversion Publishing Corp.
443 Park Avenue South, Suite 1008
New York, New York 10016
www.DiversionBooks.com

Copyright © 2017 by Mia Thompson
All rights reserved, including the right to reproduce this book or portions thereof in any form whatsoever.

This is a work of fiction. Names, characters, places and incidents either are the product of the author's imagination or are used fictitiously. Any resemblance to actual persons, living or dead, events or locales is entirely coincidental.

For more information, email info@diversionbooks.com

First Diversion Books edition December 2017.
Paperback ISBN: 978-1-63576-170-2
eBook ISBN: 978-1-63576-169-6

LSIDB/1710

CHAPTER 1

Till death do us part.

How he wished he could undo those words. Marriage was about a lot of things—sacrifice and honesty were two of them. He hoped she understood this.

"Be honest, honey." He pulled his wife's body closer to him in the chilly night. "Was that not the best pot roast we've ever had?"

"Yes." She kept her eyes on the bed of fallen pine needles that were crunching under their shoes.

The moon was full, and her short black hair glimmered in its silver light. Her pale hands shook at her sides, so he cupped them to his mouth and filled them with hot air.

"Perfect evening for a stroll, isn't it?"

"Yes." Her eyelids shut over her glossed blue eyes, and a tear trickled down her cheek.

The glade appeared between the pine trees, and they entered a section surrounded by tree stubs. He'd cut them down himself to make the perfect clearing.

Her eyes fell on the wooden table—swollen with moisture—in the middle, then on the six people in animal masks. Six tall torches had been placed in the ground behind them, and the shadows from the fires danced across the masks' hollow eyes. Her feet stopped dead.

"Wh...what is this?"

He tried to calm her with a smile and gave her a peck on the nose. "All will be right soon, just as I promised." He lifted her onto the table as he started the preparatory chant.

"Wait...no, no," she pleaded, trying to get back down as she noticed the stained table and the leather restraints.

He forced her limbs—rigid with resistance—into the straps, and as the six cloaks joined the chant, her tears turned to sobs.

"Shh." He stroked her cheek. "Just tell me who you are."

"I'm your wife," she said between weeps. "I've done everything you've asked for. You said you would let me go if I—"

He put his finger on her lips. "What's your name?"

"Alma...my name is Alma."

He gazed up at the full moon and took out the Satanic Book of Rituals from the plastic bag below the table. He read a line as his hand clutched the first syringe loaded with a mix of Adenosine and Lidocaine. "*Vos autem nuntius scientiae reditu furto et evigilare faciatis dormientis.*"

"No...no!" she shouted, her panicked eyes on the long needle. "I take it back. I'm not Alma! I'm not your wife! My name is Mary! Mary Dunnigan!"

He stabbed the needle into her neck.

Her eyes widened and her breath grew quick and shallow as the drug-mix worked its way through her system and to her heart.

Her body tensed at the pain and she let out a whisper of a scream as her heart went into cardiac arrest. Finally, her panicked gaze turned empty and her muscles turned limp. Her heart had stopped, leaving her body fresh and in perfect condition thanks to the Lidocaine and Adenosine.

He waited an extra second, giving her soul time to vacate the body, before he reached for the second needle.

He removed the shot's cap with his thumb and kept his eyes on her, feeling hope surge through his body. He looked up at the full moon and repeated the chant. "*Vos autem nuntius scientiae reditu furto et evigilare faciatis dormientis.*"

He stabbed the needle, filled with Epinephrine (adrenaline) straight into her heart.

Immediately after, he began the CPR, giving her his breath.

The instructions that went along with the chant had been clear: Only the heart of a soul willing to sacrifice himself can harbor the soul of the buried in the blaze of the true moon and before the eyes of six.

She gasped and her eyes shot wide open. Her back arched, allowing her chest to fill with air. He pulled back and waited as Mary Dunnigan's body filled with life. Hopefully, the *right* life. His blood raced through his veins, sharpening his breath. The anticipation, the nerves, the fear, caused his fingers to tremble.

He got one attempt and one attempt only per body, and he'd know if he'd succeeded right away. He'd know if it was his Alma.

Her breathing quickened and her eyes darted around her. She spotted him, standing there, smiling down at her. For a moment, she just stared at him. Then, her eyes filled with tears and her face distorted with hopelessness. "What are you doing to me?" she whimpered. "I don't understand what you want…"

The disappointment set in, turning his shoulders heavy and his spirit dark. He reached for the dagger below the table and brought it up.

"You said I'd get to go home," she cried. "You said—"

He stabbed her in the heart and watched her try to scream and hold onto life. Then, in an instant, she was gone.

The bloody dagger fell out of his hand and into the pine needles on the ground.

He inhaled, then screamed at the moon, at the six souls, at the realization that he'd failed once more. He'd thought he got the right woman this time, but perhaps her body wasn't strong enough for Alma, or maybe she hadn't *truly* committed herself to the sacrifice. Or perhaps the full moon wasn't powerful enough. But if a full, half, new, blue, or quarter moon wasn't the *true* moon, what was?

He tossed the satanic volume to the ground with a cry. It seemed like he was doomed never to succeed.

"Leave me!" he yelled, leaning on the table.

He didn't know how long he stood there, slumped over yet another body, but when he looked up they were gone, and he went to bury her.

After he disposed of the body, he stepped inside, blood still on his shirt. Rosie sat in the puffy chair, watching the movie. He said the words he always spoke, and her neck turned to him so quickly that the chains holding her in the chair rattled.

Feeling despondent, he walked upstairs and straight to the calendar hanging next to his desk. The circle he'd made around the full moon was a taunting finger pointing at another failure, another day without her. He ripped the calendar off the wall and threw it to the floor. Nothing had worked. *Nothing.* Perhaps this should be his last attempt.

Shaking with grief, he sat down at his desk and pulled out a blank piece of stationery. The only thing that could make him feel better was writing another letter. He wrote one every time he'd failed, and every time the memories overtook him. It was a small beacon in his otherwise dark world.

He ran his finger down the crossed-out names and went for the next in line on the infinite list.

Dear...

As always, the words poured out of him.

He'd just licked the envelope when the calendar on the floor caught his eyes. It had opened up to a few months ahead, to December of all months. The moon's light, penetrating through the window, illuminated it in the darkened office. He cocked his head and moved to pick it up.

Amazing. Never had it lined up so perfectly. It couldn't be a coincidence.

This was it, the day he'd waited for. He'd tried every month, every day of the week, and every moon imaginable, and here it had just aligned on its own. The tiny circle in the corner of *the date*—the anniversary—featured a blood moon.

He had to get everything right this time. *Just* right. If it didn't work then, it wouldn't work at all; he knew this in his heart. This was his last chance. He put the calendar back on the wall, studying the date. It was much sooner than he was used to.

He would only have a few months to find her, the *right* Alma. But, he had to do it. He had no choice.

He circled the big event.

By the next blood moon, December 23rd, they would be together again.

Till death do us part, no more.

• • •

A piercing wail filled the dark studio.

Shit. Sapphire Dubois dropped the cell phone back on the nightstand and closed her eyes just as her husband roused next to her.

He groaned as the cry continued. "Your turn."

"I got up twice in a row last night," Sapphire mumbled, faking drowsiness. "It's your turn twice in a row tonight."

The wail grew more urgent and Aston groaned again, then kissed her and got up. "We need a better system."

He shuffled across the studio, opened the window and shouted: "Would you shut the fuck up! It's three in the fucking morning!"

The screaming ceased for a moment, then a drunken girl yelled, "Fuck you, grandpa!"

Laughs filled the parking lot.

"Oh, you mother—" Aston slammed the window shut, then turned the lights on. He scrambled for his gun and he hopped into his boots.

"What are you going to do," Sapphire asked, propped up on her elbow, "massacre a bunch of college students?"

"We'll see." Aston vanished into the hallway.

She cranked her neck after him. "You're not wearing any pants!"

He was already gone.

This was not the first time he'd gone for a "chat" with their new neighbors. Sapphire was surprised it was still going on; Aston could be intimidating when he wanted to.

They'd returned from Las Vegas and their honeymoon to find the owner of Aston's apartment complex had been arrested and the IRS had ceased and sold the building. The prices got so low even a college kid could afford an apartment. Turned out, *many* college kids could afford one. Students from UCLA poured in and there was a party every night, and a confrontation between Aston and the students every other night. So far, he'd put nine of them in the Beverly Hills Police Department's drunk tank, locked one in his trunk, and dropped two in the community pool.

The students didn't care. They were as adamant about keeping the party going as Sapphire had been in college...if you replaced *partying* with *hunting serial killers* that was.

She listened for Aston's footsteps, then launched toward the bathroom—the only private room in their studio apartment. She lifted the porcelain top off the toilet and pulled out the Ziploc bag she'd taped to the inside. She quickly copied down the new research from her phone.

The front door slammed. He was back.

Shit. Shit. Sapphire put the papers back in, then flushed to drown out the sound of colliding porcelain. She tapped out of the site and hid the phone in her pocket before exiting.

"I wasn't wearing any pants," Aston mumbled, scrambling for his jeans.

Sapphire leaned against the door frame. "We can't keep living like this. Your lease is coming up and you know my mom said we could move in—"

"Saph, come on. If it was anyone *but* Tits McGee, I would."

"Really? How about Chrissy?"

"Okay, if it was anyone but Tits McGee *and* Face Von Surgery, I would." Aston's eyes landed on her bulging pajama bottom pocket. "Is that your phone?"

Sapphire fought to hide the guilt. "Yeah?"

"What were you doing with your phone in the bathroom?" The anger on his face became concern.

"Fine. You caught me." She tossed the phone on the nightstand. "For the past few weeks, I've been…" she took a breath. "Playing Pokémon."

Aston's face filled with cynicism. "Name one Pokémon."

"Well, there's…" Sapphire cleared her throat. "Bill?"

They stared at each other as the unsaid words hovered in the air. Aston's thoughts were blatant. *What's on that phone? Blood, murder, victims?* That was what the formerly wanted vigilante known as the Serial Catcher would have on her phone. Sapphire Dubois had spent the last few years hunting, trapping, and anonymously handing over So-Cal's most wanted serial killers to the authorities. After being put on trial and barely dodging a decade exclusively sporting prison orange, she'd officially retired from her non-official business. And Aston, the cop who'd spent the last year on the Serial Catcher's tail trying to arrest the vigilante, had also opted to retire his chase since he decided to marry her instead.

His eyes drew to the phone on the nightstand, and Sapphire's followed. They leaped for it at the same time. He snatched it from under her and went straight for her history.

Aston stared at the screen in shock, then at Sapphire who held her breath.

"You…you bought a house?"

Sapphire let out a sigh. "Merry Christmas, asshole."

She watched him, looking down at the image of a four-bedroom cottage-style home, a hidden gem in the hills.

"It's supposed to be ready in a few days. We'll be moved in before the Holidays." Sapphire kept her sullen eyes on Aston.

"Any idea how hard it is to keep a secret in this tiny place? I've had to hide paperwork all over the place. What the hell did you think I was doing?"

"Ah, nothing...nothing."

They both knew *exactly* what he was thinking.

Aston shook his head in awe. "The house looks great. Really...*normal*."

Normal, i.e. unpretentious, i.e. nothing like the Dubois Mansion Sapphire grew up in. She'd inherited the mansion, along with a percentage of DubCorp, when Charles Dubois, her uncle/stepfather, passed. When she and Aston returned from Vegas, she signed the house over to Vivienne Dubois. Partly because she didn't want it. Partly because she hoped it would work as an emotional Band-Aid for when her mother learned Sapphire had eloped to marry a 45k-a-year cop. She was sure the woman would freak.

When they told her they'd gotten married, Vivienne stared at the newlyweds from the other side of the couch, her face straight. Aston had discreetly pulled a pillow to "cover the nards" in preparation for her going ape-shit.

"Well," Vivienne Dubois said, turning her iced tea glass on its coaster. She broke out in a smile, held her arms wide, and launched at Sapphire. "Congratulations!" She leaped at Aston who stiffened in her embrace. "Son."

Sapphire glared at her mother. "Congratulations? Really?"

"Yes!" Vivienne beamed and sat back down. "I'm sure you two will be very happy together."

"Oh, *O-kay*." Sapphire wiggled a finger at her mother. "I see what you're doing here, and I'm not going to play along with whatever twisted game you've planned."

Vivienne's eyes grew with innocence. "I'm not playing a game, Sapphire. I mean it. All I want for you is *happiness*. And anyone within ten feet of you two can see you're meant to be."

"Mhm," Sapphire stood. "Keep up the sarcasm. See where it gets you."

"I'm not being sarcastic!" Vivienne assured. "Congratulations!"

Aston stood up as well and shook his head at his mother-in-law. "Sick."

They marched right out of there.

Now, Sapphire had to admit that, while she wasn't thrilled at the idea of living with her mother while they waited for the final repairs on the house, the lack of space and lack of sleep were starting to get to her.

"I turned in our notice for moving next week, but we could leave now and stay at the mansion until the house is done. Get a good night's sleep."

"Why?" Aston shrugged, trying to look chill. "It's not that bad here. You're exaggerating."

Smash! A beer can hit the window and foam exploded against the glass.

Sapphire cocked her head and waited in amusement.

"See. Totally cool." Aston held his tranquil expression as he backed toward the door, gun in hand. "I'm just going to go outside for…no particular reason. Definitely not to beat up anybody in sight."

Sapphire smiled as he turned and rushed out the door. The moment it closed, her smile vanished.

She hurried back to the bathroom and removed the toilet's tank cover. She'd planned on revealing the house to Aston in a different way, but this was better than him seeing what she was actually doing. He must've been so shocked when he spotted the realty site that he didn't notice the other searches. She'd make sure to delete her history from now on.

Sapphire stared down at her hidden notes and the picture, featuring the face that had grown familiar to her during her research.

Mary Dunnigan.

CHAPTER 2

She stood in the doorway of Ghost's attic, her long dark hair falling down over her shoulders. She then looked down at Ghost with kind, confident eyes. "*Come on. Let's get out of here.*"

Ghost woke up from the sound of the truck's door slamming shut.

She shivered in the cold as she hobbled over to the boarded window and pressed her dirty hands against the wood, feeling the hunger burn her stomach. Her once yellow shirt, now brown and holey, pushed against the cold, leaking in from the window, as she put her eye to the crack in the wood.

She watched him pack his truck and knew. It was starting again.

She was happy he'd be gone for a few days—it was the only time she didn't have to be scared—but, she was also sad because unless the woman with the long dark hair and brave eyes from her dream was next to arrive, a new woman would come and die just like Mary Dunnigan, Susan Bills, Carrie Sutterway, and the others. She knew their names well because they'd shout until they didn't have the strength to shout anymore. Then, when they gave up, and gave in, it was over.

Ghost hated the word he used when he got back without them: accident. She was little, but she knew accidents were not on purpose.

Her own mommy died and it wasn't an accident either. It happened while Ghost was in the closet. That's where her mommy put her sometimes. "Be absolutely quiet," she'd say. "You're nothing but a ghost." Then she'd put the headphones on her and give her the tablet so she could watch her princess movies in the dark.

Ghost watched him get the last bag in the truck, then dragged her chained foot back to her spot, thinking about the one with the dark hair and fearless eyes. She first had the dream when Mary Dunnigan got here, but it was such a long time ago that the season had changed. Ghost was starting to doubt what kind of dream it was.

Sometimes, she had special dreams—dreams which came true. Other times, she had regular dreams or almost dreams. Now and then, she had wish-dreams. She would sit in her corner and pretend she was a princess like Cinderella or Tiana, who was on her shirt. The shirt used to be too big for her, but it cut in on her arms and neck now. Perhaps the woman with the long hair was an almost dream, or like her princess dream, nothing but a wish.

The door flew open so hard it smacked into the wall.

She slid her back to the protective, cold wood panel and as far from him as her chain allowed. Her knees pulled to her chest and her arms wrapped around her legs.

She kept her wary eyes on him as he filled the bowls to their edge. This was all she got until he returned. She looked at the kibble, eager to eat it and stifle the hunger's bellow. The only upside of his terrible game was that she'd get to eat pot roast instead of kibble and drink soda instead of dusty water. Then there was the dessert, apple cobbler. Her mouth watered just thinking about it. She remembered when she would eat warm foods all the time before she was put in this attic.

He stood straight, kibble bag resting in his arm crease. "Behave yourself, Rosie."

She nodded. "Yes…sir?"

His mouth twitched at the word. She'd called him the wrong thing, again. It was so hard to know when she should call him *sir*, and when she shouldn't. Things weren't easy in the house of horrors. Rules changed, names changed, women showed up and vanished.

A long time ago, on that really good day at the amusement park, Ghost's mommy took her into a place called just that, the house of horrors. The darkness, the ghouls and skeletons taunting and screaming, was like walking through a nightmare. Then, they finally made it to the exit and everything was okay again. Now, Ghost was there all the time, and this house of horrors had no exit. She just went round and round, forever stuck, forever frightened.

"What did you call me?"

Ghost held her breath, staring up at his reddened face.

He dropped the kibble bag. She cowered into a ball, but he grabbed her by the ears and lifted her. The pain exploded in her head as he smacked her into the wall, over and over, until she cried.

"Why?!" he roared through his clenched his teeth. "Why can't you just learn?"

He let go and she crumbled to the ground and sobbed as he walked away.

"She's coming to save me," she whispered with hope, trying to comfort herself.

"What did you say?" He turned around. "Who's coming?"

Ghost swallowed, her throat felt thick. She only meant to say it in her mind.

"Who's coming?!" he yelled, taking a step forward.

She peered at him through her fingers.

"Nothing hurts more than having your hopes dashed, Rosie." His face softened and his shoulders sank. "No one is coming for you. Not now, not ever."

He turned toward the door.

Ghost looked at him, her lower lip still quivering. She had to say it, not for him but for herself. "You're wrong."

"You're wrong, what?" He looked at her with cold, determined eyes.

Ghost's eyes drew to the dusty floorboards. "You're wrong …Dad."

He gave her a tired smile, then left.

When Ghost fell asleep that night, she dreamt a different special dream. The fearless one with the long hair and dark eyes *did* come.

But when she did, she was put in the ground, just like the others.

• • •

"What do you say we pop out for a smoke?"

Detective Aston Ridder longingly eyed the pack, then popped a second Nicorette gum into his mouth. "Nah. I'm good."

"So Aston Ridder *doesn't* smoke and he's married?" Chief Wendell asked, leaning against the bar.

"Yeah."

When Sapphire made the argument, "the rest of our lives would be much more fun if you weren't dead," it made sense. So he chewed the gross gum vigorously, his mind on her. Of course she hadn't gone back to her old ways. She'd told him she was done months ago in the desert.

Sapphire's old man, a serial killer, had told Aston that Sapphire would always choose the hunt, and that she would never really be his. The dude clearly didn't know what he was talking about. Aston and Sapphire were solid. He'd never been happier. Fuck, he'd never been happy at all before and he was terrified that this warmth he woke up to every morning would be taken away from him. *Fear.* That was all it was. The moment he saw that picture of the house, he realized he'd projected his fears onto her.

"I thought you wanted a big career," Chief Wendell continued. "Get into the FBI, not play house?"

"Well…" Not sure what to reply, Aston took a swig of his beer.

Chief shook his head. "Wilson told me you'd changed, but I had to see it for myself. An *heiress*…I thought you hated rich people? Thought you said 'they're all the same.'"

"I do and they are, but she's not like the rest of them," he chuckled. "Trust me."

His old chief would shit bricks if he knew Sapphire was actually the vigilante Aston had been so obsessed with catching, even back when he was just an officer with the LAPD.

Wendell glanced down, noticing Aston's pink shirt. "Jeez, Ridder. Where did you get that shirt, Barbie's dream house?"

Aston studied his old LAPD chief of police, sniggering at his own joke—the man was nothing like his new boss at the Beverly Hills Police Station. Chief Anderson was a mild-mannered family man, and much like the father Aston never had. Meanwhile, Wendell was like the brazen uncle he never wanted. Nonetheless, the man was a vicious interrogator, and a great policeman who looked twenty years past his age. He blamed his wrinkles on his failed marriages, and he'd had more wives than a polygamist. But his appearance was more likely due to his taxing years at the LAPD.

"So, your last words to me before we parted last year were, if I recall correctly: With all due respect, Chief…screw you." Chief Wendell smirked, "If you're happy…perhaps I could get a *thank you* now for transferring you to Beverly Hills?"

Yes, *screw you*, were indeed the last words Aston had uttered to his old boss before storming out of the LAPD last year. If he could do it over, he may have taken the high road.

"Yeah, yeah." Aston smiled, then set his bottle down. "So, you've been around the marriage block, what, six, seven times? Any advice?"

"Deny. Lie. Deny. When that fails, get a good lawyer." Wendell raised his beer. "Nothing puts hair on a man's chest quite like his first wife."

"*Only* wife." Aston refused to clink the glass. "I'm not going to need a lawyer."

"I'll bet a hundy you will," Wendell said. "I'm starting to think you just *had to* settle down because you finally lost that godforsaken charm of yours."

Aston scoffed. "Me? Come on. I still have it."

"Oh yeah?" Wendell challenged. "Tell you what, I'll bet a hundred you can't walk up and kiss any girl like you used to."

"Forget it." Aston shook his head.

Wendell clucked like a chicken.

"Jesus." Aston turned in annoyance and spotted a gorgeous woman just as she entered the bar. "Any girl, you said?"

"You got it." Wendell placed a hundred on the bar counter, and Aston moved toward the girl who had her back to him. He placed a hand on her shoulder and leaned in to whisper in her ear.

She looked at Wendell, then back at Aston, and leaned in for a kiss. Aston closed his eyes, enjoying the hell out of the smooch, then brought her over to Wendell.

"I hope you saw that." Aston put his arm around the girl. "Otherwise, I'm sure this lovely lady can attest to my tongue being in her mouth."

Wendell slid the money over but, just as Aston was about to grab it, he held a finger up. "Actually, if you recall, the first bet I made was that you'd need a lawyer. And the way you just kissed this girl and cheated on your wife, it's clear you will. So I win." He pulled the hundred back.

Aston looked at his old boss and laughed. Then the woman at his side laughed. Chief Wendell looked at them both in confusion, then read Aston's face and sighed. "This is your wife, isn't it?"

"Sure is." Aston grinned, snagging the hundred. "Sapphire, this is my old boss. Old boss, this is Sapphire."

"Nice to meet you." Sapphire shook his hand, then turned to Aston. "We better go. We're already late."

Aston groaned. "Remind me why I agreed to this again?"

"Because ever since October you've had five work emergencies, nine family tragedies, and the swine flu, twice. I'm out of excuses."

October. Bad memories.

"No." Aston shook his head. "That's not it."

Sapphire thought about it. "Open bar?"

"That's the one." Aston snapped his fingers, then froze halfway up from his seat. "Please tell me she's not in the car."

Sapphire had gone Christmas shopping with Chrissy earlier, then came to pick up Aston for the shitty event. It wasn't that Aston *minded* Christina Kraft. He just couldn't stand her voice, her face, and everything about her.

Sapphire rolled her eyes. "No. I dropped her off earlier."

He looked down. Having never gone Christmas shopping, Aston wasn't an expert, but he was certain Sapphire's hands weren't supposed to be empty. "Looks like the shopping trip went well?"

"Hmm? Oh, right." Sapphire pursed her lips. "I dropped the bags off with Chrissy. Ready?"

She moved toward the door and Aston turned to his old boss with a smirk. "Nice catching up with you. Thanks for the Benjamin."

"Keep the hundred," Wendell said with an air of arrogance. "But you're still going to need a lawyer."

"Why?"

"Because…" Wendell nodded over to Sapphire, making her way to the door. "We both know she never went shopping."

Aston's jaw tightened, and his stomach turned to ice. The reason his old chief was such a vicious interrogator, was because the man was a human lie detector.

"Well," Wendell said and reached his hand out. "Best of luck with that one, Ridder."

"With all due respect, Chief," Aston said and took his hand. "Screw you."

His phone beeped.

He took his eyes off the road, and looked at the picture they'd sent him. Short dark hair, blue eyes.

He frowned. Her nose was too big, her eyes too close together, and she weighed about twenty pounds too much. The mother of his child would not be pleased.

He texted back *N*, then placed the phone in the cup holder.

He spotted a woman with shoulder-length red hair, pacing the side of the country road. It was her short skirt and high-heeled boots that caught his attention. Her cell phone was in her hand but, based on her trounced body language, the battery had run out. Her car sat a few feet back, steaming with its hood up. *Easy prey*, he thought.

Did he have time to pull back around, he wondered, weighing his options.

He pulled his phone from the cup holder and dialed.

"Yes. There's a girl stranded on highway 5, seven miles up the road from your shop. Mind sending a tow? Thanks."

Good. He felt better. It was cold outside and worse, that skirt could attract the wrong kind of man. There were a lot of sick people out there, men who killed for pleasure, and she was easy prey. He would've towed her himself, but he didn't have time.

Four pictures had already come in, and none of them were good enough. He'd never make the deadline if he couldn't find her before the end of the week. It took time for her to concede to the sacrifice, and she had to be ready on December 23rd and for the hour of the blood moon.

His eyes drew to the mirror and he readjusted it, catching a glimpse of himself in the process. His dirty blond hair curled at the top, away from his gray eyes. He'd started getting some crow's feet around them now, but he didn't mind. He'd just passed forty after all, and it added character.

Looking at his reflection, he held the image of his wife in mind and smiled. It was amazing how Rosie had come out. She'd gotten neither his golden locks, nor his wife's black strands, but ended up with a shade somewhere in-between. Her eyes were neither gray nor blue, but brown. Alma would always say that their baby looked like neither of them, but was instead a brand new product of them both.

Beep! He looked down at his cell. He had a text from the location in West Hollywood. He opened up a photo.

"Oh…there you are."

Her short charcoal hair, her round chin, her blue eyes—it was so close. His wife would not be disappointed.

It was the same place he had met Susan Bills and, more recently, Mary Dunnigan. And that last one was only a few months ago. He never went to the same location more than once in a year as it could attract attention, but he could almost see the grains of sand slipping through the hourglass and this one was *just* right.

It was too dangerous. Unprecedented. He knew he shouldn't do it. He drew a breath and texted back. *Y.*

CHAPTER 3

Sapphire gazed at Aston from across the Beverly Hills Country Club's ballroom. He was so uncomfortable in his tux it hurt to watch him.

She wasn't sure what was worse for him, returning to see everyone after the October incident, or the excessive Christmas decorations. Aston hated anything in excess.

He stood among a group of businessmen and two actors. He hated this too, clearly. Perhaps that's why he'd been so strange on their way home to change. He'd shut down all conversation with the pop of another Nicorette gum. Granted, Sapphire didn't want to be there either, but DubCorp had sponsored the event so it was obligatory. Most events were nowadays.

Her cousin, Petunia, the 51 percent owner of the family company, stood next to her chatting with the group from Apple. She laughed and smiled, fitting into the position she'd been raised for, like a wolf in its fur. Sapphire, on the other hand, felt more like a zebra in snakeskin.

"Isn't that right, Sapphire?" Petunia kicked her leg. "Wasn't I *just* saying how much I loved discussing the new software line with them?"

Nope. Petunia's exact words had been, "*Can't wait to close the deal with these boring bitches so we can move on. Smart people are the worst.*"

"Er...verbatim." Sapphire smiled, unaware they even had a new software line. She spent most of her time in her lavish office pondering about Mary Dunnigan and playing Candy

Crush. In her defense, Petunia, although a terrible human being, was on top of everything DubCorp.

"Excuse me, guys." Sapphire put her untouched eggnog back on one of the passing trays and moved toward Aston.

With Christmas being only twelve days away, the country club was decked out to the max. It looked like somebody had eaten ten Christmases and regurgitated them all over the ballroom. Seth MacFarlane was singing songs from his Christmas album, Martha Stewart was showing everyone how to make Christmas sweaters out of tinsel, and there was a famous psychic stashed in one of the corners so people could get their reading for the coming year.

Sapphire scoffed, glancing at the back of a woman, currently getting duped by the fraud. *Who'd be stupid enough to believe in that crap?*

The woman at the table turned and spotted her. "Oh-oh, Saph! C'mere."

Of course. Chrissy.

Christina Kraft, Sapphire's best friend, was at the top tier of heirs, something that had made her naïve and spoiled. While she was often still the former, Chrissy had changed drastically since she was kidnapped by Sapphire's father a few months back. She now treated people "below" her class with respect, and went out of her way to help. When Chrissy and Sapphire were out and about in L.A., the heiress would now abruptly turn and chase after homeless people yelling, "Hey Mr. Homeless maaaaan," much like Dennis, yelling at Mr. Wilson. She'd shove cash into their hands, and tell them about her new foundation, where she was developing solar-powered mini-homes for families below the poverty line. The problem was, Chrissy, being a Kraft, couldn't always tell the difference between homeless people and others. Last week, she'd run up to give a man in a trench coat a wad of cash. He'd turned out to be a flasher.

Sapphire chuckled at the memory. Yes, Chrissy had

changed a lot—her common sense just hadn't caught up to her heart yet.

"O-M-G, Saph!" Chrissy squealed. "It's, like, freaky how accurate she is."

The supposed psychic woman placed a tarot card on the table, adding to a pattern. "I can see you are very wealthy."

"Oh my Gawd, I totally am."

Sapphire stared at the woman who was conning her friend. "Yeah, amazing. People in Beverly Hills rarely are.

"I can see that you're in a tumultuous relationship," the psychic continued.

Chrissy turned to Sapphire. "Goose. Bumps."

Sapphire pinched the bridge of her nose. Chrissy's on-again-off-again boyfriend was John Vanderpilt, a man easily distracted by shiny things, laser pointers, and three syllable words. He also happened to be Sapphire's ex-fiancé. Since John and Chrissy got together in September, they'd broken up forty-six times. *Forty-six*! Once because John glanced at Scarlett Johansson's boob. Yes, singular. Once because John's jacket clashed with Chrissy's pumps. And once because they'd realized they stood on opposing sides of a matter splitting the nation down the middle: Mayo vs. Miracle Whip.

"Everybody knows about you and John, Chrissy," Sapphire said. "You were in *In Touch* last week for Christ's sake."

The psychic's eyes narrowed at Sapphire. She scooped up Chrissy's cards and motioned for Sapphire. "You don't believe? Then sit."

Chrissy clapped with a squeal, then pushed Sapphire into the seat. As the woman made her cut the deck, Sapphire looked back at Aston again. He stared into his eggnog as if he'd rather have a conversation with the drink than the people around him.

"I can see you're married and very in love," the psychic said after placing a few cards on the table.

Chrissy fake gagged behind her as Sapphire held up her hand with the wedding band. "Impressive. How *do* you do it?"

The woman gave her a fixed stare, then placed another card on the table. "I see a female with the initials R.H. close by. You don't know her but she...she knows you."

"You don't say," Sapphire yawned into her fist.

The psychic frowned as she placed a card with a burning tower diagonally over a card featuring a dude who looked like the Grim Reaper...or Uncle Fester. "I can't see what, but something big is coming your way. Something that will annihilate your world as you know it."

Sapphire deadpanned the woman.

The psychic squinted. "And I see a...cof-coffi..." She scooped up the cards. "Um, there are a lot of people waiting. You're done."

Sapphire looked over her shoulder. "There's no line."

"Well, I'm closed. Goodbye." She put a closed sign on the table and started packing up.

Sapphire walked off, feeling snubbed. If there was anything worse than receiving a bullshit psychic reading, it was to be rejected from a bullshit psychic reading.

And bullshit it was. Sapphire didn't believe in destiny. As her murderous father once pointed out, how could he perform so many random acts of violence if there was a grand plan, a controlling entity? People made their own paths and their own horrors. Sapphire had seen too many things now not to agree with her father. Still, she couldn't help but look back at the table. The woman was staring at her.

Sapphire's phone chirped.

Finally, her fake account had a new message. She opened it, praying it was the invitation she'd waited for since the day she scoped the place out. The same day she'd told Aston she went Christmas shopping.

She eyed her profile pic, matching the pictures of the two previous victims, then clicked on the new message.

Ms. Stone,
Can you come Friday night?

• • •

"I really can't stay…" she sang.

"But baby it's cold outside…" he sang.

Aston stared at the stage where a rendition of a particularly terrible Christmas song was taking place. Basically, the dude wanted to get into the chick's pants, so he was trying to convince her to stay: it was cold outside, her eyes were like starlight, he'd get blue balls if she left. Meanwhile, the chick replied no in different ways: the neighbors would know, her sister would be suspicious, her herpes was acting up.

It was a stupid fucking song, but it beat listening to the douchebags next to him. It was one of the few groups Aston had found who didn't recognize him from October.

"So, Ashton," said Douche #1. "What are you in? Software? Oil?"

"It's As-ton, actually." Aston popped another gum to stifle the craving. "And law enforcement."

"You own a security firm?"

"No. I *am* law enforcement. I'm a cop."

"Oh…"

The group fell into awkward silence until an actor cleared his throat. "I…I played a cop once."

"Yeah," Aston nodded into his eggnog. "That's the same."

"If you don't mind me asking," Douche #2 said. "How did you and your wife even meet?"

Aston took a swig of his eggnog. "On a bus strapped with a bomb, set to explode if the vehicle's speed dropped below fifty miles per hour."

"Wow!" Douche #1 gushed.

Yeah. Wow. Aston buried his nose in his glass.

A newly arrived douche on Aston's right studied him,

then pointed. "I'm sorry but, aren't you the one...at the Krafts' party, in October, who—"

Uh-oh. "Ah...yeah."

Some glared at him, some turned their backs.

"You know," one of the douches said. "Maybe you'd be more comfortable by the kitchen entrance."

Aston looked over to the buff, mid-twenties guys, the men who spent their days drinking protein shakes, man-scaping, and holding bags while their rich wives shopped. Aston had a *job*, one he loved. He had a *purpose*. He was beyond insulted but still, he stayed by them. It was better than having to socialize with Sapphire's inner circle.

The only person in Sapphire's life Aston actually liked was Elsa—mostly because she was a baby and spent a lot of time pooping—one of Aston's own favorite pastimes. Elsa's parents weren't bad either. Though, when they first told Julia they'd eloped, she spent fifteen minutes yelling at Sapphire in Spanish. After which, she spent twenty minutes crying and hugging her. After which, she spent another ten minutes yelling in Spanish. After which, her husband, Antonio, explained that Julia was knocked up again and a little hormonal. *A little*?

Aston sighed as the D-bags continued their D-bag conversation, and scanned the place once more. Chief Anderson was the only one from the station—aside from Aston—who was a member of the country club, but he hadn't seen him yet.

Aston reached for another eggnog on a bypassing tray and eyed the snoods around him. There were many downsides to being married to an heiress. For one, Sapphire had zero idea of how to do everyday things, but liked to pretend she did. Aston came home one day to find that all his white shirts had turned pink.

"I did our laundry," she'd beamed. "Ta-daa!"

She'd looked so proud standing there by the terribly folded pile, he didn't have the heart to tell her the obvious.

Laundry wasn't the only thing that made it clear Sapphire

had grown up with Julia as a maid. She couldn't cook for shit and she laid her clothes *everywhere*, as if she expected a magical fairy to scoop them up after her.

Despite all this, despite the fact that he had to stand here at this douchey Christmas party, it didn't bother him much. His old boss's words were what bothered him.

"Detective."

Aston turned to see his only ally in the cesspool of snobbery.

"Oh, thank God! If I had to spend another minute listening to these ass-wipes, I would've blown my brains out."

The D-bags behind him gasped as he pulled the chief away.

"Everything alright?" Chief Anderson wondered.

"Fan-fucking-tastic."

"Well, I'm glad you're here," the chief said. "I wanted to get a chance to talk to you before I address the guys tomorrow."

"About what?" Aston asked, taking a new nog from a tray.

"About me…retiring."

Burning whipped liquor lodged halfway down his throat, then sprayed out Aston's nose. He wiped it on his tux sleeve and stared at the chief. "But…you're only, like, fifty-five, aren't you?"

The chief's mouth turned to a line. "I'm forty-nine."

"Really?" Aston frowned. "You sure?"

"Pretty certain. Listen," the chief put his arm around Aston and walked. "Mona has sewed toilet covers as a hobby and sold them online for years. Suddenly, they took off and a major corporation wants to buy her out for nine million dollars. Nine million."

Aston looked at his boss, incredulously. "Toilet fucking covers?"

"Really nice toilet fucking covers." He winked. It was clearly a special occasion for him; the chief rarely cussed.

"What about your kids?" Aston was bummed. He'd really grown to like Dylan and what's-her-face.

"We're not moving. You can come by whenever you want. And, let me tell you the best part. You are going to love my replacement. He's just like you. Used to working in the inner city of Chicago. Comes with a lot of experience. You guys are going to get along great."

Aston opened his mouth to argue, but realized he was actually *excited* to work with someone with experience again. After more than a year of being surrounded by Beverly Hills folk, the thought of spending time with someone who *didn't* think forty-dollar parking was a "fair price" was exhilarating. Hell, he might even want to hang out with the guy *off* duty.

Aston must've smiled because the chief patted his arm. "See. You'll be fine without me."

"Of course I'll be fine," Aston hurried, awkwardly. "It was um, Barry I was worried about."

"Well, tell *Barry* that he has come to mean a tremendous amount to me." The chief winked. "I'll see you tomorrow, Detective."

Aston nodded, and as he watched the chief walk away, he noticed Vivienne Dubois noticing him.

"Aston!" she chirped and waved. "Yoohoo!"

Fuck. Realizing there was nowhere to go, Aston bent his knees and vanished below the surface of heads. He spotted Sapphire as he emerged from the crowd and straightened himself.

He placed his hands on her hips and turned her around. A smile spread on her lips and they kissed. Worries faded along with the sound of douchebags and their douchebaggery. The world was right again.

When they pulled away, Sapphire opened her mouth, hopefully to say the three magic words that would simultaneously melt his heart and give him a semi—*let's go home.* Then *she* happened.

"O-m-g, you're not going to believe whose boob tape just

snapped!" Chrissy Kraft rushed up to Sapphire, then saw Aston. "Oh. If it isn't," she made quotation marks, "'the *husband.*'"

"If it isn't the famous Christina Kraft," Aston said, then squinted. "Or wait, is it? Your face is like a smorgasbord of plastic surgery. I can't tell the difference between you and Mickey Rourke anymore."

"Hey!" Chrissy gasped.

"Hey!" Mickey Rourke huffed from the crowd beside them.

Chrissy put a finger in Aston's face. "Just because you…" her eyes landed behind him and her lips puckered. "Excuse me."

Sapphire and Aston watched Chrissy elbow her way to John Vanderpilt who was talking to a model, or actress, or possibly porn star.

Chrissy knocked on John's shoulder. When he turned, she tossed her eggnog in his face.

"You bastard! I can't believe you!" she yelled and stomped off.

"I'm *very* handsome!" he yelled back, following her. "I can't help that I attract people."

"Off again?" Aston asked, watching the spectacle.

"Off again," Sapphire confirmed. "What do you say we go out for some air and don't come back?"

Thank God. "Hear. Hear."

She disappeared out the door to the valet. Aston was just about to follow when he nearly smacked into a woman in hippie get-up—the party's so-called psychic.

"You're the husband," she said, eyes frantically searching the ballroom.

"I suppose?"

"Your wife had a reading with me earlier, and I…I saw something, but we're not supposed to say those sorts of things."

"Oh, come on. Lay your bullshit on someone else. There are plenty of gullible people here." Chrissy and John stormed past them. "Those two for instance."

The woman grabbed his arm. "Don't let her go."

Aston laughed. "Too late. She went to get the car."

"Not now, but soon. Don't let her go." Her expression turned grave. "I saw her. I saw her in a coffin."

She hurried toward the exit and Aston stared at the door long after her stonewashed skirt had fluttered out. He'd never believed in psychics, and he was surprised Sapphire had gone to one. Still, his stomach turned at her words.

He passed the coat room where John and Chrissy were dry humping, just as Sapphire returned. "Car's here."

Aston forced a smile and followed his beautiful wife.

His beautiful, lying wife.

CHAPTER 4

Riiiing. Riiing. Riiiiiiiiiiiiiiiing.

The day was here.

Sapphire opened her eyes to see the stacks of moving boxes. It was only hours away, but ever since the Christmas party Aston had been acting weird, and Sapphire was having second thoughts. Did he know? Should she not go?

Riiiing. Riiing. Riiiiiiiiiiiiiiiing. Sapphire reached for her phone, fingers stretched to their fullest. Aston lay behind her with his arms wrapped around her stomach, eyes squeezed too tightly—classic fake sleeping.

Sapphire used the knob on the headboard to pull herself closer and Aston's rigid body slid with her across the mattress.

"Hello?" Sapphire said into the phone.

"Hi, doll. Tiny, itty, bitty problem. Actually, it's *so* small, it's not even a dilemma."

"What?" Sapphire tried to sit, but Aston kept her down.

Noah, Vivienne's personal shopper/realtor/part-time Tina Turner impersonator, cleared his throat. "Remember when I said the inspection was pretty much done? Well, that might've been a tiny exaggeration. How do you feel about pests?"

"Ah, not a fan?"

"It's fine," Noah continued. "It's just a tiny, minor, but very extensive termite problem."

"Termites?!" Sapphire said.

"Termites?!" Aston repeated, suddenly wide awake.

"It'll be fixed in a jiffy," Noah chirped. "Two days for sure. Three months at the most."

"Three months?" Sapphire said, sitting up.

"Three *months*?!" Aston repeated as he got out of bed and reached for his clothes.

"But we're moving tomorrow! They already have a new tenant," Sapphire panted. "It takes three months to get rid of termites?"

"Oh no, doll," Noah laughed. "It's the black mold that will take time."

"Black mold?!" she yelled.

"Black *mold*?!" Aston repeated.

"Apparently, there's a minor mold problem in a few, almost every single, wall. They'll have to rebuild them from scratch. No biggie. Anywho, gotta run. Call you back with deets. Kisses."

Noah hung up and Sapphire turned to Aston. "The hotels are going to be booked up this close to Christmas. We're going to have to—"

"Don't say it."

"Move in with my mom."

"Ah, you said it." Aston banged his head against the wall.

"I survived twenty-three years with the woman. You'll live." Sapphire jumped up to pull her jeans on. "What's your problem with her anyway?"

"This, that, you know," Aston mumbled, as he studied her. "Where are you going today?"

She got that feeling again: he knew.

"We're meeting with Apple."

Her heart beat faster as she secured her long brown hair with bobby pins. "We're taking them to dinner, so I probably won't be home until late. But you're working late too, aren't you?"

"Yeah." Aston gazed at her as he put his gun in his shoulder strap and grabbed his cuffs.

She looked away, swallowing the guilt. She didn't think it would be this hard. *Go? Don't go?*

"Why don't we both ditch work today instead?" Aston grabbed her by the waist and pulled her closer. His lips leisurely worked their way up her neck.

"I have to go, and isn't your new boss coming in?"

"I'm sure he won't mind," Aston mumbled, wet lips still on her skin. "And, last I checked, you own the company so... who's going to fire you? *You?*"

Sapphire closed her eyes, enjoying the escalating tingles.

"We could order Thai food," he spoke slowly, deeply as he walked her backward, toward the bed. "Stay in bed all day..." His lips moved to her mouth and he lifted her onto the bed.

"I *can't*," Sapphire said again, but didn't fight his motions.

Aston's hands slid over her arm and pushed her wrist up to the headboard. His other hand slid down the sensitive skin on her stomach and between her legs. The heat spread through her body, and she moaned in anticipation, knowing this move usually preeeded the...

Click.

Click? Sapphire opened her eyes and looked up. "Are you kidding me?!"

Aston smiled, then slid off the bed and put his sports jacket on over his blue t-shirt to cover his shoulder strap.

"Seriously!?" Sapphire pulled on her hand, cuffed to the headboard. "I have to go to work!"

Aston turned on the TV and scrolled through the guide. "Would you rather watch *The Price is Right* or," he squinted. "That reality show where everyone is naked? Oh look, he's squatting! No, wait, don't look."

"Aston," Sapphire warned.

"*The Price is Right*, it is." He put the remote down, then placed a glass of water and her phone within her reach.

Sapphire gave him a fixed stare as he leaned down to kiss her.

"I'll try to get home by ten. I'll bring Thai food from that one place you like with the guy with the hairy mole."

"Aston!" Sapphire yelled as he moved toward the door.

"Or is it the Italian place who has the guy with the hairy mole?" He shrugged and turned.

"You son of a bitch!"

"Love you too." He closed the door.

"This is abuse!" Sapphire shouted at the door. "Aston?!"

She waited until she could hear his footsteps on the stairs outside before she dropped the panicked face, and reached for one of the bobby pins in her hair.

"Amateur," Sapphire mumbled, sticking the pin into the cuffs. She'd been picking locks since she was sixteen. Cuffs were child's play.

Aston's little stunt actually worked to her benefit. If he believed she was locked in the studio all day, he was less likely to have Barry shadow her and/or put a tracker on the bottom of her Range Rover. He'd done it before, he'd do it again.

Click.

Sapphire smiled.

• • •

Officer Barry Harry yawned as he stood by the door with a caramel macchiato in hand.

The class ran late last night, but it was worth it. He got to fly a good hour before the instructor had him take the bird down.

Barry looked at the time again, waiting.

Of course, he didn't *have to* stand here with a macchiato in hand, but it was important to have his arriving colleague remember Barry as his partner today.

Aston Ridder was the coolest guy he'd met. He wasn't scared of anything. Barry, on the other hand, was scared of everything.

His father, an accountant, had always said: "Find the best person at your job and then learn from them until they see you as their equal." Of course, when his father said this he thought Barry would join his firm fresh out of college and that he, himself, would be Barry's supervisor. The day Barry dropped out of USC and signed up to join the Police Academy was the first time he saw his father angry.

"Gosh darn it," he'd said and slapped his knee.

It was a rough day for everyone.

"Move it or lose it, fuck-head!" Aston Ridder cussed as he stormed in, holding a man in a Rudolph the Red-Nosed Reindeer suit.

"This is unjustified!" Rudolph slurred.

Aston handed him to two officers standing by the front desk. "Book this one for public intoxication, indecent exposure, and public urination."

The officers nodded and took over.

"Fuck you, man!" Rudolph yelled as he was dragged away.

"Caramel macchiato?"

Barry nodded and handed him the cup as they headed for the elevator. "What did he do?"

Aston took a few drinks while triple pushing the button. "I almost ran him over."

"I don't think that warrants an arrest."

"Then he peed on my car."

"Ah."

"Who do you think he'll use his one call for," Aston grinned as they stepped into the elevator. "Comet or Cupid?"

Barry looked at his partner, who was popping a Nicorette gum. *Oh God,* Aston was expecting him to say something funny. *So. Much. Pressure.* "I…the…I um…reindeer…"

"Moment's gone, Barry." Aston held his hand out. "Briefing?"

Barry handed him the report as they stepped out of the elevator. Aston had held the morning briefings since Lieutenant Grey went on an "extended vacation" i.e. rehab.

"So…" Aston eyed the stats. "What did you do last night?"

Barry's mouth opened in shock. One year. *One year* and this may be the first time Aston willingly inquired about Barry's personal life.

It was Sapphire. Every day since Aston came back from Vegas, he'd done something new that knocked the wind out of everyone. Last week, he whistled for a whole day. Yesterday, he told Officer Goldwin her new haircut wasn't "half-shitty." And now this.

"I had a lesson," Barry said as warm pride filled his chest. "Only two left before I test for my certification."

"Barry," Aston said. "You don't need a certification to pole dance. Just let your hair down and do it like all the other girls."

"Ha…ha," Barry made a face. "You know I'm getting a helicopter license."

Aston looked up, genuinely surprised. "You are? Why?"

The pride left Barry's chest like air petering out of a balloon. He'd already told Aston about it last week…and this week…and yesterday.

"I've wanted to fly one since I was a kid. It's the only thing I was never scared of, and…" Barry studied Aston's face. "Maybe it'll even help bump me up to detective."

"You getting your shield thanks to a pilot license is as likely as this coffee making me shit unicorn dust." Aston took another swig as he turned the corner. "And I already told you: I'll put in a recommendation for you…*when* you're ready."

Barry nodded, swallowing the disappointment. "So, where are we at with Sapphire? Still need me to shadow her?"

"Nope. Cuffed her to the bed."

Barry gaped at him. "You *cuffed* your wife to the bed?"

"Oh, please," Aston flipped through the pages. "She started it."

Barry sat down, shaking his head. He'd been a bystander to Aston and Sapphire's somewhat…er, atypical relationship for over a year now and the fact that they still shocked him, shocked him.

The detectives and officers around Barry silenced as Aston sat down on the desk at the front of the room.

"Alright," Aston called. "Connors, in the corner. You still have three days to go."

Connors sighed, then got up and put his hat on.

"As everyone knows, our new chief of police is coming today." Aston pointed his papers at them. "I want to make this clear to everyone. Do *not* mention loss. Do *not* mention Seal's runaway hamster. These are not problems." He groaned. "Speaking of which—and fuck my life for saying this—any updates on Princess Sofia?"

Rogers raised a finger. "I'm interrogating a witness today who may have spotted her. Of course, it could just be a rat again."

Aston took a moment to look depressed. "Anyway, as I was saying, I'm hoping the new chief will eventually realize you guys aren't the dimwits you seem to be. Except for you, Delaney. You're a fucking moron."

A knock came. The room turned to see a tall man in the doorway.

A grin spread on Aston's face and he waved the man in. "Come in. Come in."

Barry recognized the excitement. Aston hadn't stopped talking about meeting the new chief. Apparently, the guy had the same background as him. Beverly Hills didn't see much "real" action as Aston often said, and Barry, himself, was exceptionally green. When he first started at the BHPD, Barry used to eat alone whenever he wasn't on patrol. The other officers would get up if he sat down with them and roll their eyes if he stuttered his way into a conversation. Sometimes, he'd overhear them joke about his acne or his skinny arms. Chief Anderson was the only person in the precinct who seemed to like him.

Then one day, Aston Ridder walked through the door and Barry's life changed. Eventually, Aston didn't only expect to have lunch with him, he also let him come along on the Serial Catcher investigations…which turned out to be the *Sapphire Dubois* investigations. Now, Barry was officially *Aston Ridder*'s partner and the other officers went out of their way to talk to him and waved at him to sit with them. What would happen if the new chief and Aston got real close, Barry wondered. He could see himself fading into the background again. He broke out in sweat and felt like he may vomit as the new chief walked up and grabbed Aston's hand.

"Chief Brett Calloway."

"*Aston* Ridder. Welcome." He always did that. Everyone mispronounced his name.

"Aston," Calloway repeated, looking him up and down. "Interesting."

Aston cleared his throat. "It's As-ton, actually."

"I know. That's what I said."

"Oh…" Aston looked stunned.

Calloway's eyes glued to Aston's jeans and sports coat. "I was under the impression it was mandatory for your lieutenants to suit up."

"I'm a detective. Technically, they want us suiting up too." Aston gave him an elbow nudge. "But you know how these cushy places work; they nag just to have something to do, am I right?"

Barry's gaze moved to Calloway, who frowned at the room. "Is there a reason a detective is leading your briefing?"

"Our lieutenant is on *vacation*, if you know what I mean. Clunk, clunk, clunk." Aston pretended to chug from his thumb and pinky, then winked.

"Please don't wink at me; I'm not a fan of office gossip." Calloway motioned to Connors and the white cone on his head. "May I ask why one of your officers is facing the corner, wearing a hat with the words 'sandwich thief' written all over it?"

"He ate my sandwich," Aston said matter-of-factly. "He's being punished. Three days to go."

"Three," Connors confirmed, holding three fingers up behind his head.

A dense awkwardness settled in the room as Calloway stared at Aston. Barry felt the desire to cover his eyes and watch the rest of the conversation the way he'd watch a scary movie, through his fingers.

"Have a seat, Detective," Calloway finally said. "I've got it from here." The new chief took the report, asked Connors to leave the corner, and stole Aston's seat on the desk.

As the chief introduced himself to the group, Aston sat down next to Barry and leaned into his ear. "Could he be more of a dick?"

"He's not that bad," Barry whispered. On one hand, Barry figured, if Aston didn't get along with the new boss: friendship saved. On the other hand, if Aston didn't get along with the new boss: possible trouble.

"Barry," Aston said, glaring at him. "Go fuck yourself."

"Excuse me?"

Aston and Barry turned to an appalled Calloway.

"Did I just hear you speak to a colleague in an unprofessional manner?" He looked at Barry. "Has this happened before, Officer?"

"N…n…" Barry felt like he was going to die, like his words were suffocating him. "Uh…"

"In my defense," Aston chuckled, "Barry really should go fuck himself. God knows nobody else will. Hey-oo!" He raised his hand for Detective Furlong to high five him. Furlong discreetly shook his head, eyes to the floor. The room fell silent as Calloway stared at Aston.

"I think you and I need to have a chat later, Detective."

"Alright."

"Alright, what?" Calloway demanded, raising his chin.

Aston threw the room a glance. Everyone's eyes were on him and the tension grew with each second.

Just say it. Barry urged telepathically. *Alright, sir.*

Aston's lip twitched. "Alrighty then."

No one spoke, no one breathed as Calloway took a stance and crossed his arms.

Barry looked from his partner to his new chief of police. Neither of them broke their gaze, neither of them wavered.

Instinctively, Barry knew. Things at the Beverly Hills Police Department were about to change.

• • •

Sapphire looked at the time. 8:30 p.m.

It was okay. She'd make it back before Aston came home. She was nearly done and, after all, she was only here to check out a very weak lead. Not to catch anyone. She *couldn't* catch anyone anymore. She couldn't trap and leave an anonymous tip for the cops like the Serial Catcher would've. As far as the world knew, the Serial Catcher was Shelly McCormick and she was locked away in a mental institution. The girl, who had once been kidnapped and tortured by a serial killer just because she happened to look like Sapphire, had unknowingly developed a split personality after her rescue. While Sapphire was away in Paris and later on trial, Shelly's second personality had taken over Sapphire's job. She called herself the True Serial Catcher, but opted to kill the men she trapped instead of hand them to the police like Sapphire had. In the end, Shelly managed to get momentary control over her alternate personality and confess, not only to her doings, but Sapphire's as well.

In short, Sapphire had been cleared and Shelly was locked up. Should any Serial Catcher activities start back up, all eyes would go straight back to Sapphire.

"Ms. Stone," the manager said. "Would you like to meet our bar staff next?"

"That'd be great."

As Sapphire approached the bar, a woman in the mirror's reflection stopped her in her tracks. It took her a beat to realize she was looking at herself—a perfect replica of Mary Dunnigan and Susan Bills. Her short, black wig made her face look rounder, and her makeup along with the blue contacts made her look older.

Sapphire rubbed her tired eyes, feeling the contacts itch. It had been a long day and she'd been all over the place. She wasted a lot time debating her decision to come today, but once she'd been convinced, she hadn't looked back. It was her last stop that drained her.

Sapphire had stepped out of her Range Rover and stared up at the mansion when it hit her. "Oh…crap."

When she started looking into Mary Dunnigan months ago, when the woman first went missing, she never meant for it to go this far. But the more she looked, the more everything pointed toward the work of a serial killer. The fact that Susan Bills, a woman with the same description as Mary, had vanished from the same location nearly two years earlier, locked it in.

Since she and Aston burned her old hunting gear in the desert when she retired as the Serial Catcher, she had to get some new stuff. The only thing she still had, and the reason she was at the mansion, was tucked away under the loose floorboard, next to her dead father's wallet. The tranquilizer gun… just in case. What she hadn't thought of until now, the day of, was *how* to get to the location. She used to have a beat up and unregistered VW, but she didn't anymore, and she couldn't stay undercover in a bedazzled custom-made Range Rover.

"Uber?"

Sapphire turned to the car slowly rolling by with the window down. The guy inside looked at his phone. "Are you the Charlie who ordered an Uber?"

"No, that's mine!" Charlie Sheen came running out of his house. "Sorry, Sapphire."

Sapphire gave her old neighbor a half-assed nod as he put his bag in the trunk. Generally, Ubering or cabbing anywhere as a vigilante was a no-no—cabs had cameras and lift companies stashed your route and credit card information. However...

"Charlie could be a girl," Sapphire said, eyes on the Uber.

"Ah, yeah?" Charlie said, sounding peeved.

Sapphire squinted in thought. "Charlie *could be* a girl."

"Yeah, please stop saying that."

Sapphire hurried inside the mansion, happy to find Vivienne gone. The woman left her three voicemails daily about urgent matters, such as Christmas plans and how to set the new DVR.

Sapphire tip-toed past her mother's new help, then rushed up to her old pink bedroom, and hoisted herself up to the attic. It used to be filled with files, articles, tools, clothes, wigs, makeup, contacts. Now, after the Great Desert Fire, the walls were depressingly bare.

Sapphire stepped on the loose floorboard, and it sprung up. She stuck her hand into the cubby, and pulled out the tranq-gun she'd gotten *after* Aston confiscated her stuff last spring. She put it in her purse, then reached back in.

Her father's old wallet.

William Dubois had returned to Beverly Hills after spending the last two decades traveling around the country killing people. Convinced Sapphire was just like him, he'd come back to recruit her and have her join him on the road. After almost getting Sapphire, Aston, and Shelly McCormick killed, William Dubois was ultimately shot by Aston.

Sapphire opened his wallet to see the picture of her and her mother, taken before he abandoned them to be a full-time killer. She sneered and shook her head at it. Moments before he took his last breath, something in her father's eyes switched, as if he'd had a change of heart. He'd left her with one final plea: "*Don't do what I did. Don't choose the hunt.*" The notion angered her now. Like she would ever abandon a family the way he had. Like she was *remotely* like him. She'd proved that to herself when she let go of him, along with her unhealthy obsession with serial killers. William Dubois was a victim to his desires. Sapphire was not.

Her fingers slid over the wallet's contents, leaving the fake IDs and pulling out his credit card collection as she went. She was looking for a unisex name. Michael. Peter. Alex! *Perfect.*

She put his wallet back together, and was just about to drop it back in the cubby when she noticed an edge sticking out behind the picture of her and Vivienne. She pulled at it until the photograph slid out. It was taken from a distance and featured a woman coming out of a store. A red circle had been drawn around her head.

Sapphire flipped to the back. No date, but there was a name: Rita Hayes.

R.H.

The psychic's word bounced around in her head like a pin ball for the rest of the day. Even now, standing by the bar in the middle of trying to spot a possible killer, Sapphire had trouble letting go of it. Had the woman in the picture looked familiar to her? And what was her connection to William Dubois?

The bartender cleared his throat. "So…they said you had questions?"

Sapphire snapped back into reality, realizing he was waiting for her. "Right. Sorry."

She asked him the "safety" questions she'd asked the fifteen other staff members. Was the place safe from intruders? Hadn't two women vanished from there?

Sapphire only half listened to the answers. She was more interested in his eyes where she looked for:

A) Guilt.
B) Sociopathic detachment.
C) Knowledge of other person's guilt.

So far, none had failed her test.

By the time she was done with the bar crew, it was 9:15. *Crap.*

Sapphire grabbed her purse and went to say goodbye to the manager when she spotted a man in his forties, standing by the other side of the bar, gazing at her.

"Who's that?" Sapphire asked the manager.

"Mr. Silver. The owner." The manager answered. "He doesn't come in much. Owns a lot of locations, so he just pops in a few weeks of the year at a time."

"Really," Sapphire said. A contender? His travels would explain the two women in two years, two different dates.

She looked at her cell. *9:18*. She didn't want to lose the opportunity to talk to him so she'd have to be fast.

"I would love to meet him," she told the manager.

"Ah...I'll try." He got a strange look on his face. "Remember the events room I showed you before? Go wait there and I'll see if I can get him to sit down with you."

Riing. Riing. She looked down at her phone as she moved to the back.

She ignored the call, but kept the phone in her hand. The guilt hammered her once more, but she'd be home soon. Just one more interview and she'd be with Aston, arguing about whose turn it was to pick a movie—it was totally Sapphire's—while they gorged on Thai food.

She stepped inside the empty room and left the door ajar so she could watch him approach. The manager walked up to the owner, who reminded her of a mobster.

Goodfellas. Definitely an Aston movie.

Sapphire rejoiced as the man set his drink down and nodded. *Score.*

As he moved toward her room, she opened her purse to check the tranquilizer, just in case. Loaded and ready to go. She put it in the outside flap so it'd be accessible, and looked through the crack in the doorway. The owner, Silver, took a sharp left and disappeared into the kitchen.

"What the..."

A squeak escaped a door behind her. "There you are, honey."

She turned just as a white cloth was placed over her mouth and nose. She reached for the tranq-gun, but it was too late. The chloroform had her. She fell to the ground in a drowsy haze, watching her purse and her phone fall out of her hands.

Riing, Riiing. The last thing she saw was the name on the blurry screen.

Aston.

• • •

Aston hung up again at the sound of her voicemail.

He wasn't worried. He knew his wife was safely cuffed to the bed. Still, he picked up the pace.

"S'up, dude," a college guy put his fist out as he met Aston in the staircase.

"Fuck off," Aston mumbled, passing the fist bump.

"Narc," the kid shouted, then hurried down the staircase.

Aston moved toward the studio, clenching the white bag of Thai food. He got both her favorite vegetarian dishes, and he'd let her pick the flick tonight, even though it was totally his turn. When they hadn't spent their nights naked in bed, since returning from Vegas, Aston and Sapphire had spent them switching movie favorites. Every other night, Aston would be forced to endure one of Sapphire's. And every other night, Aston would bestow her eyes the pleasure of classics as *Raiders of the Lost Ark* and *Die Hard* 1 and 3. The extra movie pick was technically Sapphire's loss, but Aston hoped that and the Thai food would make up for being cuffed.

Though the second to last person he wanted to stay with was Vivienne Dubois—the first being Christina Kraft—Aston felt somewhat relieved that they were moving into the mansion tomorrow. He'd have an extra set of eyes on Sapphire. She couldn't tell him she'd been home all day when her mother could confirm she'd left.

It would be good for them, he thought.

He couldn't wait to set up the food, crack open two beers, and tell her all about the new asshole he was working for.

When the time for the "chat" came, Chief Calloway had stared at Aston's file in silence across the desk as the minutes ticked by.

"Hmm," Calloway finally hummed. "You've worked here for little over a year, correct? Your history is quite…something."

"Thank you." Aston had glanced down at his phone and sent another text to Sapphire. She still hadn't responded. Perhaps, one shouldn't cuff his wife to the headboard. Perhaps this was not a good way to start a marriage.

"It wasn't a compliment, Detective. What I'm wondering is…" Calloway flopped the folder onto the table. "What the hell have you been doing for the past year?"

Aston's eyes shot up. "Excuse me?"

"All I see here is that you brought in the Serial Catcher, Shelly McCormick, and then, a few cases involving a woman named…Sapphire Dubois."

"Uh, right?"

"Elaborate please."

"She was suspected to be the Serial Catcher but was found not guilty when Shelly McCormick confessed." Shelly had opted to take on Sapphire's trappings as well, fearing that her split personality—the True Serial Catcher—would harm her family if she didn't lock herself away.

Calloway shook his head. "That doesn't explain all the unrelated cases. Trackers. Cut-off limbs. Patrols at her address. Full protection. I mean, who is this woman?"

"She is, um…" Aston shifted in his seat. "My wife."

Calloway's brows went up while his chin went down. "You were married to the suspect?"

"No, no…we got married after. All that was before."

"So," Calloway's forehead crinkled. "You basically used taxpayers' money to stalk and woo your future wife."

"Er…what can I say?" Aston laughed and held his hands out. "You should see her ass."

Calloway didn't laugh, didn't even break the crinkle on his forehead. He stared at Aston, long and hard, before inhaling. "This won't be our last chat, Detective. I've got my eye on you. Please see yourself to the door."

Aston left that room feeling peeved, no, sodomized. The feeling hadn't left him all day. He touched the studio's door handle, knowing it would all wash off him the moment he saw her face. She had a way of un-shitting shit.

"I got both your favorites!" Aston pushed his way inside. "And a fifteen point list of why my new boss is the mother of all dicks."

Aston stopped. Aside from the TV's cerulean glow, the studio lay dark.

He flipped the light switch and stared at the empty bed. The cuffs lay open, spread across her pillow.

"Sapphire?" He checked the bathroom. "Saph!"

Empty.

He moved back to the living room/bedroom and fished his phone up again. This time, her phone was off. His finger frantically swiped through the contacts until he found the number.

"Kevin," he hurried the moment Sapphire's secretary answered. "I know you're off by now, but I need to know where Sapphire was meeting the Apple people tonight."

"What are you talking about?" Kevin asked, tone frantic. "They already closed the Apple deal. She *specifically* told me to clear her calendar today!"

"Oh…my bad," Aston pushed out, his voice tainted with alarm. He hung up, staring at the studio. It had never looked as empty as it did tonight.

He dropped the phone, then the Thai food to the floor, hearing the psychic's words tumble in his mind. Aston knew it before he had the evidence.

His wife was missing.

CHAPTER 5

The icy air woke up Ghost.

She hugged herself tighter as she curled up on the floor. The nights were the worst. He blasted the AC in the summer, never ran the heat during the rest of the year, and would even turn the AC on if a mild winter day happened to come along. The chill from outside got worse during the night and made it hard to sleep. The attic was hauntingly dark as she opened her eyes to the sound of her clattering teeth.

On nights like this, it was better to dream of what had been, not what would be. Ghost dreamed back to that one Christmas when her mommy was still alive. It was still dark when she woke her up that morning.

"Merry Christmas," her mommy whispered with a smile. "Time to wake up and see if Santa came."

Her mommy wrapped a warm robe around Ghost, and put a pair of slippers on her feet, then they both tip-toed to the living room, where a small Christmas tree cast colorful glows around the dim room.

"Be quiet," her mommy warned. "We don't want to wake him up."

Ghost promised, then sat by the windowsill and looked out. The stars were still out and the twinkle from the Christmas lights was just enough to illuminate the world outside.

Soon, her mommy left and came back with two cups of hot chocolate and a present wrapped in red paper. "Well… open it."

Ghost looked at the gift, wide-eyed. She took it carefully in case it was a mistake, and not really for her.

"You know," she said, eyes on the chocolate. "I wish I could protect you from it all—everything that happens, everything that hurts. But…you know I love you, don't you?"

"Yes, mommy," Ghost said, savoring the rustling sound the paper made when she unraveled it. Inside lay a princess doll. "Belle!"

"Shh," her mommy hushed, and her eyes shot to the hallway. "Quiet."

They sat silently, staring intently at the living room arch. When nothing happened, her mommy exhaled and pulled Ghost over to her side of the windowsill. They cuddled under a blanket, and sat there until the Christmas lights faded against the rising sun.

That was the only good Christmas Ghost remembered, and the last time she remembered feeling that way: happy.

The sound of tires on gravel pulled Ghost far away from that feeling. She sat up just as the headlights from outside flashed against the wall.

He was back.

Scared and anxious, Ghost got up. In her dream, she'd seen a strange red moon appear while the woman with the long dark hair lay dead inside a coffin, and she didn't want it to happen. But…a small part of her, the very selfish part of her, still hoped the woman would come and that Ghost could save her from the red moon and the coffin. Because, without her, Ghost's whole life was just one long cold night.

She hobbled toward the plywood. Was it the woman with the long dark hair and the fearless eyes that would bring an end to Ghost's life in the house of horrors, or was it another Mary?

She pushed her eye against the crack and drew a breath.

• • •

"Home at last."

He pulled down the truck bed's cover and smiled at her sweet face. He'd burned her purse and belongings on the side of the road about halfway home. Not the phone, of course. He was never sure how those damned things got tracked, so he'd left it for the manager to deal with. As he'd poured the lighter fluid over her purse, her ID had peeked out. It suggested her name was Sapphire. *Wrong.* This was *not* Sapphire. Her innocent eyes. Her jet-black hair. This was his good-hearted, gentle Alma.

She was still knocked out. He'd never had to reuse the chloroform so many times before. It was as if her body was fighting it.

He swung her up on his shoulder and carried her inside.

He was more than pleased when they had sent him the picture. It was as if she'd been tailored just for him. He knew why it was all coming together this time. The woman. The anniversary. The blood moon. The dark lord had something to do with it.

"Aaam," she mumbled, slowly awakening.

"Shh," he hushed as he undid the four locks on the cellar door. "You need your rest."

She mumbled something inaudible as he carried her down the stairs. When he placed her on the floor, her eyes cracked open then closed again. He chained her foot and sighed in relief.

"Oh Alma," he whispered. "Welcome home."

He had to start quickly so that she'd play the part perfectly when it was finally time. He was used to the stages now: the fear, the crying, the begging, the panic, and finally, the surrender and the sacrifice. His words, their tears, each step was like a dance sequence he knew so well, his body automatically went through the motions.

Her lids fluttered and her eyes rolled to the back of her head as she tried to speak. "Am-he."

"What was that?" He leaned in closer.

Her head weakly pulled back, then she launched forward with force and smacked it right into his nose. He pulled back, alarmed at her sudden speed and strength.

"I said," she hissed, darkened eyes on him as she stood up on wobbly legs. "Let me go, you son of a bitch."

He pulled a stunned breath, then backhanded her. Her face whipped to the side. After a beat, her head turned slowly, and she backhanded him right back. His face whipped to the side. He touched his burning cheek in shock and stumbled backward with maladroit steps.

"Listen up, buddy," she said with poise she should not have had. "I'm feeling generous today, so I'm going to give you two options. One, you let me go now and I'll only give you an ass-kicking. Two, I get out on my own and…" she whistled. "You're gonna wish for the ass-kicking."

He fumbled toward the stairs.

"Hey!" she yelled. "That's a onetime offer. No backsies!"

He locked the door, still hearing her dulled lashing on the other side. He leaned against the thick metal as his panicked, wide eyes stared into space. "What the hell just happened?"

• • •

"Michaels, Rogers, and Fatso, take every traffic cam south of my apartment."

Feverish worry pumped through Aston as he paced the Beverly Hills Police Station with a firm grip on his phone. "Guadalupe and Barry, take the north side to see if you can get a direction of which way she was going…" Aston paused as the ringtone broke to voicemail again.

"You've reached Chrissy," her message said. "If you're calling for my new charity, The Kraft Foundation, please leave a message. If you're John Vanderpilt, why don't you call Scarlett Johansson's boob instead, since you love it so much."

A pause. "Unless we're back together, in which case, text me, snuggle bear."

Beep.

Aston swallowed the stress, and asked her to get back to him ASAP. He'd called everyone he could think of now. Julia, Vivienne, the uncle, the aunt, the secretary, even the cousin, Petunia…though, she hung up before he could ask her when she last saw Sapphire. *Fucking October.*

He hung up, his heart rate going off the rails. The precinct bustled with life. Everybody had a task. Everybody knew who had to be found.

Aston went to pop another nicotine gum, but the container was empty. *Fuck.*

"Detective," Officer Fatso called. "I got it."

Aston and Barry ran up to the computer, showing the image of Sapphire's white Range Rover.

"The traffic cam on Wilshire and Santa Monica recorded this at 11:04 a.m."

Minutes after Aston cuffed her. His only comfort was that she'd gotten herself out of the cuffs and hadn't been taken by a serial killer. It happened before with Richard Martin, and it could've happened again.

As Officer Fatso ran to the printer, Aston pointed at the screen. "She's in the left lane. I bet she's going for the 405 South. Check all the exits off that freeway from there to fucking Timbuktu."

"What's going on here?"

Aston turned at Calloway's voice.

His new chief stood in the doorway to the hectic precinct, looking confused. He snagged Officer Fatso's print out. "Grand theft auto?"

"It's Detective Ridder's wife, sir," Fatso replied. "She's missing."

"The wife. Again. Why am I not surprised?" Calloway said

dryly. "I assume it's been twenty-four hours. And that you've filed a proper missing person report."

Aston's jaw tightened as the chief approached him. "No, but…"

"It *hasn't* been twenty-four hours?" the chief said. "Then may I ask why you're using the entire precinct to find a person who may as well be at a spa somewhere?"

The tapping of the keyboards ceased. Officers froze in place. The head-down rummaging came to a stop at every desk.

Aston's anger catapulted from his gut to his mouth. "She's not at a fucking spa."

Chief Calloway squinted at him, and put his face to Aston's. "Is that the language to use with a superior?"

"Oh, that wasn't language," Aston explained. "This is language—"

Barry stepped in between them with his hands up. "What Detective Ridder meant to say, was that he is extremely worried about his wife, and that the likelihood that she would be at a spa is very small, sir."

Aston closed his fists, trying to lock in the rage.

The chief looked at the photo of Sapphire in her Range Rover. "This was taken at 11:04, and it looks like she is leaving willingly, does it not? I assume you have reason to believe someone wanted to harm her?"

"Yes," Aston said.

"You said she was accused of being the Serial Catcher once, but she was freed." Calloway pushed. "So unless she *was* in fact guilty—in which case she should be in prison—I don't see why she would be in danger. So, please tell me, who would want to harm your wife?"

Aston blinked at his new chief, and shook his head. "No one."

"Good," the chief said. "Then perhaps she's just trying to get away from you, Detective. Am I presumptuous to assume you had a fight the day she disappeared?"

"I wouldn't call it a fight—"

"Then, once you wait the appropriate amount of time to file a missing person, should your wife *actually* be missing, I will personally oversee every step of the entire investigation."

If Sapphire had been hunting a new serial killer, this chief of police would not look the other way, as Aston suspected his old chief had. In fact, it seemed this chief would do his best to put Sapphire away.

Aston faked a smile. "Of course."

"Good." Calloway turned to Fatso. "Now, where are we on that hamster?"

Aston smacked the doors open and left the station.

Somehow, he had to find Sapphire without his team. Somehow, Aston had to get her back.

• • •

Sapphire tried to ignore the cold as she put the pin back into the ankle's shackle lock.

It was her sixth go. Luckily, she'd used bobby pins to keep her hair up under the wig. Without them, she'd have nothing to jimmy the lock with. This time it would work, she thought, letting the pin search for the sweet spot. It *had* to work.

She had no idea where she was. She didn't know how long she'd been out, maybe an hour or so, maybe more, before she fully regained consciousness last night. If it took him an hour to drive her from point A, where he took her, to point B, she could be in L.A. County, Ventura, or even O.C.

It was fine. Aston was probably pissed beyond belief by now, but she'd get out of here, throat chop the dude upstairs, and be on her way. Hell, she'd probably be home in time to heat up the leftover takeout and watch Aston pretend to hate *Billy Elliot*.

Yes. She felt the bobby pin slip into position and twisted it slowly, carefully…

Almost there…

Snap!

Snap? Sapphire's head perked. It was supposed to say click. *CLICK.* She pulled the pin out and stared at it, broken in half.

Damn. She'd need something thin, yet sturdy for this lock.

Her body tensed at the rustle of a keychain, preparing her for battle. She smiled, tossing the broken pin aside and moving on to plan B.

She listened to lock after lock and devised a plan as he closed the door and worked his way down. She would use the chain to choke him out, steal the keys, undo the shackle, and stroll out. *Super.*

His eyes were on her the moment his head appeared from the divider.

"If it isn't my gracious host," she beamed. "Thanks for a lovely night. Who needs warmth and a bed when you have arctic cold and a rock floor?"

He grabbed a chair from the side of the wall, then placed it in front of Sapphire, three feet out of her reach. *Not super.*

"Why do you speak like that?" he asked and sat.

"With words…or?"

"Like you're not afraid." He titled his head. "Why aren't you crying?"

"Like this…" Sapphire fake cried. "*Why are you doing this to me? Wh-hy-hy?*" She deadpanned. "Not my thing."

He studied her. "It's not that I want you to cry. I'm just curious how this is going to work."

Sapphire studied him right back, taking in his expression. Something was off about this guy. Something was missing. It took her a beat to realize his eyes lacked that psychopathic light of depravity. *Odd.* Killers often masked that light until they had you. There was no reason for a mask now, or to look so *normal.*

"I'm going to be honest with you. You weren't what I expected." He shook his head. "I was up all night thinking, and…with the time constraints, you will have to work very hard over the next few days to not be…you. Can you do that?"

"Who is it that you want me to be, exactly?" Sapphire asked, an edge to her voice. *Mary Dunnigan? Susan Bills?*

"I will not hurt you and I *will* let you go, if you promise to do as I ask, and be…who you are supposed to be."

"Really?" Sapphire laughed in skepticism.

"I swear in the name of God." He held his hand up. "So from here on out, you will only refer to yourself as Alma and me as Mer."

He took out a thin manuscript and pushed it over to her. "When you are invited up for dinner and asked questions, you will follow these answers. You will not deviate. Are we clear?"

Ah. He wanted her to be this Alma person. Assumedly, his dead wife. If he found out she was wearing contacts and a wig, he'd probably kill her on the spot. However, if playing along was all one had to do to get free, how come Mary and Susan never returned? Playing along didn't get you free, it got you dead. She had to walk a very fine line and choose neither.

Sapphire inhaled. "I'll think about it, champ."

"No." He glared at her. "Mer."

Sapphire held her hands up. "Alright…"

He nodded and got out of his chair.

"…pal."

He stopped, shoulders tensed, fist clenched. "Mer. *Mer.*"

"Won't happen again, boss."

"Stop!" He yelled. "No boss, no pal, no champ!"

"What about chief?"

"No boss, no pal, no champ, *no* chief!"

"You got it, bucko."

"Mer!" he yelled. "Me—" he suddenly stopped. "Your mind may be a mystery to me but your body, I can crack." He lifted his chin. "You haven't had food or water for a while. Two more days without it, and you'll be begging to please me."

"Oh yeah?" Sapphire said coolly.

He moved back upstairs. "I'll see you in forty-eight hours."

"Good luck. I'm the Gandhi of L.A. I had two grains of rice on Sunday so I'll be good till March!" She paused, hearing him open the door. "And by the way, I was just being polite before! I'm giving you one star on Yelp. Worst B&B *ever*!"

The doors closed with all four locks, and Sapphire leaned her head against the cold concrete, trying to ignore her parched throat and the howl of her empty stomach.

Forty-eight hours? Self-doubt slithered around her like a boa constrictor. Aston would be worried sick by then, wondering what had happened to her. The guilt she'd felt before didn't hold a candle to what she felt now. What if this was the one time she couldn't fight her way out? What if she'd never see him again?

Sapphire looked up at the small, boarded-up basement window, and knew.

This was a mistake.

• • •

"What the hell are you doing with my shit?!" Aston ran up the stairs to stop the two men on their way out of his studio.

Resting a box on his chest, one of them handed Aston a paper. "Moving company. Your wife gave us the spare key. This is her signature, right?"

Aston stared at Sapphire's handwriting. She'd ordered a moving company for a *studio*? Rich people.

"We'll meet you at the new address," the mover said, and vanished into the elevator.

Aston stepped inside and stared at the empty studio. He didn't have time to deal with this. Still, he needed somewhere to work. Thick-minded and full of worry, Aston drove to the mansion.

The moment he put the gear in park, he got a text from Barry.

Still no news on the RR.

His partner was keeping an eye on the incoming reports for her Range Rover. If a claim came in on the car being abandoned anywhere in L.A. County, at least he'd have Sapphire's last location.

A *tap-tap-tap* from a long fingernail came on his window, and Aston turned to face Vivienne Dubois. She looked back to the movers, and her dulled voice sounded through the glass. "Yes! Put everything in the garage!"

Aston looked away, feeling the familiar shiver. There were normally two reasons he avoided Sapphire's mother, and they were the reason why he didn't want to move into the mansion to begin with. Today, there were *three*. Reason #3: he hadn't told her Sapphire was missing. He'd hung up the moment Mrs. Dubois said she hadn't seen her daughter.

"Hellooooo!" She tapped the glass again and waved, as if to make sure he actually saw her through the *glass*.

He held back the urge to drive off and stepped out of the car. Reason #2:

"Darling!" Vivienne exclaimed, then leaned in with pouty lips.

This.

Aston continuously moved his face to dodge the kiss, but her lips kept hounding him.

"Moaw," she said, ending up kissing the air of his chin.

Over a year ago, Mrs. Dubois had hit on Aston. It wasn't a subtle hit, but a full-on oops-I-dropped-my-kimono hit. Aston turned her down, and it hadn't bothered him much until he and Sapphire got married and he realized he knew the exact shape of his mother-in-law's nipples. Gross. Worse yet, she kept trying to kiss him every time she saw him, and he feared it would happen again. *The kimono-moment.*

He nodded awkwardly. "Mrs. D."

"I wish you would stop calling me that." Vivienne rolled her eyes. "Can't you call me mom?"

Aston didn't have time to swallow the gag.

Mrs. Dubois eyed the empty car. "Where's Sapphire?"

He scratched the back of his head. Reason #1:

Last time he told Mrs. Dubois that Sapphire had been kidnapped, the woman acted as if he'd announced that her pet rock was missing. She also happened to be a terrible mother, the kind that drugged her daughter to get her to walk down the aisle with someone she didn't want to marry. Of course, Vivienne had gotten off the sauce now and had "changed," but it didn't matter to Aston. Anyone who'd ever made Sapphire miserable could go fuck themselves for eternity. That said, he needed to keep Mrs. Dubois with her newfound "care" from blabbing to Calloway. An investigation on Sapphire would end up in a two-word combo: serial killer. Aston was sure of it now.

"She…is…" Aston said. "At…"

Mrs. Dubois waited.

"A…retre…at?" Aston nodded at the idea, approving it. "Yes, Sapphire is at a retreat."

"Now? Which one?"

Aston looked toward the sun. He knew of zero rich people retreats. "That one place where they do the…thing, and the stuff?"

"Richmond Hills?"

He snapped his fingers. "Right."

"Oh, thank God." Vivienne moved toward the house. "I've been begging her to get them enlarged for years." She turned. "She did the boobs, right? Or did she do her ears? I hope not. She's young; she could still grow into them."

Aston looked at her in bewilderment.

"Richmond Hills," Vivienne circled her hand. "Is the discreet retreat you go to after you've had work done to heal in private. Didn't you say that's where she went?"

"Oh," Aston said, "Yeah, yeah, the boobs. Big ol' knockers."

"Hey," one of the movers came up. "If you want us to put the stuff in the garage, you're going to have to move your car."

"I don't use the garage." Vivienne pointed at her town car in the driveway.

Aston pushed past the movers and marched up to the garage. He stopped at the opening.

Sapphire's Range Rover.

CHAPTER 6

Two days didn't sound like much. Forty-eight tiny hours, right?
Wrong.

Sapphire's cheek lay pressed to the cold floor as she stared at the thick safe on the other side of the basement. To keep her mind off her various pains, she pondered what it may contain. Money? Body parts? An obscene amount of Hello Kitty stickers?

Her lips, burning from dehydration, brought an end to her distraction. Forty-eight hours without food was bad. Forty-eight hours without water was torture. People could die from three days without it, but Sapphire felt like she was already there. The parched throat and dry mouth were just the tip of the iceberg. Her tongue had swelled and painful smarts shot through her muscles and insides. Yesterday, she'd sweated even though the room was freezing. Today, her body shivered uncontrollably.

His plan was obvious. When he returned, he would offer her food and water in exchange for her compliance in his little dinner game. Knowing compliance likely led to death—just like it had for Mary and Susan—Sapphire would not give in. She would hold her ground. No matter *what*.

She closed her eyes, trying to put her mind, which was going mad with thirst and hunger, to rest. She wished she was home with Aston. She never meant for this to happen.

Nausea rose in her. Sapphire pulled herself up and crawled away from her corner. She retched again and painful, burning bile came up. She collapsed, her throat burning like fire. There was no water. No thirst-quenching, cold, fire-exterminating water.

"Let me guess," a voice said. "Sweating. Burning throat. Shivers. Vomiting."

Sapphire pried her eyes open. He was back. She should put herself in a defensive stance, but knew her legs wouldn't hold her.

"You know why the body sweats?" he continued. "And why we vomit the last of our liquids when we're dehydrated?"

Sapphire opened her mouth to say something sarcastic, but groaned instead.

"As much as your body is trying to save you, it's also trying to kill you quicker to spare you from a long, painful death." There was oddly no satisfaction in his voice; he just wanted her to know what was happening to her.

"I'm here to offer you something," he said.

Sapphire lacked the energy to do jazz-hands and say *oh, I'm sooo surprised*, but mustered a snort.

"A practice run. Frankly, in your case, I think it's necessary. So, if you're not ready to concede, I'll leave. If you *are* ready to do as I wish, you can come up for water and a dish."

Sapphire lifted her heavy head and used every bit of strength to form her dry mouth. "Thanks, Dr. Seuss."

She fell back down, exhausted. *Worth it.*

He stared at her in cold disappointment. He probably thought she'd fold right away. *Sucker.* He got up and Sapphire watched his feet move away from her.

"See you in another twenty-four," he said, back still turned to her.

The thought was overwhelming and panic hit her. Twenty-four hours might as well be a hundred. Her stomach howled at her, stabbing its way through her body like poison. The thirst burned her throat and tongue worse each second.

"Wait," Sapphire said, her voice feeble.

He stopped, but didn't turn.

"Wait…" Sapphire closed her eyes. "Mer."

He turned around with a big, victorious grin.

• • •

"Cream puff."

Aston looked away from his notes and up at Lurch, Mrs. Dubois's butler. "What did you just call me?"

"Nothing, sir," he assured, holding out a plate of pastries. "Cream puff?"

"None for me, Lurch."

Lurch gave him a strained smile. "If I may remind you just *once* more, sir. My name is Radison. Perhaps, if it's easier for you, you can think of Radisson the hotel, hospitality, myself, Radison."

"Mhm." Aston went back to his notes and put his feet up on the glass coffee table.

Lurch sighed, spraying the table around his shoes with Windex.

It had been two days since Aston found the Range Rover. Two days of sleeping in his wife's old pink bedroom and avoiding Tits McGee. He'd spent an hour and a half hiding in the pantry yesterday, waiting for her to leave the kitchen. Two days and still no clue as to why Sapphire's car was here, and she was gone. He'd gone up to her attic, thinking maybe she'd started her old collection again, but the walls were still bare.

Lurch cleared his throat.

Aston stared at his work. He'd started the investigation where he assumed Sapphire would've—with serial killers. Unfortunately for him, but fortunately for the citizens of L.A., there were no *known* serial killers running around at the moment. There were always a few too slick for the police to catch onto. He'd also talked to almost everyone Sapphire knew, and no one could offer him any clue as to what she'd been up to in the days before d-day, or disappearing-day.

When Aston looked back up, Lurch was staring at his shoes, then sprayed them and rubbed them with his rag.

"Are you... Windexing my shoes?"

"Yes, sir."

"M'alright." Aston shrugged and looked at his phone, vibrating off the hook, showing an odd number: *000-000-0000*.

Hope immediately overtook him and he picked up, yanking his feet off the table. "Saph?"

"Hi," a chipper voice said. "My name's Marla and I'm calling about—"

Of course. Aston hung up, sick with disappointment. *Fucking sales.*

The front door slammed shut. She was back. Aston scrambled for his paperwork and hopped up.

"Hellooooo!" she called. "Aston?"

Aston hurried toward the kitchen as the sound of her heels traveled toward the living room. He slid in against the wall and peeked around the corner of the kitchen's hallway entrance. She disappeared into the living room and Aston moved to slip out the kitchen exit.

"Sir."

Aston turned to face Lurch.

"I believe Mrs. Dubois is looking for you," Lurch said, unreasonably loud.

Mrs. Dubois's heels headed toward the kitchen as Aston stared at Lurch, staring back at him. "Did you do that on purpose?"

"I haven't got a clue what you mean, sir." Lurch vanished and Mrs. Dubois entered, boobs out and about.

"There you are." She tried for a cheek kiss again, but Aston dodged it. "I've barely seen you. If I didn't know any better, I'd think you were avoiding me?"

She stared at Aston, waiting for him to dispute her claim. He stared back at her in awkward silence, then cleared his throat. "So, what's up?"

"Coffee?"

He nodded with reluctance. Perhaps the caffeine would kick his mind back in gear; he'd been so worried about Sapphire he'd barely slept since she vanished.

Mrs. Dubois pressed the button on the crazy-ass coffee machine, then pulled a lever and twisted a knob. Aston watched with interest as the coffee started up. He was frankly surprised she didn't have to tickle its balls, too. The fucking thing was like something out of a steampunk novel.

Mrs. Dubois turned and played with her locket as she studied him.

"Um…" Aston said, "you wanted to talk about something?" It could be his imagination but it looked like she was leaning her giant knockers into the coffee machine's steam. A sense of déjà vu hit him, followed by unease.

"Has anyone ever told you, you have that…*je ne sais quoi*?"

"No," Aston shook his head. "A girl once called and told me I had Chlamydia, but…turned out I didn't."

She approached him slowly, eyes skating down his body. Okay, he was *not* imagining this. Aston slid away along the kitchen counter, but she followed.

"You know," she continued. "Some people don't believe a man and a woman can live together platonically."

"Some people are morons."

His back hit the kitchen corner, trapping him. *Mayday. Mayday.* He knew it would come to this. He fucking knew she'd do it again.

"Some people think that wild, sexual energy between the two individuals is inevitable." Mrs. Dubois pushed her body against his. "Do you agree?"

"Not even a little."

Vivienne closed her eyes and leaned in.

Aston pressed himself into the wall, hand defensively up. He didn't know what to do. What was the protocol when your mother-in-law hit on you: Run? Knock her upside the head? Play dead?

"Aaaaand there." Vivienne opened her eyes and pulled back. "How was that?"

Aston blinked. "What?"

"If you were a single man, would you not have ravaged me after that speech?"

"Wh...how...*what*?"

"I walked up to him, just like that, and said everything, just like that." She picked up the ready coffee cups.

"Who?" Aston held his hands out.

"Radison, of course. Can't you tell, I'm terribly attracted to him?"

"To *Lurch*?"

"Of course!" Vivienne gushed. "The man obviously oozes of raw sexuality."

They both leaned forward to peer into the living room where the butler Windexed the table then, after a moment of thought, Windexed the Windex bottle.

"Obviously," Aston said, turning back. "So...let's just be clear. You're *not* hitting on me?"

"That's disgusting, Aston." She handed him the coffee cup. "You're my son-in-law."

"Well, right, but—"

"Please," Vivienne's hand flew up. "Stop talking before you make this uncomfortable."

"Before *I* make it uncomfortable?"

Vivienne sighed. "I did exactly what I showed you and nothing. He didn't even blink. What do you think I should do?"

Aston drank his coffee in annoyance. He didn't have time for this crap. "I guess...you could always try the oops-I-dropped-my-kimono move."

"How do you know about that...oh, right." Vivienne's eyes widened, then she laughed at the memory. "You know, I *will* give that a go."

He studied his mother-in-law. He could cross cougar attack off the list of reasons to avoid her, but it didn't matter. After all the things this icy trophy wife had done to her daughter and her late husband, Aston would never like her. Sure, unlike Joe Ridder, Vivienne Dubois had provided her daughter with a ridiculously large closet, a maid to care for her, and a custom-built Range Rover, but it didn't make up for...

Aston's mind paused and rewound. He swallowed the coffee and looked at Mrs. Dubois. "Sapphire's Range Rover, what exactly makes it custom made?"

"Oh, I put in all sorts of stuff." Vivienne took a sip. "Italian leather. Massaging seats. Pre-loaded music system with—"

"Did you," Aston closed his eyes, praying, "by any chance, happen to purchase a built-in GPS system with a tracking unit?"

Her long fingernails tapped the counter as she pondered. Aston held his breath, waiting. If the car had it, he could download the data, and go through every step Sapphire made before she vanished. The unit could hold the key to her whereabouts.

His mother-in-law held up a finger. "No."

Salted fuck-nuts.

"The guy threw all that in for free," she continued, beaming at the memory. "I'm not going to say it was because we had a sexual relationship...but we did."

"That's fan-fucking-tastic!" Aston's pulse surged as he rushed to chug the coffee and be on his way. "Great coffee."

"It should be," Vivienne said as Aston took the final mouthful. "They ferment the beans in elephant stomachs then pick them out of their feces. One ounce costs a fortune."

Aston slowly spit the elephant shit coffee back in the cup and pushed it away from him.

After a quick puke, he ran for the Range Rover.

• • •

Crack…

Crack…

Cold.

Ghost was pulled out of her strange, fragmented dream and opened her eyes. She stared at the door, the weight of disappointment still crushing down on her.

The new woman had been here a few nights now. The moment Ghost put her eye against the plywood and saw that short black hair instead of the long hair she'd dreamed of, she cried.

It must've been an almost dream. Almost dreams were of events that nearly happened but then didn't. The second dream where Ghost would live and run, while the woman was buried in a coffin, must've been an almost dream, too. At least, this meant the girl with the long hair wouldn't face the coffin.

Her body stiffened as his sounds arose from the staircase. He unlocked the attic and opened the door as she held her breath.

"Good evening, Rosie," he said, unlocking the chain on her foot. "You look nice."

"Thank you, Dad." It was the dress he always laid out for her for the dinner, the red one with snowflakes.

He took her hand in a firm grip and brought her down to the second level.

"Wait here." He placed her on top of the staircase and hurried downstairs.

The moment he was out of sight, Ghost's tired eyes moved to the bathroom. The door was cracked. He usually left all doors in the hallway closed, but he must've forgotten.

Her eyes landed on the jar of pills on top of the sink. They looked just like her mommy's old pills. Pills that would make you sleep forever if you took too many and the paramedics didn't wake you.

Ghost stared at them. Maybe if she got her hands on them, she could find a way to put him to sleep.

Her eyes bounced down the staircase. She had only a few seconds. She moved quickly, knowing he'd beat her if he caught her straying. Three steps to the bathroom sink, and the three steps back. She hid the bottle in her dress just as his voice sounded.

"Rosie! Dinner's ready!"

"Coming!" Ghost chirped and hopped down the steps.

"Mommy made pot roast tonight." He opened the door to the dining room, and Ghost passed in under his arm.

As always, the table was lit by candle, decorated with multicolored gourds, and full of food: pot roast, vegetables, gravy, and potatoes. The cobbler stood in the middle, still steaming.

Her eyes drew to the woman at the head of the table seat. Ghost's heart was weighed down by the knowledge that she would soon be dead. This woman was definitely not the one from her dreams. Besides the short black hair and blue eye color, there was no power in her gaze, just blank nothingness. It meant he got to her too, already.

Ghost swallowed the tears, and forced the wide smile. "I love pot roast. It's my favorite."

The woman shot her an evaluating glance, then eyed the script. "I know it is."

Her neck and back had been chained so tightly to the chair that it looked uncomfortable. Ghost saw her notice the glass of water next to her plate and reach for it.

"Not yet." His voice was a firm hiss. "Or I'll take it away."

This is how he spoke when they strayed.

The woman clenched her jaw and pulled her hand back. She looked so sick, she might fall over without the chain's restraint.

"Who wants to say the prayer tonight?" he asked. "Rosie?"

"Yes, Dad." She bowed her head and clasped her hands. "Dear heavenly father, please bless this food and my family, and bless this house with your love and guidance. Amen."

"Amen."

Silence.

He kicked the woman's chair.

"Amen," she growled.

He pushed her glass to her: the reward. She launched for the water and chugged the whole thing. He refilled it for her, then used the big fork and a knife to carve the pot roast and serve everyone.

"Eat up, honey."

The woman drank her second glass of water at a slower pace, watching him intently.

"Save room for dessert, Rosie," he said.

"I will, Dad," she smiled between chews. She noticed that the woman's plate was still untouched, and felt a burst of panic. She had to eat it. That was the way the game worked. The women had to follow the rules or things got worse for them.

"Oh, listen!" he said as always, and went to the music player by the windowsill. "You like this one, don't you, honey?"

"Yes…Mer." She *sighed* his name, as if it was a hassle to speak it.

As he turned up the volume of the Christmas song, the woman turned to Ghost and whispered. "Are you okay?"

Ghost kept her smile, holding the horror inside. Sometimes, he watched them in the reflection from the small mirror above the cabinet.

"Is it poisoned?" the woman whispered. "The food?"

Ghost glanced over, unable to tell if his eyes were on them or not.

"Dad," she smiled. "She's talking all sorts of funny. I think she's hungry."

He turned and glared at the woman, admonishing her with his eyes. "I think so too, Rosie. Eat, honey, *eat*."

He took two long strides to shove the woman's plate closer.

The food was not poisoned. Ghost wanted her to know it, but she didn't dare. The woman brought a fork full of mashed potatoes to her mouth. She held it there for a while, her hand shaking from strain. She shoved it in and chewed. As she downed more water, she glared back at him angrily, fearlessly.

Ghost blinked. It reminded her of the woman from her dream, but it couldn't be. They looked completely different from each other. Ghost watched the woman eat everything on her plate but the roast.

"Remember, you *love* pot roast, honey," he said.

The woman stared at the meat, seeming disgusted, then brought it to her mouth and forked it in. The two watched in astonishment as she chewed, gagged, chewed, and gagged. The woman twisted her head, swallowing the meat by chugging water.

Ghost saw it: the strand of dark brown sticking out from under the short hair. The black hair wasn't real.

"It's a wig," Ghost gasped before she could stop herself.

• • •

The words seemed to reverberate in the room. *It's a wig-it's a wig-it's a wig.*

Sapphire's head whipped toward Mer. He sat still, seeming fearful, or panicked. Then he marched over to her. He grabbed a fist full of her wig and yanked it off. Sapphire's dark mocha strands fell over her shoulder.

The creepy smile finally left the daughter, Rosie, as she covered her mouth and looked at her father who stood still, shaking with anger.

"Do you know what you've done!" he yelled. "Do you have the slightest idea of what you've caused?!"

"No," Sapphire said, then brought her finger to her eyes. "But I suppose I can take these out too. They've been itching like crazy."

His eyes widened with shock as she flicked the contacts away. The jig was up, so…screw it. Sapphire reached for the water and took a gulp. "Aaah. Refreshing."

He took the glass from her and threw it to the wall. It smashed and the water trickled down the wallpaper. Sapphire didn't flinch, didn't blink.

"You've ruined everything! *Everything*!"

Finally, there was the blatant psycho she'd been waiting for.

"Rosie, go to your room." He paced the floor. "Now!"

Sapphire watched his daughter hurry upstairs. When she was gone, he grabbed Sapphire's chair and tossed it, along with her, to the ground.

At least, Sapphire thought as she lay squished to the floor, he didn't smash her head in while his daughter was still in the room. Not that it made him Father of the Year or anything—the man and his cray-cray dinner game was a major Social Services case.

He grabbed Sapphire by the shoulders, swung her around, and shook her. "Who the hell are you?!"

"Alma."

"No. *Who* are you? Why the wig, the eyes? You *knew* I was going to be there that night somehow. You did this on purpose!"

"I have no idea what you're talking about, *Mer*." She smiled.

"Stop it! Stop it!" He paced again, manically banging his palms against his forehead. "This is not good. There's no time. I'm out of time. You were supposed to be her."

Sapphire watched him. Despite the fact that he sounded crazy, talking to himself, he still didn't sound murderous. Even the whole insane dinner thing had seemed like it stressed him out. Like every word he said, every piece of this "play" made him nervous. He didn't enjoy this. *None* of it.

His creepy daughter was equally hard to decipher. Sapphire had watched her closely to figure out what kind of danger she was in. But she'd smiled throughout the whole thing, like it was just any ol' day.

Mer stopped pacing and grabbed a photograph of a woman from the mantel. The real Alma, she realized as his shoulders started shaking. He was crying.

"Um," Sapphire said. "This seems like a personal moment. It's probably best I leave."

The shaking stopped, and there was a beat of stillness before he turned. He strode up to her and grabbed the whole chair, surprising Sapphire with his strength, then carried her down the staircase.

He sat her down in the corner of the basement. Within a second, he somehow managed to hook the chain back into the wall, unravel it from around the chair, and use the thick lock to refasten her before stepping out of her reach.

She stared at him. "So, what you going to do now, old fart?"

He looked at her, confused for a second, then exhaled and left, locking all four locks behind him.

Sapphire waited a beat, then leaned forward. She pulled out the long, pot roast fork from her pant lining and smiled.

Thin, yet sturdy. Sapphire was getting out.

CHAPTER 7

"What the hell?"

Aston stood in the parking lot, looking up at the building, then down at Sapphire's routes that he'd downloaded to his phone.

This was the first place she went after leaving the studio? A college?

He moved inside and toward the receptionist, a woman in her thirties, who was crying as an older guy patted her hand.

"Then he dumped me," she sniffled, "and stole my tablet."

"I know it's hard, sweetheart," the old guy said, "but a man who steals one's pills is not a man one should be with at all."

"Tablet," the woman corrected, blowing her nose.

"Pill, tablet, doesn't matter. He shouldn't be stealing anyone's medication."

"Excuse me." Aston smacked his phone onto the desk. "Have either of you seen this woman?"

The receptionist, still teary-eyed, looked at the picture of Sapphire.

"Can't say I have." She turned toward the old guy. "Have you—" she looked at the empty spot next to her in confusion.

Aston noticed the man, looking over his shoulder as he speed-walked down the hallway and past a long line of students.

"Next!" the man yelled at the line before hurrying into his office.

"Is she enrolled here?" the receptionist yelled after him as he followed the old guy.

Yippy! The Counselor Is In, said the sign on the door and Aston yanked it open.

"Hey!" the bawling girl next in line yelled. "No cutsies."

Aston slammed the door behind him. He marched up to the desk where the counselor and a boy with a sweaty forehead stared at him in shock.

"You know her, don't you?" Aston planted his hands on the desk.

"I don't know what you're talking about?" the counselor said.

"Dude," the boy with the sweaty forehead said. "It's kind of my turn."

Aston pulled up his wallet and handed the kid a six pack of condoms. "Here. Enjoy. Don't overthink it."

The scrawny kid looked from the condoms to Aston. "How did you know?"

"The odds were like ninety to ten, so."

The kid grinned and headed for the door, condoms in hand.

"No, Marcus," the counselor shouted after him. "Sex is only meaningful when it's with someone truly speci—"

"He's gone," Aston said.

The counselor sighed, then gave Aston a penetrating gaze. "I won't tell you anything. You're one of her sickos aren't you? I've already pushed the button for security; they're on their way."

Sickos? Aston studied the man. "How well do you know Sapphire?"

"Why?" The old man's facial muscles twitched. "How well do *you* know her?"

Aston raised his chin and studied him. "Do you know what I think you know?"

The man raised his chin, too. "What if what I think you think I know, is not what *you* know?"

Aston raised his chin farther. "I think we both think what I think we know."

As they sat there—chins in the air, tapered eyes on each other—a security guy with a stained napkin tucked into his collar, burst in.

"Everything alright, Counselor O'Riley?" he asked, out of breath. "You pushed the alarm button."

O'Riley peered at Aston. "Yeah, sorry. Thought it was the intercom…again."

"Happens all the time." The guard forced a smile then left, muttering, "not like I was in the middle of lunch or anything."

O'Riley turned to Aston. "So, who are you?"

"The husband."

The counselor's demeanor changed at once: suspicion became joy; narrowed eyes turned wide with delight.

"The officer." He took Aston's hand and shook it vigorously. "I've heard a great deal about you. Pleasure."

"Detective," Aston corrected. "Afraid I can't say the same."

"Oh." O'Riley pulled back. "I've known Sapphire for a few years now. We meet up a few times a month. I used to be a priest. Still help out at the church every now and then but, this is my new job. Just getting used to being called counselor instead of Father O'Riley and…"

Aston stared at the man giving him the novel-length version of his life. She'd never mentioned an O'Riley, Father, or Counselor, yet clearly, this blabbering man knew her well enough to know her secret. Aston shook his head and interrupted. "I'm here because Sapphire is missing."

O'Riley gave him an astute smile. "You know, she goes off on her little adventures, and comes back when she's done. She always does. That's what she's like."

Aston laughed. This old dude seemed to think he knew Sapphire better than he did.

"I *know* what she's like," Aston said slowly. "This is different. It's been days since I've heard from her and as opposed to you, her twice-a-month check in, she wouldn't leave without telling me."

O'Riley nodded, letting it sink in. He got up and walked over to the window. "I last saw her on Friday."

"About what?"

O'Riley turned and leaned against the windowsill. "A new fellow she was chasing."

Aston exhaled. It was confirmed. She *was* back to her old habits. He felt a tug at his stomach, but he ignored it. "What did she know about him?"

"I don't know the details. I usually only half listen. Can't understand what she's talking about most of the time. But…" O'Riley closed his eyes, trying to remember. "I do recall her saying she was going somewhere in L.A."

"So you've narrowed it down to *all* of Los Angeles. Good job, O'Tool."

"O'Riley."

"Whatever. She didn't mention any names, any people?"

"No," O'Riley said. "Wait, yes. She mentioned that somebody was helping her. Seemed quite excited about it."

This was good. Aston took one of O'Riley's business cards and plugged the number into his phone, then scribbled his own on the back of the card. "No name?"

"No."

Aston slid over the card with his number and got up. "Call me if you remember anything else."

O'Riley looked at the card and Aston turned toward the door. "You know, I told her to talk to you. That honesty is a vital part of marriage. Interesting story: when my wife and I first met—"

Aston shut the door behind him and moved toward the parking lot. *A helper.* He reached for the Nicorette, just to remember he was still out. He headed for his car, trying to suffocate the shitty feeling in his stomach and focus on what he had. "The helper" was the answer. This person seemed to be the only one who knew what the hell Sapphire had been up to. He clicked on his phone to look at the next address on the map. Perhaps, this would lead him there.

He'd just turned the ignition when his phone rang. It was Barry.

"Aston," his partner peeped with urgency. "You need to come to the station right now."

• • •

Old fart.

He tossed the pharmacy bag in the passenger seat and headed toward town. He should show his face today. Not that he had to. The benefit of being the man in charge was that nobody questioned him. He could come and go as he pleased, something that had come in handy more than once with his trips and attempts.

Old Fart. He was only forty, not even ten years her senior. Or was he? He'd been certain she was thirty when he took her, but the way she'd looked last night—no wig, no contacts, makeup rubbed out—she'd seemed so much younger. Perhaps as young as twenty.

He glanced at the pharmacy bag and exhaled. Age he could do nothing about, but this—his new plan—had to work. He owed it to Alma and he refused to disappoint her again.

Last night may as well have been the apocalypse. He'd cleaned up after the failed dinner in a trance-like state, then gone upstairs and fallen straight to sleep, clothes still on, emotionally exhausted and distraught. When he woke up this morning, she was standing by the window, gazing out.

"I'm sorry, honey. I'm really sorry."

Alma didn't reply. Her arms remained crossed and her mouth was a thin line.

"I didn't know she'd done this," Mer tried, close to tears

as he got up. "Please don't be angry with me. There's nothing I can do."

He'd tried to come up with plan. He wondered if he could just get rid of her and get a new one? He'd only ever killed the women *after* a failed attempt before—couldn't very well let them go and have them tell the whole world about him—but what choice did he have? The problem was the timeframe. He was only days away from the blood moon and it didn't seem possible. He wished he could just use the woman he had and transform her in some way...

His head perked. "Maybe I could..."

Alma's angry gaze didn't waver so he clasped his hands and stepped in front of her view.

"Yes. I will make it work! Only the heart of a soul willing to sacrifice himself, can harbor the soul of the buried in the blaze of the true moon and before the eyes of six. I have a plan and I *will* get it right this time."

Alma turned her pale face away from him and stared at the wall. She didn't believe him. She never did. No matter how hard he tried.

He held his hand up, just an inch away from her white cheek, wanting to touch her. Of course, he couldn't.

He pulled his hand back, and his eyes drew down. Her red wound was a stark contrast to her pale skin that had been tainted by death's kiss. Her blood was still as fresh as the day she died, but the rest of her was not. Her eyes, hauntingly furious, lay deep in their sockets, and her mouth was gnarly and cracked, as if life had literally been sucked out of her.

"I love you. And I will get you your body," he'd whispered, then left to go to the pharmacy and do exactly what he'd promised his wife.

He'd gotten almost everything he needed. Since her body seemed to resist the chloroform, he'd gotten something else to keep her docile. And, realizing that an actual dye process would be difficult, even with the medication he was going to give her, he bought a jar of ink instead. Once Alma took over the woman's body, they could work on coloring the hair more permanently.

Mer pulled up outside of work. He really needed to go in, catch up on some paperwork, but…something didn't feel right and his subconscious was running overtime.

About to override it as paranoia and put the gear in park, Mer froze.

He hadn't noticed it last night, but now that he thought back, he saw it. It had been on the table during dinner. When he'd gathered everything to do dishes, it was no longer there.

The pot roast fork.

Mer reversed and raced back home.

• • •

The lock popped.

Sapphire exhaled and stood, letting the chains fall off her.

She held the pot roast fork firmly, eyes aimed on the staircase.

It had taken her all night to bend the fork just right and to tease the lock open. She could see daylight break through the tiny cracks in the plywood, blocking the rectangular basement windows.

She'd heard what she assumed was the front door close about twenty minutes ago, so she hoped he was out. Nonetheless, she'd take him down with the fork if she had to.

She worked her way up the staircase, letting her feet regain circulation. She pulled out the bobby pins still in her hair and assessed the door. The four locks were basic, easy work.

When the last lock clicked, Sapphire could feel freedom within her reach. Her plan was easy. Get out of this godforsaken house. Then borrow someone's cell to call Aston, so he could come get her.

She pushed the door open and held her fork up, as if she were wading through water with a spear, ready to impale a fish.

The house was dark. All curtains were drawn, and all blinds were shut. She hurried over to the front door and undid the lock, ready to charge for freedom.

She pulled the door handle, but it didn't budge. She yanked harder, but nothing.

"Shit," Sapphire mumbled. He'd deadbolted *the outside*.

She ran over to the window and pulled on the blinds. The windows were barred with such fine margin she could neither smash the glass nor see outside. Sapphire inhaled, calming herself, then noticed the black cord running from a phone jack.

Aston.

She followed the cord up the narrow staircase and into a hallway. She looked inside a room, clearly belonging to the little girl. There were roses everywhere—wallpaper, ornaments, lamp shades. Above the red bed was a framed embroidered cloth with the words: *My Rose.*

It was empty; the little girl must be in school. If Mer only went to drop his daughter off, he could be back any minute.

Sapphire moved on, following the cord toward a study, right next to an even narrower staircase leading upward. That attic door had a deadbolt on the outside as well.

She ignored the chilling sensation the attic gave her, and stepped inside the darkened office. Thick curtains were drawn shut over the windows. Everything in the room, the bookcases, the chairs, the paintings on the walls, was caked in dust. Everything except the desk, its chair and the…phone?

"Oh." Sapphire stared down at the device and poked it. The chubby phone with its rotary dial, perhaps once white, was an off-yellow. She'd never seen one in real life. This place was like the house that time forgot and it was creeping her out.

Sapphire grimaced at the old phone, then picked up the receiver. She put her finger in the hole and pulled at the one before she could start putting in his number.

Once the one reached the end, it made its way back with painful leisure.

"Oh, come on!" Sapphire yelled at the lazy number, then eyed the door, watching for Mer. Every time she spun a new number, the ancient device seemed to slow down further. Finally, she finished and waited as she stared at a calendar in front of her.

It rang, and rang, and rang…

• • •

Barry sat at his desk, biting his nails as he stared at the big clock above the entrance of the bullpen.

He had to get to Aston the moment he walked in, before Chief Calloway did.

Their new boss wasn't actually that bad. He was friendly and fair with everyone except Aston, and knew how to rotate assignments. If they could only get along, Barry was convinced his partner and his new chief of police could bring the BHPD to new levels.

"Are you going to release me or what?"

Barry took his eyes off the elevator to look at the formerly drunken Rudolph, who was going through the final paperwork.

Ding.

The elevator doors opened and Aston stepped in. His eyes moved over the glass wall in search of Barry. Aston thought he was here because Barry had information about Sapphire. He didn't.

Barry shot out of his desk and took long steps across the bullpen, toward Aston. He, unfortunately, wasn't the only one who'd kept an ear on the elevator's ding.

Chief Calloway was taller, his legs longer, and he strolled toward Aston at an alarming speed.

"Detective!" Calloway cut Barry off and stopped Aston. "Where have you been?"

"Excuse me?" Aston asked, then glanced at Barry, standing behind Calloway.

Family. Family. Barry mouthed, hugging himself, the way a family would hug you.

"I assume your wife returned since you never filed a report," Calloway continued. "So, what is your excuse for your absence?"

"Ah." Aston squinted at Barry's motion. "Hugging? Cold? Cold! Yes, sick."

Barry shook his head, but it was too late.

"You never called in sick. You simply didn't show up for work. Would your old chief have tolerated this behavior?"

"Frankly?" Aston said. "Yes."

"Well, I have zero tolerance for a no-call, no-show." The chief held his thumb and index finger up. "I was this close to suspending you, until Officer Harry told me you'd had a family crisis and that you'd be back today. But *you* just told me you were sick, so which is it?"

Aston sent Barry a glare, then looked back at the chief. "Didn't say *I* was sick. My family was sick. Hence the crisis."

"Your *whole* family was sick?"

"No," Aston said. "My dad. The light's on but nobody's home." He rolled his finger over his temple. "If you know what I mean."

"Your father is mentally ill?" The chief asked with apprehension.

Aston picked up his phone to dial and put it on speaker.

"Joe Ridder here," a whiskey-and-cigarettes voice said.

"Hey pops, it's me," Aston said, eyes on the chief.

"Oh, good," Joe Ridder said. "Maybe you can get me Hoover on the line."

"The vacuum company?" Aston asked.

"The vacuum...what the fuck is wrong with you? The *president* of the United States, you moron."

"Ah," Aston said and hung up.

Barry stared at his partner. His own father would never talk to him that way. He couldn't imagine what Aston's childhood was like.

"Alright, I'll let it slide," Calloway said. "But one more incident from you, Detective Ridder, and I *will* suspend you."

Aston's narrowed eyes followed Calloway as he marched off, before he, himself turned and headed for his office.

"Why didn't you tell me it wasn't about Sapphire?" Aston roared over his shoulder. "Any idea how much time I've wasted now?"

Barry hurried after him. "Had I told you why you needed to come in, you wouldn't have come and you would've gotten suspended."

Aston turned into his office. "My wife is missing, Barry, *missing*. I have more important things to do." He held his phone up. "*And* I just missed two unknown calls while dickface was blabbing. It could've been information." His hands shuffled through the paperwork on his desk. "I need the folders of all young females between 18-30 who've gone missing in L.A. County. I know, I know, there's a million of them, but who knows, right?"

Aston's office phone rang as Barry leaned against the doorframe. "But the chief said…"

"I don't give a shit what the chief said."

Ring. Ring.

Aston pressed the speaker button, hand still searching for the paperwork. "What?"

Silence, then: "Aston?"

Barry knew the voice. Aston closed his eyes, and exhaled as if he'd been holding his breath for days.

"Saph." Aston grabbed his hair. "Thank God. Are you okay?"

Barry stood frozen, as if moving would cause her voice to disappear.

"I'm okay," Sapphire hurried. "This guy locked me up in his house. He's killed before. At least two victims. I'm loose now, but the downstairs windows are barred and the door's locked. I'm upstairs in some office, but I can't get out."

"Do you see an address anywhere?"

"No," Sapphire replied. "But there's a calendar on the wall and December 23rd is circled. If it's about me, I don't think it's because he's planning to throw me a surprise party."

"Are there any windows upstairs?" Aston asked. "See if you can see any buildings and I'll find you. I know L.A. like the back of my hand."

"Hold on." The crackle of a cord followed; it sounded like she was dragging along an old school phone carrier. The swoosh of curtains, then nothing. Barry and Aston stared at the phone.

"What?" Aston held his hands out. "*What?*"

"I…" her voice trembled. "I'm not in L.A."

"Where then? O.C.? Ventura? Where?"

"I'm not in California," she panted. "There's snow everywhere. There's a chain of mountains around a forest. There's a huge cedar tree outside, and…" she paused and screamed. "Oh my God, he's—"

Click.

"No." Aston stared at the office phone, reverting to dial tone. "NO!"

Sapphire's last words, last scream, lingered in the room, and they were both thinking the same things. She could be anywhere in the states and worse, the man could've just killed her.

Barry suddenly noticed the dark circles under Aston's eyes. His hair was a mess, and his unshaven face made him look forty instead of thirty. His eyes flew to Barry, and there was an ocean of pain in them. He slowly pushed a button and the dial tone ceased.

Aston cleared his throat then pressed the intercom and spoke slowly. "Hernando, see if you can track the number that just came into my office."

"Got it," Hernando replied.

"Worth a shot," Barry agreed, keeping his eyes on his partner as he moved toward the door. "Are you okay? It must've been really hard to hear—"

Aston put a hand up to stop him. "I'm fine."

They moved through the bullpen, toward Hernando's desk, and passed Rudolph, who glared at Aston.

"If it isn't Officer Jackass and his girlfriend, Peggy Sue," Rudolph hollered.

Barry didn't have to ask if he was Peggy Sue. For some reason, Barry was always the girl.

Aston ignored him, putting his palms on Hernando's desk. "Anything?"

Hernando eyed his computer and shook his head. "Blocked. Sorry."

Aston closed his eyes.

"What, are you crying now?" Rudolph yelled. "Huh? You fucking wuss!"

Aston turned toward Rudolph.

Barry reached for him, but was too late. Aston ripped Rudolph out of his chair and threw him against the glass wall. He grabbed him by his long, red nose and tore the mask off, then slammed his face into the bulletproof glass, again and again until the glass was covered in blood.

Barry yelled as the rest of the bullpen rushed toward the brawl.

Aston pulled Rudolph down and punched him in the face. Blood sprayed Aston's face, but he kept going, kept beating.

"Ridder! Detective!" their co-workers screamed, trying to pull him off.

"Okay! Okay!" Aston held his hands up, taking deep breaths, still on top of the unconscious reindeer.

"Congratulations."

Barry and Aston simultaneously turned to the voice.

Calloway stood over them, his concerned eyes on the bloody Rudolph.

"Please, turn in your badge and weapon before you leave. You just bought yourself one week of unpaid suspension while the investigation of this incident is pending." He looked around the room, and his gaze stopped on Barry. "If I catch *anyone* in here aiding Detective Ridder in any way, you'll have to deal with the consequences."

He walked back into his office and closed the door.

Someone pulled Rudolph away from Aston, who stood slowly, eyes hazed with shock. The other officers and detectives withdrew from him, as if he was a leper and his touch contagious.

With swollen knuckles and a blood-covered face, Aston looked over at Barry. Perhaps because he was the only one left. Perhaps because he needed someone's actions to say *I'm still behind you.*

But for the first time since they met, Barry couldn't meet his partner's eyes.

CHAPTER 8

Sapphire touched her bleeding forehead, and looked up at Mer from the floor.

He stood tall, staring down at her with the lamp he'd hit her with in one hand, and a pharmacy bag in the other.

Her eyes drew to the phone. Before he smacked her in the head, he'd ripped the phone cord out of the phone so hard, the wires split. *Crap.* She glanced at the pot roast fork on the desk, then looked back at Mer and the uneven bulge by his left pocket. The man either had a johnson that belonged in the Guinness World Records, or that's where he kept his keys.

A plan began to shape in Sapphire's mind. Her head hurt, she felt off-center, but she could easily take him down and pull this off.

"Who did you call," Mer asked, "and what did you tell them?"

Sapphire grabbed the windowsill and pulled herself up. "My husband. Everything. And, not to plagiarize, but he *does* have a certain set of skills and he *will* find me."

Mer stared at her.

"Judging by your empty gaze and creepy house, I have a feeling the last thing you saw Liam Neeson in was *Schindler's List*." No response. "Point is, he's a cop and he's on his way here, so you might wanna let me go. He's the jealous type."

For a second, there was panic in Mer's eyes, then they narrowed. "Then tell me, where are we?"

Sapphire glanced out the window. "Canada…eh?"

"Wrong."

Damn.

Mer shook his head as he emptied the pharmacy bag on the desk. Sapphire took in the items, especially the syringe and bottle. "So you think you can turn me into Alma with some contacts, a haircut, and...*ink,* really? What, no good deals on Schwarzkopf?"

Mer glared at her as he filled the syringe with the small bottle's liquid.

How cute. He thought he'd get her to hold still while he injected her with a drug that was probably meant to make her docile so he could give her Mer's Discounted Makeover Special. Well, he had another thing coming. Sapphire cracked her neck, then brought her fists up and put her feet in defense position.

He raised the syringe. "I don't like to hurt women, but I will when I have to."

He came at her and Sapphire gave a spinning crescent kick straight to his head. She leaped past him as he stumbled to the ground and grabbed the pot roast fork from the desk. Mer got up and touched his bleeding lip, looking staggered.

Sapphire emulated his demeaning tone. "I don't like to hurt men, but I will when I have to." She corrected her position to en garde in annoyance. "Just FYI, this woman took four years of fencing, five years of gymnastics, and three years of MMA."

Mer attacked again and Sapphire sneered. She sprung up to the desk and jumped back down, fork out. Before she connected to Mer, he moved as he grabbed a hold of her arm, then slammed her down on the floor, sending the fork sliding.

"I may be a bit rusty," Mer hissed as he put her arm and neck in a lock, "but I did four years of wrestling and two turns in the army."

Sapphire groaned and clawed at his face with her free hand. His move had caught her off guard. He wasn't in bad shape so she'd expected some strength, but not skill. He brought the syringe toward her neck. She felt the prick just as she moved her hand from his face to search behind her.

Her fingers slid over the desk's wood until they connected to the phone carrier. Sapphire latched onto it and slammed it into Mer's head.

The phone *dinged* as it connected.

His grip loosened and Sapphire shot up, ripping the syringe out of her neck. She hadn't gotten the whole thing, but the amount that made it into her bloodstream had an immediate effect.

Sapphire stumbled toward the swaying door, hearing Mer scramble up behind her. Her muscles were weak, her vision was jacked up, and her equilibrium was off. She staggered through the hallway, grabbing anything in her path and throwing it back at Mer, coming after her.

The headbang must've gotten him off balance, too, because he stumbled after her, holding his palm to his bleeding head.

Sapphire nearly tumbled down the stairs as she clutched the railing.

"Stop!" Mer yelled behind her.

Sapphire launched for the front door. Mer was inside, so it couldn't be dead bolted. From behind, Mer grabbed her by the hair and yanked her back. He threw her to the floor, and Sapphire crab-crawled backward, the open basement door gaping like a hungry mouth behind her. Mer moved toward her slowly, eyes burning with rage.

"I'm tired of you," he growled. "Of your lack of compliance. Of your every effort to ruin the thing that is most important to me!"

"Well, you know what..." Sapphire stopped her crawl. "I'm not too fond of you either."

She sent a kick to his crotch. Not very creative, but always a fan favorite.

Mer toppled forward and Sapphire grabbed a hold of his pants pockets, then shot a foot to his stomach and used her last bit of strength to pull him over her head. He dove through the open basement door, and plummeted down the stairs.

Sapphire pulled herself up by the doorframe, and squinted down as he lay on the floor, palm still pushed to his head. He looked up, seeming disoriented and like he was about to pass out.

Sapphire smiled and held up the keys she'd snatched.

Mer's face dropped and his hand went to his empty pocket.

"No!" he shouted just as she slammed the door shut.

• • •

Aston yanked on the door to the Dubois mansion. Locked.

He repeatedly rang the doorbell, but no Lurch came to his rescue.

"Fuck!" Aston leaned against the door. His body felt as heavy as his heart. He had no idea where to go from here and he was running out of time to find her.

Everything got worse after he turned in his gun and badge, the items that could've gotten him in anywhere to question anyone.

He'd gone to the second address on Sapphire's GPS map. The moment he stepped out of the car, he knew who she'd gone to see. This had to be the helper; it wasn't a coincidence.

The institution before him held Shelly McCormick. As far as he knew, Sapphire hadn't seen her since that day in court when Shelly took the fall, the whole fall, and nothing but the fall.

He walked in, relieved to see it was visiting hours. With his badge, he could've seen her anyway. Without it, Aston could demand nothing.

Shelly McCormick came out, looking stunned. Of course she was. The few times she'd seen him was either right after she was rescued from Vincent Parlov, or during the debacle with her split personality after being captured by Sapphire's father.

"Detective Ridder," she said and sat. "Hi."

"How are you?" Aston asked. Though her other personality was a psychotic bitch, he often found himself pitying Shelly McCormick. She'd had her whole future ahead of her, then she was taken by Vincent Parlov and was tortured in a basement for days. Now, here she was.

"Nothing much." Shelly shrugged. "That girl over there, with the big ears, is trying to kill me because she thinks I punched her for eating all the Tootsie Rolls."

"Did you?"

"Me? No. She's crazy; I hate Tootsie Rolls. Anyway, something tells me this isn't a social call."

"No," he admitted, and breathed out the next words. "Sapphire's missing."

Shelly eyes went wide with worry. Aston hoped it meant she knew something; he needed every clue he could get his hands on. He'd stayed up all night, studying maps of the obvious states—Colorado, Utah, Alaska—but mountain chain, snow, and big cedar tree was vague as fuck, and he had no coffee to help him focus. Elephant shit was where he drew the line.

"I know she was here," Aston continued. "Why?"

"Which time?"

"*Which* time?" Aston felt the same gut-stab he'd felt at O'Riley's office.

"How often does she come?"

"Once, twice a month. Sometimes to talk about me, sometimes about her." She lowered her voice, eyeing the security guard by them. "Sometimes we talk about our common interests."

The guard must've noticed the whispering, because she stepped closer to them.

"You know, our love for, uh…" Shelly's brows twitched twice, "*donuts*."

"And what did Sapphire have to say about…donuts."

"She had a new donut. Wasn't sure if she should," she eyed the guard, "eat it or not."

The guard looked from Shelly to Aston, then gave a kill-me-now eye roll and moved on.

Aston pulled out the pen and paper he hid during the security pat-down. "Tell me everything she told you about the case. In detail."

"She was going to a club. She thought the guy might've worked there. Two women, with the same description, went missing from there."

"Names?"

"Didn't say."

"Club?"

Shelly shook her head. "Maybe O'Riley knows. Did you talk to him?"

"No, he doesn't..." Aston stopped. "She told *you* about O'Riley?"

Shelly shrugged and nodded.

Aston leaned back in his seat, perplexed. "If that's all you know, what exactly were you helping her with?"

Shelly's mystified expression mirrored his, then she realized it. "Oh! You think *I'm* the one helping her? No. And I don't know who is. Just that the person could get her full access to the club."

"Oh shit," Aston said. Who did Sapphire know with that type of influence? "Chrissy!"

She was the only one who hadn't called him back. He hadn't worried about it because he figured Chrissy, like in all aspects of life, knew nothing about this.

Shelly closed her eyes, then let out a chilling, full-hearted laugh.

Aston gave her an askance glance. "Okay, calm down, tiger."

"But it's so sad, it's hilarious," Shelly smirked and leaned back. "You, the husband, have to come to someone like me, to learn about your own wife."

Aston's jaw tightened at her darkened eyes; she'd flipped personalities.

"I've heard every word Sapphire has said to Shelly, and guess what?" She leered. "There's only one thing on that girl's mind, and it's not you, my friend. She has to do this, it's in her blood. Nobody knows that better than I do. I'm sorry to be the one to tell you, but if it's between you and them, she won't choose you in the end."

After the initial slap-in-the-face feeling, anger washed over Aston. "And what do you know? You're not even a person. You're an echo of someone else's misery."

"Aw. Did I hurt someone's feelings?" She fake-pouted. "Be glad someone is telling you the truth." She reached over and snagged his pen. "Sorry, I gotta go kill a bitch."

Aston didn't have time to react before Shelly's alternate personality flew across the room and stabbed the big-eared girl in the arm with his pen, screaming: "That's what you get for hogging the Tootsie Rolls!"

Oops.

Visitors screamed while guards and nurses came running, and Aston slowly backed out of there.

He should feel great. This was the break he'd been waiting for, but the psychotic woman's words tortured him as he drove back to Beverly Hills. They were similar to the words Sapphire's father, William Dubois used: "*She will never be yours. She will always hunt.*"

They were wrong. She'd married *Aston*. Marrying someone *was* choosing. This, what had happened, was a one-time thing. A mistake.

Aston tried Chrissy again and again, but only got voicemail. He drove over to the Kraft Manor, but they wouldn't let him through the giant gates without a badge. Their housekeeper told him over the intercom that Ms. Kraft was away, but didn't know where. He went everywhere. The country club. The salon she always dragged Sapphire to. John Vanderpilt, but he and Chrissy were off again. The more people he asked, the less he knew. Had Chrissy been kidnapped too?

Aston stopped at the convenience store, then drove to the Dubois mansion to find himself locked out with nowhere else to go. He let his back slide down the door.

The only person who had information about Sapphire was nowhere to be found. December 23rd was less than seventy-two hours away. What if he didn't get to her in time? He involuntarily imagined her face, pale. Her eyes, hollow. Her body, lifeless. The vision sliced through his insides like knives and he felt sick.

He pulled out the pack he'd bought at the convenience store and lit his first cigarette in months.

He knew he shouldn't have allowed himself to feel happy. He knew it would be taken away from him. To be unhappy was easier, because what could you steal from a person who cared about nothing? He closed his eyes as he exhaled the cloud of gray smoke and felt the poison do its trick to his brain.

When he opened them, Mrs. Dubois's black town car pulled into the driveway, and she jumped out with Lurch in tow.

"Oh, darling," she said, seeing Aston on the ground. "I thought you had Sapphire's keys."

Nope. Sapphire's keys were in her purse. Her purse was gone, along with Sapphire.

"Radison," Vivienne gushed, "we'll have to make a copy for Aston."

Lurch pulled his head out from behind the open trunk. "Yes, Mrs. Dubois."

She turned to Aston with a low tone. "I tried dropping my kimono, and he just stood there, looking at me. Then he picked the kimono up and *washed it*. I mean, is there a reason he doesn't want to touch me?"

Aston could think of a handful.

"Oh!" Vivienne snapped her fingers as she waited for Lurch, holding a hundred bags, to open the door. "You know who has a spare key you can take until I get one made. Chrissy."

He laughed sardonically. "Nobody has any idea where Chrissy is."

"Oh, I see. Makes sense."

Aston stared at her. All that Botox must've leaked into her brain. "What?"

"If nobody has any idea where someone in Beverly Hills is…it means they're at Richmond Hills," Vivienne said, stepping through the door. "I guess she decided to join Sapphire."

Aston stood frozen in the doorway.

"Well come on, darling," Vivienne gestured, "you're letting the chill in."

He turned right back around and headed for his car.

• • •

She leaned against the wall, determined to keep her eyes opened. She'd had that strange dream again:

Crack.

Crack.

Cold. The chill had jolted her out of the dream, so she'd decided to stay awake and be ready. The woman from downstairs, with the long hair and the defiant eyes, would come soon. Any time now, that door to Ghost's prison would open and she'd be saved. And she, in turn, would do everything to keep the woman out of that coffin. Ghost refused to let anything happen to her.

She felt nervous and exhilarated at the thought of finally escaping the house of horrors. She was so excited that she dared to wish about silly things. Like, maybe Christmas hadn't passed yet. Maybe Santa would find her again. Or maybe…her mommy was right.

Her mind wandered back. Not to the Christmas when she was happy, but to the one after it.

Ghost had woken up on her own while it was still dark outside. She threw on her robe and slippers and ran into the living room. There were twenty-six rat traps on the floor so Ghost was careful to walk around them. She'd stepped on one a few days earlier and her toe still throbbed. There was no Christmas tree this time, and no Mommy in sight, but Ghost sat down by the windowsill, and waited and waited.

It wasn't snowing this Christmas. It was raining and the sky was gray with sadness.

"What are you doing?"

Ghost turned to her mommy who stood under the arch. Her hair was wild and her eyes glossed.

"Waiting for Santa," Ghost whispered.

"You don't have to whisper, he's not here." Her mommy shuffled through the living room, shoving the rat traps away with her feet. "And Santa's not coming."

The disappointment pulled at Ghost's mouth. "W…why?"

"He's forgotten you exist; you're as much of a ghost to him as you are to everyone else. You're lucky *I* can see you."

Tears burned Ghost's eye, but she forced them back and followed her mommy into the kitchen. She held her breath, watching her mommy grab two bowls that she filled with cereal and milk. Ghost exhaled in relief, but then her mommy reached for the second box and sprinkled its contents over Ghost's bowl before slamming it down on the table.

"Eat."

Ghost stared down at the cereal and thumb-tacks swimming in the milk. Thumb-tacks were sharp, Ghost knew this, so she was careful to eat around them.

The cereal turned into kibble, and the bowl into a dog dish, but Ghost still stared. The memory was sad, but sometimes she had to remember even the sad ones, or she wouldn't have many memories at all.

The front door slammed downstairs and Ghost sat up straight. *Did he leave?*

He never left at this time of the day.

She dragged her sore foot and its chain across the floor toward the plywood. She put her eye to the crack and pressed her hands to the wood. His truck was still there.

Then she saw her. The woman stumbled away in the deep snow, her body veering left and right.

No! She'd forgotten Ghost!

"Wait!" Ghost banged her palms to the wood, utter panic grabbing her. "I'm up here! Come back!"

But the woman couldn't hear her, and she didn't come back. She sprinted away from the house as fast as she could.

"Please!" Tears poured out of Ghost as she watched her leave.

It must've been an almost dream, just like the almost dream she had right after her mother died. Ghost dreamt that a tall, bald man, Social Services she'd thought, stood outside of a house, her new home with beautiful white flowers growing beside the door. They were called Christmas roses. Ghost knew this because Susie, her mommy's friend, was a florist and told Ghost all about flowers so strong, they could grow in the winter.

But the tall bald man never showed up. Instead, a Social Services woman came. She didn't bring Ghost to the house with the Christmas roses, but to an apartment where a lady named Faith had seven other foster children and mattresses that smelled. Faith liked to drink, and the other children liked to steal. Like Lila, who stole Ghost's Belle doll then took it with her to Wisconsin where her new family lived.

One day, the city held a meet and greet, and Ghost was invited. She met a nice man named Thomas, who said that his wife would love Ghost. When the event was over, the city sent Ghost back to Faith with a nectarine and a *Princess and the Frog* t-shirt. Two days later, she was walking home from school, when a truck pulled up behind her and a smelly rag was placed over Ghost's face.

Then she woke up here, in this attic, and Thomas's name wasn't really Thomas, but Mer.

Ghost wasn't good with time, but she knew she'd been in the attic for many winters now. And, watching the woman run away, she realized she'd be here for many winters more.

"Please," Ghost whispered, tears trickling down her cheeks. "Please come back."

But the long dark hair vanished into the trees of his vast land, and didn't reappear.

Ghost slid down the wall, then fell to her knees and cried. Without the woman, she was never getting out of the house of horrors. She saw no hope now. The tall, bald Social Service man never came, and the home with the white Christmas roses was gone. The woman with the brave eyes was gone.

And Ghost was still here, forever.

Unless…

She pulled on the chain, then lifted the dog bowl and grabbed the bottle of pills she'd stolen from the bathroom. Ghost knew about pills, because sometimes her mom would take them when she said she wanted to sleep forever. She was always angry when the paramedics woke her.

That's what Ghost wanted now, too…to sleep forever. She didn't want to be awake for any more winters.

Tears ran down her cheeks as she poured the pills into her hand.

• • •

I got out. I'm free. Sapphire repeated the mantra as she ran with dazed eyes and a fumbling body.

Whatever Mer had given her screwed with her whole system. She couldn't see, run, or aim properly anymore.

She stopped about a thousand yards away from the house and leaned against the giant cedar to catch her breath.

The snow-covered ground swayed before her and the sky gyrated. Sapphire pushed her back against the tree, trying to make the world stop spinning.

She took a deep breath and pushed forward. She had no choice. If Mer somehow got out of the basement, she'd lose if she fought him like this—all feeble.

She jogged in arches, feeling like her muscles had taken a vacation, leaving only soft limbs and flesh behind. A gate appeared in front of her. She stumbled forward, and grabbed onto the rods. It swung and Sapphire fell to her knees.

A massive cemetery stretched out before her.

Plot after plot, stone after stone, lined in perfect symmetry toward a mausoleum. Sapphire slowly moved through the pathway. Alma May 2016. Alma August 2016. Alma June 2015. Alma September 2015. Alma January 2014. Alma December 2013.

"Oh my God." The horrible realization hit Sapphire in the chest. She stared at the plots as she kept going. 2010. 2009. 2008.

Already dizzy, Sapphire kneeled in the snow as the never-ending lines of graves danced around her. This man, she realized, wasn't the strangest serial killer she'd ever faced. He was the worst; he'd killed *hundreds*.

Sapphire pulled herself toward the mausoleum.

Her footsteps echoed between the stone floor and ceiling as she moved up toward a marble grave. The plaque was covered in dust and Sapphire brushed until she saw the name:

Alma. The real Alma?

Sapphire read the birth and death date. It didn't make sense. How could this woman have a child who was only seven, or eight years old, if she died in…

Her eyes latched to the second door at the end of the mausoleum. She pushed it open and stared at the other side of the cemetery. Thick bile rose in her throat as she stepped out onto the snow and stared at the plots.

Rosie–2008. Rosie–2011. Rosie–2014.

Sapphire took in the cold air so she wouldn't vomit. This man, Mer, had murdered children. There weren't as many Rosie graves as there were Alma graves—on average the child graves were about 3-4 years spread apart—but there were still many.

"Oh my God," Sapphire whispered.

Buuur! Buuur!

A semi horn blasted and Sapphire stumbled toward the edge of the cemetery. There was a nearly vacant road far below the hill. A trucker stood down there, speaking to a person on the shoulder. They exchanged something, she couldn't tell what.

"Hey!" She waved her arms, noticing, what looked like a cell in one man's hand. "Up here!"

No reaction. Her voice didn't carry.

They shook hands, then the trucker hurried back to his cab and the second guy headed for the woods.

She had to go now if she wanted to get to that phone and call Aston. Sapphire was just about to take off down the hill when her body stopped her.

A lot didn't sit right about what she'd seen, but in Sapphire's doped up mind, she was having trouble pinpointing the thing that really bothered her.

Her eyes strayed back to the Rosie graves.

Presumption: the girl had followed a script at dinner, just like Sapphire.

Fact: the girl wasn't Mer's daughter, she was just the new Rosie.

Presumption: the child wasn't at school. She was locked away somewhere inside, just like Sapphire had been, behind the attic door with a deadbolt.

Fact: the girl in the attic was in danger.

"Shit."

Still dizzy, Sapphire turned her back on the man with the cell, feeling a chill run through her. The house's darkness was daunting, and the last thing she wanted was to reenter it, especially while affected by drugs that rendered her body useless.

Sapphire pushed her way through the snow and back to the house.

The front door let out a longwinded creak when she shoved it open, and the hair on her neck stood. She stepped inside the darkened manor and eyed the basement door. Still locked.

She swallowed the nausea and pulled herself up the staircase with lethargic hands, keeping the basement door in her line of vision as long as she could.

She actually feared Mer, she realized. Perhaps because he'd already taken her down once, when she *wasn't* impaired. Perhaps because she'd never encountered a man cold enough to have killed children before.

By the time she conquered the two mountain-like staircases, she was covered in sweat and her legs shook from exhaustion. Sapphire clenched her teeth and glanced back down, afraid Mer would pop up behind her.

She pulled Mer's keys out and found a skeleton key that looked like it would fit.

Click. She pushed the door open.

"Oh my God," Sapphire whispered. Sadness and empathy burrowed in her stomach. This is how the child had lived, for God knew how long.

The little girl lay chained to the wall and curled in the fetal position, wearing outgrown clothes, covered in dirt and holes. Sapphire covered her mouth when she saw the kibble and water bowls, then the reeking bucket adjacent to the food.

The little girl lay still, her hair spread over her face, hugging something tightly to her chest. Sapphire walked up slowly, not to scare her, as she located the small key to the foot shackle. She unlocked it, but the girl still didn't move.

"Hey." Sapphire placed her hand on the girl's exposed arm.

Her skin was like ice, which should've been alarming but made sense. The attic was freezing, even colder than the basement had been.

"Wake up," Sapphire whispered and shook the girl's shoulder lightly. An open jar of pills tumbled out from the girl's clutch and fell to the floor.

Sapphire took in the label, then shook the girl harder. "No. Please tell me you didn't." She put her fingers to the small, cold neck, then waited a few seconds and turned her over. She shoved her fingers down the little girl's throat and patted her back.

"Come on…come on!"

No reaction. Just when Sapphire was about to pull back, the girl gagged. Thick white slime ejected from her mouth, and she coughed.

"Yes!" Sapphire rubbed the girl's back to help her get the last out, then turned her around.

Her little eyelids fluttered and opened weakly. She stared up at Sapphire in disbelief and her bottom lip shook as her eyes filled with tears. "You came back," she whispered.

Sapphire forced the pity out of her voice and tried to smile. "Come on. Let's get out of here."

The girl let out a sound so tragic Sapphire wasn't sure if it was relief, sadness, happiness, or everything at once.

"Hey," Sapphire said, holding onto her. "I'm Sapphire. What's your name? It isn't Rosie, right?"

She shook her head. "Ghost."

Sapphire raised a brow, then flinched at the sound of two gunshots.

CHAPTER 9

"So, this is the juice bar."

The lady glanced back at him as they passed a lounge full of half-sedated mummies, sipping drinks between their bandages. "I'm sorry, sir, but aren't you that husband…from the party at—"

"Yup." He scanned the lounge for a familiar face and shook his head. *Fucking October.*

"I see." Her smile didn't leave, but it turned rigid and disingenuous.

Aston didn't care, he was just happy he'd gotten this far. Though, Richmond Hills was a pretty uptight place for a recovery retreat whose slogan was: *Come. Relax.* There were restriction signs everywhere.

NO TALKING. NO MUSIC. NO PROCESSED FOOD. NO LEMURS.

No Lemurs?

"So." The lady waved Aston on with phony politeness. "How did you and Mrs., um…"

"Still Dubois. She kept her name."

"How did you and your wife meet?"

"At a summer resort," Aston fibbed. "She was there with her rich family and I was the dance instructor from the wrong side of the tracks."

"Oh, that sounds romantic!"

"Oh, yeah." Aston searched the grounds. "We had the time of our lives."

"So this is the yoga facility," the lady said, then put her

palms together and bowed to the class of half-sedated mummies attempting yoga. "What procedure did you say you'll be recouping from?"

"I didn't. I'm having my, um, balls…lifted." Aston looked at the time again.

"Oh. I had no idea that was a thing."

"Oh yeah. Ball-lifting. Huge in Europe. So, listen," he clapped his hands, "my wife is good friends with Christina Kraft, obviously. You don't happen to know where she's at right now, do you?"

"Even if I knew where Ms. Kraft was, it would be confidential, sir."

Damn it. When he asked for the complimentary tour, he'd expected to find Chrissy by now. Since all the patients were at Richmond Hills in confidentiality, this was his only way past security without his badge. Again, investigating as a civilian *sucked ass*. He had no idea how Sapphire, the Serial Catcher, had managed it for so long.

The lady motioned to a corridor lined with curtains. "So, this is the spa and beautification area. Clients spend about 80-90 percent of their time here, recouping and re-glamming. And down here we have our rec center…"

80-90 percent? Aston stopped as the lady moved passed the curtain-lined hall. *Good odds.*

"Christina Kraft!" He turned into the corridor and pulled at the first curtain.

A naked lady, with the body of a 102-year-old and the face of someone in permanent headwind, was mid-massage when she noticed Aston and winked. "Oh, come on in."

Aston moved on, feeling his penis retract into his body. "Christina Kraft! Are you in here?"

"Oh my God! Sir-sir-sir-sir!" the lady came chasing after him. "You can't be in here."

He pulled the next curtain. A semi-naked, seaweed-wrapped Arnold Schwarzenegger looked at Aston, and covered his nipples with his fingertips.

"Sorry, wrong room," Aston apologized, then chuckled and pulled out his best Austrian accent. "I won't be baa-ck."

Arnold stared at him.

"Get it?" Aston said. "Instead of I'll be ba—"

"Yeah, I *got* it."

Aston grinned and left, hearing the actor mumble: "Every fucking day."

"Sir-sir-sir." The lady had now added a continuous shoulder tap.

A distinct scream emerged from a curtain on his left, and after a moment of processing, Aston yanked it to the side.

There she was, Christina Kraft, laying with her feet in the air and a waxer between her legs.

"Oh my God!" Aston yelled. "What are you doing to yourself?!"

"I'm waxing!" Chrissy yelled from behind a mask, covering her nose and chin. "What the hell are you doing here?"

The male waxer turned in confusion, leaving all of Chrissy's cooch for public viewing.

"Gaaah!" Aston covered his eyes.

"Oh no!" Chrissy said to the waxer. "Please don't stop mid-wax. I'll never have the nerve to continue and I'll walk around with a half-baked va-jay-jay."

"Of course, Ms. Kraft."

Aston peered at her through his fingers, careful to block out the *thing*, which he unfortunately knew looked like the head of half Ben Kingsley, and half Sideshow Bob.

"I'm *so* sorry, Miss Kraft," the lady begged. "I'm calling security."

"It's important," Aston urged. "It's about Sapphire."

Chrissy gave him a once over, then sighed. "I'll allow it."

The annoying lady left as Aston fumbled until he found

a chair, then maneuvered it around to obstruct his view of Chrissy's half-stache. "She's missing."

The heiress's eyes grew. "Since whe-EEEEEN!"

Aston cringed at the sound of the strip ripping. "Four days now."

"*Four* days, and you're just now telling me?"

Aston held his cell up. "Well maybe check your fucking phone once in a while!"

"Hello." The waxer pointed to a sign. *NO CURSING.*

"Hello." Chrissy pointed to a different sign. *NO CELL PHONES.*

"Fine," Aston said. "It's just, I know you were helping her."

Chrissy pinched her mouth shut. "I pinky swore."

"*Pinky* swore. What are you, twelve? Pinky swore on what?"

"That I wouldn't tell yo-OOOOU!" Another strip went off.

Aston put his palms over his nose, then spoke through his teeth.

"If you don't tell me, I will—I swear to God, Chrissy—*murder* you."

The waxer gasped.

"Oh, please," Aston said. "Like the guy with the vagina in his face should be the one to judge."

"Fine." Chrissy sighed. "I called this club in West Hollywood, Club Scene…"

Aston rolled his eyes.

"…and told them I wanted to host a million-dollar party there. Then I gave them my secretary's e-mail, which was Sapphire's fake e-mail, and said I wanted her to have a meeting with them and make sure all their staff was up to par."

"Okay." Finally, a real lead. "Here's what's going to happen. You're going to take me to that club and tell me everything you know. And then—"

"Alright, Ms. Kraft," the waxer patted the plastic bed, "up on all fours."

"You know what!" Aston shot up, and re-covered his eyes. "I'll wait outside."

After spending a minute tangled in the curtain, Aston emerged, feeling hopeful for the first time since the night she vanished. He *would* find her. Soon, he would wake up next to his wife with that warm feeling in his chest again.

But for how long? A tiny voice whispered.

The hope was suddenly pulled down by something heavier, like the truth.

A truth Aston couldn't admit to.

• • •

The basement door hit the ground with a whack. Two blasts to the hinges with his old rifle was all it took.

After the door had been locked on him, Mer had fallen back and passed out from the blow to the head, maybe for a second, maybe longer. When he awoke, he realized he kept his old hunting and tranquilizer rifles in the basement safe. It had been so long since he last opened it, it took him ten minutes to remember the combination.

He'd hated pulling that trigger and the heavy feel of the weapon in his hand. Guns he was okay with, rifles he was not. There was a reason they came out of the safe with a thick layer of dust.

Mer burst up out of the basement, aim ready for her, but it was too late. The front door stood wide open. She was gone.

A nagging feeling pulled his gaze toward the staircase and he launched for the loft. He knew the moment he saw the open attic door. Rosie was gone too.

He couldn't remember what time he returned home in the first place, so he wasn't sure how long he'd been passed out, but there was a possibility they'd hitched a ride and were already halfway to the neighboring town right now.

He stood in the doorway, staring at the empty attic, feeling so tired, so hopeless.

It was December 21st. December 23rd would come and go, and he would miss the blood moon. Another blood moon wouldn't fall on the anniversary until long after he was dead and buried.

It was over. Everything Mer had worked for had crumbled, and there was no way of rebuilding it. A chill crept up his spine, and he felt the presence of another person in the attic. She was behind him.

"I'm sorry. I failed you…again."

He mustered up the courage to turn. Alma stood by the attic's door, staring at him in angry silence. Her eyes moved and he followed them.

Two handfuls of pills lay on the dusty floor beside his shoes. The girl must've gotten into the bathroom and found the pills he took when that terrible night came back so vividly and nothing but oblivion could save him. He picked them up and let them lay in his palm as he moved to his office.

He placed them on the desk and grabbed the stationery. Maybe he would take one now, and fall into oblivion for a while.

He eyed the pills. Or maybe…more than one.

Reverend Tom told him that the road of suicide wouldn't lead him to Alma, only down to fire and brimstone. But forgetting how many pills the bottle had directed could be an accident, couldn't it? If he squinted hard enough, the label's instructions were almost illegible.

He clasped the pills in one hand, and grabbed the stationery with his other. He'd take them and write a letter while they worked their way through his system. He wouldn't send this one, but he needed to write it. *One last letter.*

He took the pen, allowing the memories to flood his mind.

It was December 23rd.

They'd all had dinner, pot roast. He, Rosie, and Alma.

Then the song came on. The Christmas song his wife loved. Before the cobbler had turned lukewarm, he'd stood and said the words he'd regret forever. "I'm going to go see if I can get the bobcat that's been taking the hens."

"Why do we even have hens?" Rosie asked. "Farmers have hens. You're not a farmer."

"No, he's not." Alma sighed. "Please, Mer, not tonight. The hens are locked in, and *A Christmas Story* comes on at nine. You know how much she likes to watch it with us."

His daughter's eyes lit with excitement.

"I'll be back before the movie starts."

"But it's freezing out there," Alma tried.

"It's freezing in here," he muttered. The woman kept the house cold, no matter the season. Both she and Rosie ran hot.

Rosie's eyes were on her red, snowflake dress and his wife cut up the cobbler in anger, refusing to look at him. He left anyway. He took his rifle out of the basement safe he'd installed when Rosie was born, and went out into the night.

"At least bring your gloves!" Alma shouted behind him.

"I'm fine," he muttered, and closed the door.

He must've lost track of time while tracing the bobcat, because when he finally spotted the damned animal he was almost down by the town's lake and it was ten o'clock.

He raised his rifle, then put his ice-cold finger to the trigger and got it in his aim. He fired.

The bobcat took off, escaping the bullet.

"Damn it," he cussed, hurrying after it so he wouldn't lose its trail.

He saw it move behind the bush and fired again. A thunder of wings emerged as crows took flight, spooked by the shot. There was no more movement.

"Gotcha," he smiled.

He whistled and leaned his rifle against his shoulder as he moved to get the beast.

His feet stopped before his mind could comprehend why.

His black gloves lay on the ground, and her reaching hand lay next to them.

She must've come looking for him when he didn't come back in time. She was probably bringing him the gloves. She must've dropped them by the bush, and crouched down to get them.

Her blue eyes stared blankly into the distance. Her white jacket had a hole in the chest where the bullet had hit. Right in her beautiful heart.

He remembered screaming and crying as he tried to will his beloved back to life, but she stayed lifeless in his arms.

He carried her all the way home and stood in the doorway, dead wife in his arms. His daughter, who'd sat in her puffy chair still watching her movie, turned to him.

"Mommy had an accident," was all he could say.

People in town knew he'd never hurt his wife. There was no guilt or accusation put on him by them, only by himself. He locked up the rifles in the safe and never hunted again.

He and Rosie managed for a while. But *managing* was not living. Rosie grew harder and quieter. She spent a lot of time up in the attic, away from him. She couldn't look at him without something vile escaping her mouth. One night, on the first anniversary of Alma's death, she said something particularly vile and true, and he'd snapped. He slapped her across the face, and she ran. He knew she didn't run because of the slap, but because she blamed him. She hated him for taking her mother away from her.

He chased after her, pleading for her forgiveness, but lost her in the woods.

She was only nine years old.

The town formed a human chain and searched for three days, but never found Rosie or her body. They all told him to accept the fact that she'd probably fallen into the river, drowned, and been swept away. Mer knew this was likely, but a part of him always hoped it wasn't so.

He spent years turning to the religion he'd been raised in. He spoke to Jesus when his pain was bad. He prayed and prayed for his wife and child's return, but nobody listened.

"Jesus doesn't do that," Reverend Tom had said. "It's Christianity, not necromancy."

So, Mer found someone who *did* do that.

The dark powers were the only ones who could help him. Mer was still a Christian at heart, but his new lord gave him hope when his old one had not.

Until now.

He used his pen to locate the next name from the public listings. Rosie Bakers from Louisville, Kentucky was up.

Yes, his daughter was probably dead, but Mer liked to imagine that Rosie had managed to get to the neighboring town and snuck on a bus to somewhere far away. He imagined she'd changed her surname, and eventually met a man whom she married and had children with. He imagined her walking on a beach in sunny Miami or strolling the historic streets of Boston.

There were roughly 90,000 Rosies in the United States, and Mer had gotten the listings for as many as he could. Over the years, he'd gone down the names, sending letters and crossing them off, hoping one day, one of them would be the right Rosie. He wrote them all in different ways, but said the same things: *I love you…I'm sorry. Come home.*

Of course, he wasn't dumb. The likelihood of one of his letters getting to the right Rosie was impossibly slim. And the odds of a nine-year-old surviving nature's rough elements in the first place weren't good.

A few years after he started trying to bring back Alma, he'd realized she'd be furious with him if he brought her back to the world without a daughter. Alma was a mother, heart and soul, and he had to give her a child. Since the real Rosie was gone, he had to get a replica. One whose hair landed perfectly between his wife's jet black and his blond. Obviously, Alma would know it wasn't truly her child but if he could make the child copy Rosie, perhaps Alma would get used to the idea. And, the closer to Rosie the child was, the better the reenactment became.

The problem was, he couldn't keep the child past the age of eight when Alma had known her. And, just like the women, it wasn't like he could release them and have them tell the world about him. It wasn't easy. Mer had learned to stomach killing the women, but getting rid of the children when they turned too old was hard. He kept them in the attic and treated them like vermin so he wouldn't get attached. That way, if the day came and Alma was yet to return, his heart didn't completely break. He didn't have a choice after all, he *had to* do it.

The latest Rosie had been on her last stretch anyway. Had he chosen to continue trying, and had December 23rd not been successful, he would've killed her. Had it worked, Alma would've been pleased with the similarity. This Rosie looked and sounded so much like their daughter that, at times, Mer's heart couldn't stand her calling him *dad* even though he'd asked her to. He'd forced her to call him sir instead sometimes.

Mer's eyes drew to his beloved wife, now standing in front of his desk. She'd started appearing around the time he began reading about necromancy, as if she knew a new body was coming her way.

She stared at him in anger now, as always. Of course she was angry. Mer had ruined everything.

He shoved the pills into his mouth as he wrote the familiar words: *Dear Rosie…*

Just as he brought the water to his lips to help him swallow the tablets, there was movement in his peripheral. He looked out the window.

It had only been a bird, but it was what lay beyond the crow's black wings that interested him.

They ran haphazardly over the field in the far distance.

They must've escaped only moments before he got out of the basement.

He spat out the pills and hope filled him again.

No, he had not gone to the woods and tracked an animal since that terrible night. But today, once more, Mer would hunt.

• • •

"Hurry!" Sapphire led Ghost by the hand to the main road.

Her equilibrium was still out of whack, and she tried to squint to get her sights straight as they ran. Some of the pills had made it into Ghost's system which made her drowsy, so Sapphire had to drag her along.

"Do you know where we are?" Sapphire asked as they skidded down the snow-covered hill, avoiding trees and bushes.

The girl shook her head. They stepped onto the deserted road, snaking through the icy forest, looking left and right as they caught up on air.

"We have to find a phone so I can call my husband," Sapphire said. "He's a cop. He'll find us and everything's going to be okay, alright?"

The little girl nodded up at her with big eyes.

The robust sound of an engine came from over the hill.

"Car," Sapphire said, pulling Ghost toward it as the truck hit the top of the hill.

The girl's feet stopped dead on the asphalt. "Blue truck."

"I know." Sapphire waved at the truck with her free hand. "Hey!!"

"No," Ghost said with urgency. "Blue truck!"

Right as the truck increased its speed toward them, Sapphire realized what she meant. *Mer*. "Run!"

They stumbled into the forest. Sapphire shut and reopened her eyes to make the trees stop dancing in front of her. Her body was so weak that she could hardly keep the girl's hand clasped in hers.

They staggered through the woods, both running out of air. The more Sapphire struggled, the harder she tried to hold onto the girl's hand. The moment she stood in that cemetery, her own safety had taken a back seat. She couldn't allow this man to murder another child and add another stone to that sickening graveyard. The thought of how long he'd killed, and how many women and children had passed through that house and been forced to play his twisted game, made her ill.

They emerged out of the woods and onto a narrow dirt road. A beat-up Chevy was pulled over to the side.

"Come on!" Sapphire hurried over to the vehicle. Its truck bed was loaded with animal traps, dead rabbits tied together by their feet, and a baby deer.

Sapphire dragged her hand over the rusty truck until it connected to the door handle. She closed her eyes. "Please be a trusty moron. Please be a trusty moron."

She pulled on the handle. He *was* a trusty moron. The door opened as if with magic. Magic or, perhaps, the trusty moron had no reason to lock his truck. Wherever they were, it wasn't exactly crime-riddled L.A.

Sapphire lifted the girl in, then clambered inside. Ghost slid over to the passenger side and sat silently, hugging her body as Sapphire yanked on the clips and removed the plastic panel on the steering column.

"Look for something sharp, would you?" Sapphire asked, eyeing the bundled wires, trying to remember the how-to-hotwire YouTube video. *Ignition and battery*. She'd watched it years ago and, sadly, Sapphire recalled the funny cat video she'd watched afterward better. *Stupid, hilarious cat video.*

"Will this work?" Ghost asked, eyes ballooned with hope.

Sapphire looked at the single key, a spare, in the girl's hand and laughed. "Yes. Yes, it will."

She pushed the key into the ignition and the old truck rumbled to life.

They sped off and soon the dirt road connected to the main road. Not knowing which way led where, Sapphire flipped a coin in her mind and took a right.

"Make sure to read the signs, anything with a city or state on it. Oh, and check the glove box for anything with an address."

Ghost's eyes fell to her clasped hands. Sapphire studied her morose expression and realization hit her. Ghost had probably been in the attic for a while, long enough never to have gone to school. She didn't know how to read.

"Ghost, do you know how old you are?" Sapphire tried to keep her tone light, but the girl's poignant shrug was heartbreaking. "Okay. Do you know how old were you when he took you?"

"Five."

"Do you know how many times it's been winter since then?"

"Maybe...three?"

"Okay, good." Sapphire kept her eyes on the road, trying to swallow the vile emotions. The man had imprisoned this child and fed her dog kibble for *three years*. Three years missing. Three years of sickening worry for a set of parents somewhere out there—*if* Ghost even had parents.

"Do you have...a mom or a dad?" Sapphire shut one eye to try and keep the Chevy straight.

"Yes," the girl nodded.

A bridge suspended over a river came into view just as Sapphire's eyes moved to the rearview mirror. The blue truck was speeding toward them.

"Hold on," Sapphire said and floored the gas.

They flew down the hill, but his truck was newer and its engine bigger. He was on their tail within seconds. He pulled up beside them and stared at Sapphire as he slammed his truck into the Chevy.

Ghost screamed as the truck veered. Sapphire fought against the wheel, barely managing to keep it on the road. She tried to speed past him, but the pedal was already to the floor. Then, something must've happened, because his truck pulled back and she was able to get ahead.

"Come on," Sapphire encouraged the old truck between clenched teeth. "Faster."

They pulled onto the bridge as the blue truck tailed them.

Halfway across, Mer sped up. His truck slammed into theirs at an angle, and Sapphire lost control. The old truck crashed into the railing.

• • •

Sounds of screams and rushing water amplified, as if someone were gradually turning up the volume.

"Sapphire! Wake up!" a small voice yelled. "Sapphire!"

It didn't sound like Aston. And why would anyone else be in her bedroom, yelling at her to wake up? And why was the studio *so loud*?

"Please wake up!" the little voice was crying now, desperate. "He's coming!"

Sapphire cracked her heavy eyelids. Warm blood dripped down her forehead and onto the steering wheel in front of her.

She wasn't at home with Aston. She was in the driver's seat of a truck that was teetering over a rift, lined by a wild river. The little voice belonged to Ghost, who was clinging onto her seatbelt, the only thing keeping her from dropping through the crushed windshield.

Sapphire stared at the straight plummet outside the window, and the wild river they would crash into if the truck teetered anymore. The truck creaked louder every time it doddered forward.

Sapphire's eyes landed in the side view mirror and she saw him.

"No!" he yelled.

She didn't have time to react before the passenger door opened. He reached in and grabbed Ghost. She screamed, tears bursting out of her eyes as she reached for Sapphire.

Sapphire snapped out of her haze and launched for Ghost. She got her hand.

"Don't let go," the girl pleaded.

All the motion rocked the truck and broke the balance. The Chevy groaned with strain then rolled forward. Sapphire screamed as she lost her grip on the girl's hand. Mer yanked Ghost out, then reached for Sapphire.

The truck plummeted through the air. A gut-wrenching scream escaped Sapphire's throat as her hands clasped onto the steering wheel and the truck smashed into the river.

CHAPTER 10

She tried to stifle her cries.

"Stop crying!" He locked the chain around her foot, then slapped her hard across the cheek. "*Never* run away again, Rosie. You hear me?"

Ghost looked up at him and felt a burst of anger. She hated him for taking her away from the city. She hated him because she was back in the attic. She hated him for hurting Sapphire and she couldn't hold it in anymore. She looked at him, mimicking the defiance she'd seen in Sapphire's eyes. "I'm not Rosie. I'm NOT Rosie!"

It felt good to finally say it.

He stared at her, his eyes big with shock. Then they slowly grew narrow with arrogance. "If you're not Rosie, tell me your name?"

She opened her mouth, then closed it. She knew her name wasn't Rosie. She also knew it wasn't really Ghost.

He scoffed. "That's what I thought."

Ghost felt her bottom lip shake. *Remember. Try to remember.*

"Now," Mer said. "I'm going to go out and find your mother. Then, soon, everything will change. You'll see."

Ghost was still angry. "You're not going to get her. She's not like the other ones. She's strong and smart, and brave."

"She's just a woman, Rosie. She's not some sort of hero." He stood still, staring at her as if he were digesting his own words. "Hero…"

She closed her eyes and didn't open them until he was gone.

When Ghost got here all those winters ago, she knew her name. Then, when he asked for her name and she replied, he beat her. Again and again, for seasons. Maybe that's why she couldn't remember now.

She tried to recall. She tried to picture her mommy, Faith, the other children, or even Matthew White, call her by her real name. She closed her eyes.

"*What's your name,*" he'd asked her.

Once, when it was summer, the doorbell rang and Ghost's mommy was in the bathroom.

Ghost stood in the hallway, staring at the door. Usually, her mommy would grab her when the doorbell rang, then lock her in the closet with her tablet and headphones on. There she would sit until the battery ran out, and wait for her mommy to say she could come out.

When the doorbell rang a third time, and her mommy still hadn't come, Ghost decided to unlock the door. She opened to see a man she'd dreamt of. He had a kind, but surprised smile. "Hello?"

"Matthew White," she said, remembering his name from her dream.

"Uh, yes." He clenched a bouquet of flowers as his eyes searched behind Ghost. "And who are you?"

Ghost said her name but, in the memory it came out inaudible, like she was speaking from underwater.

"Oh, okay." He crouched down to match her height and held his hand out for her. "Well, how do you do?"

Ghost giggled and took his hand.

"Where's, um…your…is she your mom?"

Ghost nodded.

"No! No!" Her mommy came running toward them. "Matthew, get out!"

"Wait," he said confused. "Who is she? Is she your daughter?"

"No!" Ghost's mommy pushed her away, then pulled Matthew out of the door and slammed it behind them.

Ghost stood still, listening to the words on the other side.

"If that's your daughter, where has she been every time I've come over? How old is she?"

"She's not my daughter. She's my neighbor's girl, and I watch her sometimes," Ghost's mommy said.

"She knew my name, and her name is…" His voice turned inaudible, too.

"Doesn't matter, and she knows all sorts of crap. She's some sort of mind-freak."

"Oh," he said, "well, I'm in town on business for a bit, so why don't I take all three of us out?"

"What? You, me, *and* her?"

"Sure. Why not?"

"You don't understand," Ghost's mommy urged. "This girl, she's not like other children and that's why I didn't want—"

"Hey," he interrupted, and Ghost heard a kissing sound. "I'm sure it'll be just fine."

They spent the day at a place called an amusement park, where they had candy, and toys, and big wheels that took you round and round. Everything but the house of horrors her mommy insisted on taking her into, was so much fun. The three of them walked around the grounds, looking just like the other families in the park, and Matthew even won a bear for Ghost.

At one point, Ghost's mommy pulled her aside and told her to keep her mouth shut all day, no matter what. So, Ghost did, besides from laughing and screaming with joy when Matthew took her on the rides. She liked him a lot. Secretly, she liked him even better than she liked her mommy.

Ghost's mommy suddenly reached for her and said. "I have to go to the restroom."

"Don't worry," Matthew said firmly, putting a hand on Ghost's shoulder. "I'll watch her. We'll go get ice cream."

Ghost's mommy cast him a nervous glance then glared at Ghost, eyes saying: *keep your mouth shut.*

She hustled into the bathroom and Matthew bought them two ice creams. They stood on the dock, eating them when Matthew looked down at her with concern. "How old are you, five?"

Ghost nodded. She was five.

"You know, I only come to town for business a few months or weeks out of the year, but I make sure to see her every time I'm here." Matthew eyed the bathroom. "Her and I, we met at a bar many years ago, almost twice as many years as you're old. About six years ago, she called me up and asked me what my favorite girl's name was. I gave her a name, *your* name."

Ghost didn't understand, but she knew she wasn't allowed to talk so she just smiled.

"It's just…" he said, eyes on her. "You look a lot like me, don't you think?"

Ghost shrugged.

He studied her intently and his voice filled with concern. "Are you okay? I like her, I do, but…that woman should not care for a child."

He looked toward the bathroom in frustration, and Ghost noticed her mommy coming out.

"Just please tell me," Matthew whispered, "by nodding or shaking your head so I know. Is she your mother?"

Ghost watched her mommy hurry to them. She didn't want to lie to Matthew, but she shook her head because she knew that's what her mommy would've wanted. Matthew exhaled, maybe looking a little relieved, maybe a little disappointed.

"Hey," Ghost's mommy said. "We have to go. I have to get her back to her parents, but…I'll meet you tonight, at Flannigan's, just you and me."

"Sounds good," he said, then gave Ghost one more warm smile. "It was very nice to meet you."

Then he walked away, and Ghost wanted to follow him.

Her mommy grabbed her hand hard and dragged her off toward the station. After a few minutes, she finally slowed down and glanced at Ghost. "You know who that was?"

"Matthew White," Ghost replied.

Her mom stopped and looked at her. "Your father."

Ghost felt her heart skip a beat. "I have one?"

"Everyone has one, idiot." Her mom started walking again. "The reason we can't tell him is because, should he find out you were his, he would never, ever want to see me again. Nobody wants a child like you, Ghost. Nobody. Say it."

"Nobody," she whispered as her mommy took the stuffed bear Matthew won her and threw it in a trash can.

It had been many days since that summer, and though Ghost had forgotten her own name, she'd not forgotten Matthew White's.

Ghost wiped her tears and shuffled over to the plywood. She watched Mer walk up to his truck with his rifle over his shoulder. Before he stepped into the truck, he looked up at her window. Though she knew he couldn't see her through the crack, she felt like he knew she was there.

As Mer drove off, Ghost watched her dream get set in motion. She'd lied to him before. She knew he would go to the woods, then bring Sapphire here, and put her in a coffin.

• • •

Sapphire clawed her way up on the rocky beach and collapsed.

She tried to catch up on air, but as her wet clothes froze, her breath sharpened with strain. She ordered her fingers to clench together and protect each other from the icy wind, but they remained frozen claws.

Once she got out of the sinking car, the current took her downstream. With all the boulders and heavy wood floating about, she should have been knocked dead. Somehow, she made it.

"Get up, Sapphire," her weak voice wheezed, as she stared into the snow-covered forest before her. "Get…up."

Sapphire groaned, pulling her sore body up from the cold, wet rocks. The biting wind whipped at her wet hair and body. She moved into the woods on shaky legs.

The easiest thing would have been to follow the river back to the bridge, but Mer could be waiting there for her.

She hugged herself and listened to her teeth's tremors as she moved, even though all she wanted to do was curl up and sleep. She was suddenly so tired.

There couldn't have been a worse person to end up in the forest. Put her in the most crime-riddled part of Downtown L.A. in the middle of the night, with drug dealers, murderers, and rapists and she'd be fine. Put her in a forest in the middle of nowhere and she was fucked.

A small growl stopped her in her tracks. Sapphire swallowed as she turned to the sound, expecting a wolf or bobcat to tear her face off. Didn't bobcats do that, tear people's faces off?

"Oh God," Sapphire chuckled.

A few feet away, two tiny bear cubs played. It was so cute, Sapphire's frozen lips drew to a relieved smile. "You don't have a cell phone, do you?"

One of the cubs sniffed his butt to show her even his own asshole was more interesting than her.

"Of course you don't have a cell. Why would you?" Sapphire gazed at the miles of nothing but woods. "No reception."

A rustle sounded from behind Sapphire, and despite her lack of attendance at the Girl Scouts, she realized no bear cubs were left to roam the forest by themselves. Unless of course they too had been raised by Vivienne Dubois.

The vicious growl sounded and Sapphire turned, slowly, feeling a sudden rush of heat run through her. Behind her stood a full grown, eight-foot-tall brown bear on its hind legs. This time it didn't growl; it *roared* at her.

Sapphire looked around. What were you supposed to do

when facing a bear, play dead? Seemed counterintuitive. So, she ran.

It turned out bears were unfairly faster with their four legs against her measly two. A sharp claw smacked her in the back and clonked her into a tree. Sapphire turned, feeling her back burn. She faced the bear as it stood back up on its hind legs.

It roared, then came off its back legs, letting out a low snarl. It swung a weak paw toward her face. The tip of its two-inch claw dinged Sapphire's nose, then the bear collapsed.

Sapphire held onto the tree behind her, and stared at the zonked-out beast, wondering if perhaps the bear had heard from another bear that you should play dead if you ever ran into a human?

Then, she noticed the three low-grade tranquilizer darts sticking out of its back. She knew those darts well; they were just like the ones Sapphire had used to sedate killers.

She looked up, and spotted a man in green. A hunter. He stood yards away, at the top of a snowy hill, still holding his rifle high.

Sapphire lifted her hand. A weak appreciation for what he'd just done for her. Another dart zoomed by her and into the tree, an inch off her shoulder.

It wasn't a hunter. It was Mer.

Sapphire bolted again. She leaped through the forest, pushing branches and bushes out of her way. Darts zoomed around her, barely missing. She was the prey, and she felt the panic she imagined millions of animals before her had felt as she dashed in random patterns, hoping to lose him. She spotted a boulder up ahead, and headed for it. She hurled herself up the rock and tumbled to hide behind it.

It would've worked, had there been a *behind it*.

Sapphire plummeted down the steep hill. Her body tumbled, arms and legs smashing into everything in its path.

She finally rolled to a stop, and pulled herself up at

lightning speed. She had to keep moving. Mer could be right behind her.

Her heart battered against her chest as she looked over her shoulder for him.

Snap!

Time stood still. The forest, and all its creatures, stopped moving to witness her big blunder. Sapphire looked down, just as time unfroze and the snare tightened around her ankle.

The rope snatched her up, rotating heaven and earth.

As the sun set and night fell, Sapphire hung there, upside down, arms dangling over her head.

An owl hooted somewhere in the distance as if he, too, knew how screwed she was.

CHAPTER 11

Aston stood in a sea of ass-shakers, arm-wavers, and crotch-grinders.

It was never going to work. Never.

People on the dance floor of Club Scene were sweaty and the heat radiating off their bodies made Aston sweat too. His new shirt didn't help. Asking Mrs. D to help him fit in at the club was his first mistake.

Vivienne Dubois had gasped, and then picked up her phone. "Noah, it has finally happened."

A high-pitched shriek sounded through the phone.

Before Aston knew it, he was on Rodeo Drive with his mother-in-law, Noah, and Lurch, who seemed to be there as a carrying mule.

"How's the house looking, Noah?" he'd asked, standing still so the tailor could keep sewing him into a pair of... women's pants? Aston couldn't tell for sure; the mirrors were behind him.

"Oh, it's going great! Flawlessly." Noah waved his hand. "Aside from the tiny water damage debacle."

"Water damage?"

"Oh, don't worry. It's only in the bathroom. And two of the bedrooms. It'll be fixed in *no time*."

"Why don't I believe you?" Aston said.

"Oh, he-llo. Look. At. You," Noah gushed. "I could just eat you *up!*" He grabbed Aston's arm and pretended to audibly chomp it down. "Ha-ha!"

"Ha-ha!" Vivienne joined in.

"Kill me," Aston said.

Vivienne gestured to his outfit. "Sapphire is just going to love it. *Love* it. Don't you think Sapphire will just *die* when she sees him, Radison?"

"I'm sure she will indeed just die," Lurch assured.

Die. Aston felt sick again.

"Could you be a darling and find us a fuchsia square, Radison?"

"Yaaaz," Noah squealed, "buh-rilliant."

"Square?" Aston repeated. He didn't know what a square was…or fuchsia.

Vivienne sighed longingly after Lurch, then turned to Aston. "So, when is Sapphire coming back from Richmond Hills?" She grabbed a skin-tight jacket and forced it on Aston. "And what are the two of you doing on Christmas Day?"

"Um, soon and I don't know, nothing." Aston exhaled so hard the button of his skinny pants popped. It shot across the room, ricocheted off the wall and hit Lurch in the eye.

"Sorry, man!" Aston yelled out, hand up.

"That's quite alright, sir," Lurch yelled back, holding his eye. "Excellent aim."

"You're doing *nothing* for Christmas?" Noah huffed into his complimentary champagne. "Traaaa-gic."

"That's not tragic," Aston said. "Tragic is someone having propped up their passed-out father in a chair and sprayed on whipped cream as a fake beard so that they could pretend Santa came."

"My God." Vivienne joined Noah in staring. "Did that actually happen?"

"No-ho." Aston laughed. Now that he thought about it, it was shaving cream.

"Anyway," Vivienne said. "I usually went up to ski in Big Bear for Christmas with, you know, whoever, when Sapphire was younger. So I want to make this one special for her. I want a big Christmas morning party. Maybe we could invite your father and make it a real family affair."

Aston's eyes widened, and it wasn't just because the tailor, who was adjusting his inner leg, had accidently poked his ball. What if he didn't have Sapphire back by Christmas?

Aston cleared his throat to force the panic out. "If you want to make it special for her, invite Julia. I mean, the woman raised her after all."

"Of course," Vivienne hurried, but her gaze turned glossy as it moved to the carpet. She then forced a smile as Lurch handed her a small pink square. She put it in Aston's chest pocket, then stepped over to Noah so they could assess him.

"C'est magnifique," Vivienne babbled.

"Oh my God," Noah wiped a tear. "It's just as good as I imagined it."

They turned Aston around to the mirror and he stared at the new him. *Fuck me yesterday.*

So here he was, at Club Scene in skinny pants, a gold-trimmed shirt, tight jacket, and a pink snot rag in his pocket, meshing seamlessly with the rest of the crowd. He looked like a seventh-generation douche who spent his weekend at the country club, tying a cardigan over his shoulders and saying things like, "*Mmm, you simply must try the black truffle bruschetta.*" What the fuck was truffle, anyway? Chocolate or fungus? People needed to make up their minds.

Yes, his clothes were the first mistake of the day, and he was staring at his second: trusting Christina Kraft. They'd spent the first half of the day together scoping out the club. Since Aston still didn't have his badge, they had to get in through other means.

The objective: get into the upstairs office they'd spotted from the fire escape outside. It was assumedly where the club kept the security data.

The plan...

Aston shook his head. The plan was going to Shitsville in a shit basket.

Chrissy stood at the bar now, seeming to have forgotten about their strategy as she flirted with the five guys surrounding her, especially a guy with an ascot.

"Jesus Christ," Aston mumbled, trying to get her attention from across the floor in a subtle manner. His gaze moved to the door leading to the upper level with the two bouncers outside. Their steroidal muscles bulged and their jaws remained tight as they kept their eyes on the crowd.

Two things were off. One, it was overkill to guard an office space. Two, Aston could see the protuberance of the weapons from under their jackets. Illegal and way fucking overkill. Something wasn't kosher, and had Aston had his gun and badge, he would've called Barry and the boys for backup. The two towns bordered each other, so the BHPD worked with West Hollywood's sheriff's station all the time anyway. But since Aston's new boss was the equivalent of the moist towel one wipes their ass with, he had to pull this off like…well, like the Serial Catcher.

Two girls and a guy came to grind on Aston as he stood there, eyes shifting between the bouncers and Chrissy. She was supposed to create a diversion and throw a big heiress fit, say she was being harassed and have the bouncers rush over. Instead, she just kept flirting. Really, Aston could suit himself. He'd basically agreed to go undercover with a banana peel.

He groaned. Just when he thought it couldn't get any worse, John Vanderpilt showed up at Chrissy's side. It was time to intervene.

Aston pushed the grinding people off him and headed toward the bar, watching Chrissy and Vanderpilt argue dramatically. By the time he got there, their tongues were down each other's throats.

Aston squeezed in against the bar, eyes ahead, and spoke out of the side of his mouth. "What the hell are you doing?"

He watched her in the bar's mirror as she tore her lips away from Vanderpilt. "I got it. Relax."

"Hey!" Vanderpilt suddenly noticed Aston and gave him the thumbs up. "Looking sharp, Ridder."

"Oh fuck me," Aston groaned, taking a second look at John. They were wearing the *exact* same outfit. New low.

"Hey, teddy bear." Chrissy turned John's chin to her. "I just want to be honest with you. While we were apart, I hooked up with someone."

"Who?" John Vanderpilt asked, mouth turned down in disgust.

Chrissy sighed. "Just that guy over there."

It was ascot guy, who had now moved on to hitting on a model, or actress, or possibly porn star.

"Him? God, Chrissy. You know that's my nemesis."

Aston raised his finger. "I thought I was your nemesis."

"Pff. Ridder, please." Vanderpilt rolled his eyes. "This is the big leagues."

"Speaking of big." Chrissy nodded toward ascot. "I'm not going to say his was bigger…but it *definitely* wasn't smaller."

Vanderpilt's mouth puckered with rage. "Ronald, Michaels, Jerry, Bieber!"

The boys seemed to come out of nowhere, as if they'd been lurking around their master, waiting to be called.

"My dueling glove." Vanderpilt held his hand out, until one of the guys handed him a yellow Porsche glove. "Let's go kick some ass."

Then they went, the boys from the mean streets of Beverly Hills.

"Go," Chrissy said to Aston. "Now."

"Nothing has happened."

A shrill scream rang out over the music and Chrissy smiled. Apparently, there was no greater insult than being slapped with a Porsche glove because ascot guy was flailing his hands, clawing at John's face. John jumped around, low-kicking the air, screaming: "You want some of this? You want some of this?"

"Shit," a bouncer said to the other, passing Aston. "Vanderpilt and Rockefeller are at it again."

Aston smiled and slipped inside the door. He moved upstairs with caution and through the corridor on nimble feet. He stopped in front of the door at the end which led to the corner office. He'd seen the manager downstairs, so it should be empty.

Inside, he located the computer and searched the footage from d-day, fast forwarding through the incoming crowd and people ordering at the bar. Chrissy had warned him about Sapphire's wig, so he knew what to look for. Except… he didn't see her. No kidnapping. No arrival. No footage of Sapphire whatsoever.

Aston leaned back. *What the fuck?* Sapphire was never at Club Scene. Chrissy had it all wrong.

He stood up, mind-boggled. He was just about to get the hell out when his eyes landed on a drawer that sat ajar. He grabbed the edge with his index finger and pushed it open. He pulled out a phone, Sapphire's exact make and model. He turned it on and waited, heart rate speeding, nostrils flaring.

The wallpaper popped up: a silhouette of two people kissing in front of the Bellagio Fountain. Despite being far past toasted at the time, Aston recalled taking the picture.

Sapphire had been here. The club must've deleted the footage…the evidence.

He scrolled through her last calls but found nothing of importance so he pocketed it.

"Want to tell me who the fuck you are, and what the hell you're doing in my office."

Aston turned to find three big bouncers and a guy in a suit. The men didn't concern him. The cocked Beretta did.

• • •

Sapphire opened her eyes. The first thing she saw was a giant moose head staring back at her. She sat up, her breath lodged in her throat, and looked around.

Location: unknown bedroom. Body: seemingly unharmed. Company: dead mounted moose.

Sapphire shot out of the bed and grabbed the first weapon she could find: a cut-off elk antler. *Gross.*

She had no memory of getting out of the trap. She'd passed out from hanging upside down, and her last memory showed nothing but a cloud of white coming toward her. So who brought her here? *Mer?* No. She'd be tied up.

Sapphire was just about to open the window, when she looked outside. There was a massive blizzard going on. Blizzard + no phone + in the middle of nowhere = Bad. Shelter + possible phone + possible food = Good?

She didn't have time to strategize more before the door opened and a small old man, who looked like he could answer to Jebediah, Jeremiah, or Jim-Bob, stepped in.

"Why good morning," he smiled, then shouted over his shoulder. "ESTER, SHE'S UP!" He turned back to Sapphire. "Hungry?"

"Uh…"

"ESTER, SHE'S HUNGRY!" He turned back and nodded to the elk horn in her hand. "We've got elk hash for dinner. Good thing since you seem to like elk. Come on out." He shuffled out of the room. "ESTER!"

"I heard you the first time!" a woman shouted back. "You don't have to shout, Jebediah!"

Jebediah. *Nailed it.* After a moment of thought, Sapphire put down the elk horn, and peeked out of the room and into the small cabin.

"If you weren't deaf!" Jebediah shouted, shuffling into the kitchen, "I wouldn't have to shout!"

"Deaf?" Ester, a little old woman with a hooked back, shouted as she stirred a skillet at an old-fashioned stove.

"I'm not deaf. I'd hear you just fine if you didn't have such a mousey voice."

"Mousey?!" he shouted. "Does this sound mousey, YOU DEAF COW?!"

The two glared at each other, ready to throw down. Ester's eyes moved to Sapphire in the doorway. She smacked Jebediah in the chest, and they both smiled at her.

"Hello!" Ester yelled. "Have a seat!"

Sapphire sat at the table in a chair, and watched Jebediah shuffle over.

"You're one lucky girl," Jebediah said, sipping coffee from a cracked cup. "I found you just before the worst of the storm hit. You would've died. You have to be careful not to step on snares around these parts."

"And where exactly are these parts?" Sapphire asked

"Tarts? We don't have any tarts!" Ester yelled as she scuffled up to Sapphire with the skillet and dumped two pounds of elk hash on her plate. "You know, you have to be careful not to step on snares around these parts!"

Jebediah turned to his wife. "I *just* said that, goddamnit!"

"MILK?" Ester screamed into Sapphire's ear.

Sapphire put her finger in her ear to ease the pain, then nodded. "Could I use your phone?"

"There's no cellular reception around here," Jebediah said, "and we don't have a landline. This is just our hunting cabin."

Damn.

"Phone? We don't have a landline!" Ester yelled. "This is just our hunting cabin!"

"I *just* said that goddamnit!"

Sapphire peered down at the elk hash. She had to eat, but Jebediah and Ester didn't seem like folks who had a freezer full of soy burgers…or a freezer. Second time Sapphire had been forced to eat meat this week. She put a fork-full in her mouth, then chewed and tried to suffocate the gag the flavor brought.

"We'll go into town once the storm settles. You can call

there," Jebediah said, then eyed her. "Don't you like the elk hash? It's good. Ester was real generous with the heart and kidney this time."

"Heart and…" Sapphire's stomach convulsed. She covered her mouth, then shot out of her chair and rushed toward the bathroom door.

"No! Not there!" Ester yelled.

Sapphire opened the door to find a room full of boiling liquids, crystalized nuggets, and…a phone on top of a desk.

She turned just as Ester clonked the cast iron skilled into her head. Her body gave out and she fell to the ground as the husband and wife stared down at her.

"I should've locked the damn door," Jebediah muttered, shaking his head.

"You should've locked the damn door!" Ester yelled.

Sapphire's sight gave out and darkness took over.

"I *just* said that goddamnit!"

• • •

Aston was tied to a chair and the man, looking like a mobster, glared down at him as his bouncer handed him Aston's wallet.

"What are you doing here," he pulled Aston's driver's license out. "Ashton Ridder?"

Aston cracked his neck. "It's As-ton, actually."

"I don't give a fuck," the mobster guy said, taking a drag off his cigarette. "Do I look like someone who gives a fuck?"

Aston shook his head. "No. You look a little like that guy from *Goodfellas*."

"Ray Liotta?" he leered, brushing his shoulder off.

"Joe Pesci."

The guy's face fell.

"Well, his name isn't Joe Pesci," a bouncer burled. "It's Lango Silver. Idiot."

Silver glowered at his bouncer. "You wanna give him my social and my mother's maiden name too while you're at it?"

"Uh…"

"Shut up." Silver flicked his cigarette butt at the bouncer, then turned to Aston. "Now, start spilling the beans or I'll have Dumb Rock here blow your brains out in three…two…"

"Wouldn't do that," Aston said calmly. "I didn't come alone, and if my comrade finds me dead, you don't want to know what would happen."

Nothing. That's what would happen. Not a damn thing.

"Oh, you mean the girl who set up your little distraction?" Silver snapped his fingers. "Boys."

Two new bouncers appeared with Chrissy, gagged with tape.

Fuckbucket.

"You thought we wouldn't figure out your little charade, did you?" Sliver said.

They sat Chrissy down in the chair next to him and tied her up.

Aston looked up at Silver. "Okay. Fine. You want the story? Last week a woman was taken from here. Just like Mary Dunnigan was a few months back. Your security footage recorded none of it. I'm assuming A, you have a conveniently shitty security system. Or B, you're purposely letting this man out with women and deleting the evidence." Aston's eyes flittered over the room. "Based on the talcum powder and scales in this room, I'm guessing the latter, and that your partnership has something to do with the fact that this club is a front for drug smuggling. Am I right, or am I right?"

"Oooo," Chrissy mumbled behind her gag and turned to Silver.

Aston looked confident, but inside he thanked his lucky stars he didn't have his badge on him. Depending on size, drug bands rarely shied away from killing a cop here and there to keep the business going.

Silver examined Aston. "In what world does the man tied to the chair with three guns to his head get to ask the questions?"

"In the world where he's sitting next to an heiress so famous that the FBI would be called if so much as a hair on her head was harmed."

Chrissy nodded.

Silver's brows furrowed. He nodded at his bouncers to search Chrissy's purse. They found her wallet and showed him the ID.

"Christina Kraft. Shit." Silver smacked the closest bouncer. "How didn't you recognize her? Moron."

The corner of Aston's mouth pulled up. Silver nodded at his bouncers, and they disappeared into the hallway to discuss their hostage situation.

Chrissy moved her mouth until the tape peeled. "You really think that'll work?"

"Sure," Aston said. "Unless they decide to shoot us and acidize our bodies instead. It could go either way, really."

Chrissy's eyes filled with fear.

He gave her a once over. "You okay? Did they hurt you?"

Chrissy shrugged. "One guy smacked me in the back of the head, but I'm on some crazy good pain meds from the surgery, so I barely felt it."

Aston gazed at her. "Do you have a stamp card over there or something? Pay for nine, get the tenth tit free."

"Hey! *You're* the one who said I looked like Mickey Rourke. I had to do something to look more natural."

Aston passed on the obvious oxymoron and stared at the ever-confident heiress, not so confident at all. Much like the rest of the world, she was a self-conscious mess. He felt a sting of guilt. "Look...I didn't actually mean it. I was just sick of your snide-ass comments."

Chrissy pouted, then sighed. "I just say those things because, you know...what if Sapphire would start loving you more than she loves me?"

"That's ridiculous," Aston said. "*Of course*, she loves me more than she loves you."

Chrissy huffed. "Fact: I've known her longer and I know her better."

"Sapphire has been missing for *five* days, because you knew what she was planning and you didn't fucking stop her. Why? *Why*, if you cared remotely about her in that bratty brain of yours, wouldn't you stop her?"

Chrissy's eyes narrowed. "Because, you idiot, Sapphire would've done it anyway. And if this is what she wants to do, who am I to stop her? Unlike *some people* I don't try to keep her on a leash. No wonder she comes to me instead of you."

Aston opened his mouth to cuss her out, but the words lodged in his throat as he stared at the heiress. Her comment felt like a bat to his stomach. It was true. And it was exactly what had bothered him so much. Sapphire had gone to Chrissy, Shelly, and O'Riley, but not him. She'd spoken to everyone but her own husband.

Chrissy must've caught onto what he was thinking because her voice turned softer. "I mean…that's just how she is. She does what she wants to do, so you either get with the program or…"

"Or what?"

"Or get out of her way." Chrissy paused. "I didn't make the rules. I just follow them."

They looked at each other and their silence said what they could not. For the first time, Aston found himself somewhere he never thought he'd be with Christina Kraft: in the same boat.

The bouncers and Silver reentered and positioned themselves in a crescent around Aston and Chrissy.

"What are your terms?" Silver asked, pointing at Aston with his phone. "And what is my insurance you won't blab to the cops."

"Untie us, then tell me everything you know about the

guy on the tape," Aston said. "And you have the addresses on our licenses. What more insurance do you need?"

Aston had just moved and the Kraft Manor had security coming out the yin-yang, but Silver didn't know that.

He nodded to the bouncers and they started undoing their ropes.

"I don't know what he does with the girls. He just showed up one day, forcing us to send him pictures of a certain type of girl when he asks for it, because he had evidence of our… merchandise. He says it'll automatically go to the cops if something happens to him. It seems like we're not the only ones on his list. His name is Mer."

"Mer what?" Aston asked.

"Just Mer."

Chrissy turned to Aston to explain. "Like Adele."

Aston took a few seconds to stare at her, then turned back to Silver. "So, what else you got?"

"He communicates with us only through text, and he has a new number every time."

"So, you don't have a last name." Aston rubbed the rope burn off his wrist. "And you don't have an address or a way to reach him. What *do* you have?"

"One of the guys saw him drive off once," Silver said, "and he got the license plate number."

The bouncer pulled up a folded note and reached it out to Aston.

"Ooh," Chrissy said, stepping closer. "Can you put that in at the station? Like in the movies?"

Fuck…me. Aston closed his eyes and closed his fist as the bouncer pulled the note back. *So close.*

Chrissy looked around the dead silent room. "What?"

"The station…you're a cop!" Silver hissed.

"Oooh," Chrissy said, then nodded. "I see what I did there."

All the goons simultaneously re-raised their weapons at

Aston and Chrissy, and Silver cocked his gun. "She's probably not even the real Christina Kraft. It's probably a fake ID."

"She is!" Aston held his hand up to Silver and used his other hand to usher Chrissy behind him. "And I promise, if you let us walk with that note, I *will* leave you alone."

"Bullshit. I'll never trust a god damn pig. Tank 'em, boys."

The bouncers stepped in front of Aston and Chrissy.

The heiress screamed, pushing her face into his back, and Aston stared down the barrel, as if it magically held the answers to his problem.

"Okay!" he yelled as the idea came to him. "You're right. You're right. She's not really Christina Kraft…"

Chrissy gasped behind him.

"She's a cop, too. We're both cops," Aston said it with such conviction even *he* believed it. "In fact, I'm wearing a wire. And I hate to tell you this, Silver, but in a minute our colleagues will be at that door, and it'll be over for you."

Chrissy stepped up from behind him, one hand on her hip, the other pointing at Silver. "That's right, so stick 'em up…freeze. Yippee-ki-yay, mother fucker."

Oh Christ. Aston fought to keep his face straight. "She's part of our special unit…like, glue-eating special."

Silver eyed Chrissy with doubt, then nodded to the bouncer. "Check him for the wire."

The bouncer checked Aston's lapel for pins, then ripped his shirt open to reveal a bare chest and stomach.

"Well, isn't that something," Silver smirked.

"Thanks," Aston said. "I do work out."

Silver glared at him. "I mean the fact that there's no wire, wise guy."

"Oh, there's a wire. It's…well, we don't put them *outside* of our bodies anymore."

"What? If it's not on the outside…where is it?"

Aston cleared his throat, looking over his shoulder and down.

Silver, the bouncers, and Chrissy's eyes slowly drew to Aston's ass. He clenched it, giving a slight grimace.

Best case scenario, they'd get grossed out and take his word for it. Worst case scenario, he'd get to reenact the *Mooooon River* scene from *Fletch*. Win-win.

"With all due respect, boss," the bouncer said, staring at Aston's ass. "I ain't checking that."

Silver's eyes turned slim. "I think you're full of shit, but you said a minute, right? So, here's the deal. If nobody shows up at that door in the next..." he checked the time, "thirty seconds, my boys will blow your brains out."

The bouncers pulled a gun each to Aston and Chrissy's head, who stood frozen, palms showing.

Shit!

Silver looked at the time, eyebrows raised. "And that's five...four...three...two...hey, what do you know, *one*."

"Oh my God," Chrissy shrieked, then started wailing.

A loud knock came on the door.

"Hey! We know you're in there!"

Chrissy immediately stopped bawling and looked at Aston as Silver turned to the door in shock. It was Vanderpilt.

"Everybody saw you come up here with them!" Vanderpilt continued. "There are five of us out here and we're not afraid to kick ass."

John Vanderpilt had to be talking about Chrissy, coming upstairs with Silver's men in tow.

"Er...yeah!" Aston yelled back, eyes on Silver. "We're all in here, Serg!"

"Wha—*Ridder*? What the hell are you doing in there?" Vanderpilt yanked on the locked door. "How many times are you going to take what's mine?! *Not* cool, man!"

"Yeah, sorry, I know this was your *case*!"

"Shit, boss!" one of the bouncers said. "We're going down."

"Just...don't panic," Silver hissed, clearly in panic.

"Who was that?" Vanderpilt yelled. "How many guys are in there with you?!"

"A lot! And things are really...*heating* up," Chrissy yelled, then looked at Aston and winked with her whole face.

Aston rolled his eyes. The goons were luckily too busy freaking out to notice.

"This door better be open in three seconds!" Vanderpilt yelled. "Or we'll break it down!"

"Here's the deal," Aston said to Silver, "because I like you, we'll go out and tell them that you're giving yourself up. It'll look good for the judge, shave off a few years even. You'll probably be out in one to two for good behavior. Okay?"

Silver and the bouncers reluctantly nodded.

"Just need this. Thank you." Aston snatched the note out of the goon's hand and headed for the door with Chrissy in tow.

When Aston unlocked it and grabbed the handle, the heiress turned dramatically behind him and sighed. "I'm getting too old for this shit."

"Jesus." Aston yanked her out the door. He quickly closed it behind him and turned to the Beverly Hills posse and John Vanderpilt, who had his fists up and was one mustache, and a pair of high-waisted tights away from looking like an old timey boxer.

"Ridder, you son of a—"

"Unless you guys want a bullet between the eyes when those guys realize no one's coming for them," Aston whispered, "I suggest you follow our lead and *haul ass* out of here."

Chrissy and Aston took off. Soon John and his boys followed, and dove into their Porsches the moment they exited.

Aston and Chrissy didn't stop moving until they reached his car. Chrissy leaned against it to catch up on air as he unraveled the note. "Idaho."

"Is that the license plate state?"

"No, I'm just naming my favorite kind of potato. Yes, it's the fucking state." Aston picked up his phone and dialed.

"Barry, are you at the station like I asked? Good. In one minute, you're going to get an anonymous tip, suspecting Club Scene in West Hollywood as a drug front. Before you move on it, look up Idaho license plate number Alfa 376-901 and text me the info."

Aston hung up and a minute later, his phone beeped. He stared at it, taking in the information.

"What?" Chrissy asked, walking up to him. "What does it say?"

"Weird." Aston stared at the text. "He says the vehicle is registered, but the information pops up blank."

Chrissy sighed. "So, what now?"

"We have a first name, we have Idaho, and Sapphire's description." Aston opened the passenger door and held it for Chrissy. "We're going to get help, more minds on this, and then we're going to find her."

"How do you know?" Chrissy hopped in.

"Because we have to," Aston said and shut the door.

CHAPTER 12

"I suppose you're wondering why you're here," Aston said. To call this meeting, at an institution for the criminally insane, had not been easy.

"Oh-oh." Chrissy raised her hand. "I know."

"I know you know, I'm talking to them." Aston looked at Shelly McCormick and O'Riley. He explained the description Sapphire had given him over the phone as he unfolded the map and pulled out the non-fatal box of crayons security had allowed. He circled the map with purple. "This is the state of Idaho. So far, I've found ten towns surrounded by mountain chains. We need to narrow it down to one. And, due to Shelly's visiting hours, we only have thirty minutes to do so."

They gathered around the map and brainstormed.

"Christ," Aston said after a while, looking at the time, "even if we do figure it out in the next ten minutes, it's going to take me fifteen hours to drive to Idaho."

"What about flying?" Chrissy asked.

"All these towns are too small," Shelly said, "the closest airport is in Boise. It'd take him hours to fly, and he'd *still* have to drive. Can I borrow your phone?" Shelly took it before Chrissy could answer and plugged away.

O'Riley looked at Aston. "Why's he going all the way from Idaho to L.A. to get women? There's been what, three including Sapphire."

"Oh, it gets weirder." Shelly brought the phone up. "He doesn't just go to California. I just typed in the missing women's description with random states, and look."

Aston took the phone and scrolled through the articles. Countless women, different dates, different years, same five states, same five cities. Salem, Oregon. Havre, Montana. Aberdeen, South Dakota. Roswell, New Mexico. Los Angeles, California.

"But why those towns?" Shelly asked as Aston drew a dot on every city. "Why go two states over to get something you can get fifty or a hundred miles away?"

They sat in silence, staring at the dotted map.

"So…" Chrissy said, "what about flying?"

Aston, Shelly, and O'Riley looked at each other, then turned to Chrissy.

"Chrissy, go wait in the car," Aston said.

"But…"

"For the love of Jesus, Mary, and Joseph, *go* wait in the car!" O'Riley yelled. "We only have three and a half minutes left!"

Aston glanced at O'Riley. He must actually care for Sapphire. He didn't seem like a dude who raised his voice often. Chrissy pouted and stormed off.

Two and a half minutes later, they were all panicking. Shelly was chewing her hair. O'Riley was praying for an answer. And Aston was two seconds away from lighting a cigarette inside.

"Visiting hours are up!" The guard's voice came too soon.

"We still have twenty-seven seconds!" Shelly yelled.

The guard rolled his eyes. "By all means, use your twenty-seven seconds as you wish."

"Wait…" Aston looked at the map, and saw it. It was a pattern he'd seen years ago on his old sergeant's whiteboard, when Aston was still green at the LAPD.

He grabbed the crayon and drew the lines between the dots. It took his sergeant months to catch the satanic worshiper, killing people based on locations that formed this very shape.

They all stared at the symbol.

"A pentagram," O'Riley said.

Two of their mountain towns landed within the pentagram's center: Pleasant Pines and Shadow Falls. Pleasant Pines was more centered than the latter.

"That's it!" Shelly pointed. "That has to be the town."

Pleasant Pines. Aston stood, quickly thanking them, then headed for the elevator. O'Riley slipped in right before the doors closed. They stood in silence as the floors dinged downward.

"Give me a ring when you find her, won't you?" O'Riley said. "Or shoot me a text. I'm getting very good at it. W…T…F: Wow That's Fantastic."

Aston frowned and stepped out of the elevator. He reached for the main door, then froze. "Will she stop?"

"Excuse me?" O'Riley said.

Aston swallowed the emotion clawing its way up his throat. "If she lives, when this is all over…will she stop?"

"I wouldn't know."

"Come on…"

O'Riley's eyes drew to the floor, then back at Aston. "I wouldn't bet on it."

Aston's heart sank. It wasn't the answer he wanted. The old man left and Aston moved toward his car, blood rushing through his ears. A *pentagram*. This undoubtedly involved some sort of deadly ritual. The date Sapphire had seen circled on the calendar, became vivid in his mind and he knew. Unless Aston got to Pleasant Pines in time, Sapphire was going to be *sacrificed* on December 23rd.

He'd be lucky if he got there with any time to spare. He jumped into his car to find a pouting heiress in the passenger seat. *Right.* He'd forgotten about her.

"You gotta get out," Aston said, eyes on the GPS on his phone. "Get an Uber."

"What? Why?"

"One, you're not coming. Two, I have a fifteen-hour drive ahead of me and I can't afford the time it takes to drop you off."

Chrissy inhaled, then spoke calmly. "But…what…about…flying?"

"Seriously?!" Aston yelled. "Did you not hear Shelly? Small mountain towns like that don't even have a place for planes to land!"

Chrissy glared at him. "FYI, *helicopters* can land wherever they want."

"You have a helicopter?" Aston blinked at her. "Of course you do. Of course you have a helicopter." He broke out in a smile.

"I do…but it's out today. My dad took it to San Fran."

The disappointment knocked Aston back to earth.

"But DubCorp has one too."

Oh, good! Aston thought, then realized it. *Oh, bad.* He reached over and opened the door. "I still need you to get out."

"Why?" Chrissy squealed, then counted on her fingers. "I helped you at the club, I helped you figure out how to get there, *and* I'm good company."

"That's…mostly true," Aston said, "but I almost got you killed last night. This is as far as you go."

Chrissy's mouth gradually un-pouted and she gave a reluctant nod, then got out and turned to him. "Just…bring our girl home, okay?"

Aston gave her as much confidence as he could muster. "I will."

He drove away, focused on his next challenge. Once more, October had come back to bite him in the ass.

• • •

"*Sapphire!*"

Sapphire tossed her head from side to side, fighting to get control of her wandering mind. She had to get up. She had to get away, but her eyelids felt as heavy as bricks and reality was slippery, like a greased article that she couldn't hold onto.

It slipped further…and further…until…

"Sapphire!" Chrissy launched in for a hug. Sapphire

stepped inside and pulled Aston along. The Kraft Manor was bursting with life. It was October, the Krafts were holding their annual Halloween party, and hundreds of dancing and drinking guests wore extravagant costumes. It was the first time Aston and Sapphire stepped into a party as a married couple. It had taken her a week and a half to convince him, but he'd finally agreed to come.

Her best friend noticed Aston. "Oh…great, you brought *him*."

Chrissy wasn't making it any easier.

"Well," Aston replied, "fuck you very much."

Neither was Aston.

"Tsk." Chrissy turned dramatically, then pranced off in her eight-inch heels, matching her slutty nun costume. "Walk this way."

Aston looked back at Sapphire then imitated Chrissy's dramatic turn, and pranced off after her. Sapphire shook her head and suffocated her laugh.

"What are you guys supposed to be anyway?" Chrissy eyed them over her shoulder. "Gangsters?"

"Told you no one would get it," Aston whispered to Sapphire.

"Nick and Nora Charles." Sapphire held up the stuffed animal, Jack Russell dog. "You know, from the old Thin Man movies."

Last week, while arguing about whose pick-night it was, they'd stumbled upon the black and white movie series about the alky private investigator and his wife, an heiress, solving crimes together, and binged it till the sun came up.

"I don't watch old movies. They're too old." Chrissy eyed Aston. "Like your husband."

Aston's face twisted and he took a step toward Chrissy.

"Hey." Sapphire grabbed his arm and led him away. "Let's see if we can find some martinis." She wasn't sure why the two couldn't get along, but she'd given up on the fact that they ever would. "Okay, so, first rule of the Beverly Hills Survival Guide: don't linger by the bar."

"Why," Aston said, "is that where Chrissy is?"

Sapphire gave him an exasperated look. "That's where the freshest batch of trophy wives hang out." She nodded to the women with identical blonde hair, boobs, and pouty lips, huddling around the Krafts' bar, tended by a zombie in a bowtie. "They get into fights a lot and you don't wanna get caught in the crossfire of those nails. Exhibit A," Sapphire pointed at the tiny scar at the bottom of her chin.

"Duly noted."

"Second rule, stay clear of the kitchen entrance." Sapphire nodded over to kitchen doors where a group of buff, mid-twenties men had gathered. The moment the door opened and a zombie emerged with a tray of hors d'oeuvres, the men jumped on it like a pack of wolves fighting for a rabbit. They dispersed two seconds later, leaving the zombie with an empty tray, looking confused and molested.

"Who are they?" Aston asked.

"Trophy husbands," Sapphire explained. "It's said that if they don't eat protein every fifteen minutes, they deflate like balloons and turn rabid."

"Trophy *husbands*?"

"Sure," Sapphire said matter-of-factly, "what else do you think the trophy wives do once their first husbands die and they get their inheritance? It's the circle of life, Aston. Try to keep up."

Aston exhaled with a head shake. "I'll go get the martinis."

Sapphire watched as he headed for the bar, noticing how uncomfortable he looked among her peers. She, herself, had grown up feeling like the black sheep of her society, but it was different with Aston. He couldn't hold a conversation with anyone for longer than thirty seconds before he excused himself to use the bathroom—the general Beverly Hills public now believed he had a prostate problem. He didn't belong in

Beverly Hills and it wasn't fair to force him, but what was she supposed to do, never see her family and friends again?

Sapphire turned toward the window and frowned.

A nurse, not the classic slutty nurse, but in scrubs, stood outside in the street. She stared up at Sapphire with an unyielding gaze.

"Your drink, Mrs. Charles," Aston said with the pace of a 1920s reporter, seemingly in a better mood, and handed her a martini.

"Thank you, Mr. Charles," Sapphire said, matching his tone, then eyed the three glasses as he set them down on the table. "Thirsty?"

"Getting into character," he replied, then swallowed a martini in one gulp. Sapphire looked out the window again. The nurse was still there. Still staring.

"What is she doing?" Sapphire said.

"Who?"

She turned to him. "There's a nurse out there."

"And there are fifteen nurses in here," Aston chuckled, moving onto the next martini. "It's Halloween."

"No, she's different, and she's staring at me. Look." Sapphire turned back to the window and pointed. She lowered her finger, and her eyes darted around the empty street. She was gone.

"Okay, crazy." Aston's last martini sloshed out of the rim as he grabbed Sapphire by the shoulder. "Let's dance, Mrs. Charles. I assume you foxtrot."

"Of course. What do you take me for," Sapphire joked, but couldn't help look back toward the window.

Out on the dance floor, they attempted the foxtrot. When that didn't work, since neither of them actually knew how to foxtrot, they switched to the Charleston, a dance neither of them knew either. While in the middle of accidentally kicking each other, they heard the whispers.

"Left a Vanderpilt at the altar…"

"Can't believe she married a *policeman*."

"Obviously some sort of mental breakdown…"

Sapphire laughed, but Aston glared drunkenly at the people casting looks and whispering. "How are you okay with this? Don't you wanna go over there and punch them?"

Sapphire pointed from person to person. "Mrs. Tingsworth drinks because her husband had an affair with her brother. Judge Gold is addicted to his son's Adderall. Minny Hopper's nose is 90 percent rubber and keeps falling off." Sapphire continued for a while, telling him everyone's secrets. "Point is, I don't have to punch them; they're already miserable people."

Aston didn't look convinced.

"If you're going to be annoyed every time someone talks about you in Beverly Hills," Sapphire continued, "you're going to spend the rest of your life annoyed."

Aston's face flickered with a new displeasure. "So…we're going to stay here for the rest of our lives?"

Sapphire shrugged. "Where else would we go?"

"*Of course* he doesn't really love her," a familiar voice sneered. "I know love and that isn't it."

It was Petunia. Sapphire pressed her mouth to Aston's ear. "Said the woman whose first kiss was with her second cousin James."

"She's a mental case," Petunia continued. "Think anyone would wanna marry her if she didn't come with a billion?"

"That's it," Aston slurred and stormed off.

"Aston!" Sapphire called, but he'd already plowed through the crowd and was halfway across the room.

He jumped up on the stage and stole the microphone from Taylor Swift, pulling a Kanye.

"Woooh!" he hooted. "How's everyone tonight?"

The band looked around confused and stopped playing, letting the speakers fill with only Aston's voice. The crowd silenced as their heads turned to the stage.

"Do you guys know what the difference between a porcupine and a Porsche is?" he slurred and waited. "The porcupine's pricks are on the outside." Aston pointed at the drummer behind him. "Ba-dum-dum-tsh."

The motionless drummer gaped at him.

"No?" Aston nodded down to the crowd. "You get it, don't you, Vanderpilt?"

John Vanderpilt stared up at Aston with an open mouth and Sapphire covered her face with her palm.

"Well *I* thought it was funny." Aston pointed at Judge Gold. "Almost as funny as a drug-addicted judge." His finger moved on. "Or your husband bumping nasties with your brother."

"Oh no." Sapphire pushed her way through the horrified crowd and toward the stage, passing the judge and Mr. and Mrs. Tingsworth, all beet red with embarrassment.

"What else do we have? Spoiled rotten, obviously." Aston pointed at Chrissy, then moved his finger as he went through Sapphire's list. "Perv! Broke! Embezzler! Masochist! Rubber nose! Fucked the nanny! Toe fetish!"

He looked over at Petunia and pulled his arm back, as if winding it up.

Sapphire's cousin froze, champagne glass halfway to her mouth. Sapphire vigorously shook her head at her husband. *No-no-no.*

"Aaaaaaaaaand cousin kisser!"

Petunia's cheeks turned maroon.

"The bottom line for all you rich ass-wipes..." Aston's finger swept over the crowd. "Get off your high fucking horse!"

Sapphire pushed her way through the crowd as Aston bowed.

"Thank you, Beverly Hills. Goodnight!" He dropped the mic into the guitarist's glass of whiskey, then strolled off the stage, leaving an angry mob in his wake. Some gestured wildly, while others stood in shock. A few criers were scattered throughout. Sapphire reached Aston's arm, and yanked him toward the exit as the outrage grew. Loud complaints followed forceful booing as they passed people.

"Are you kidding me?" Sapphire hissed at him. Then her eyes landed on the window.

The nurse was back, and she was staring at Sapphire.

A blunt force took Sapphire by the collar and yanked her out of the manor, out of October, and away from Aston.

No. No. The anxiety was painful. She didn't want to leave him. She hadn't *meant* to leave him. It was all a big mistake.

Sapphire opened her eyes to find Ester shaking her. Skinned animal carcasses hung all over the room, medicine bowls boiled with liquid, and everything was spinning.

"How much did you give her?" Ester yelled, giving Sapphire's cheek fast, hard slaps.

"Mer said to make sure to incapacitate her until we hand her over," Jebediah yelled from over by the window. "So…a lot."

"A lot!" Ester yelled back. "Well, let's just hope she doesn't die then!"

Sapphire felt sick. She was drenched in sweat, her mind was a jumble, and as she stared at the warped, old faces, she knew that she was high out of her mind.

"Call him," Jebediah said, peeking out the window. "Storm's settling."

• • •

Aston stormed into the Dubois Mansion, cussing himself out. He should've expected this.

An hour ago, he'd stood in his wife's office. That's where Kevin sent him to wait for the she-devil. While he waited, he went through her drawers, but found nothing about Mary Dunnigan or the case she'd been working on.

Aston's phone vibrated and looked at the screen.

000-000-0000. Marla, that salesperson again.

"Jesus," he muttered and rejected it.

"What do you want?" Petunia Dubois's cold voice cut through the room.

Aston held his hands up to show he came in peace. "Look. I know you're not a fan of mine. Especially after…you know."

"Oh," Petunia Dubois said, "you mean that time you told all my neighbors, friends, coworkers, and business partners, that I kissed my second cousin?"

"Yeah." Aston cleared his throat. "Anywho, I was wondering if there was any way I could borrow DubCorp's chopper and pil—"

"No."

"You don't understand. Sapphire's in tro—"

"No."

"But you don't even know—"

"No."

Aston studied her. "There nothing I can say to rectify—"

"No."

She had turned her heel, leaving him with one option.

He ended up back here, at the Dubois mansion. Aston moved through the hallway, hearing her voice escape the living room. He rushed into spot her by the fireplace, holding a cup of tea.

"I can't tell you why, but I need you to call Petunia and tell her you need DubCorp's helicopter and pilot. I know you're busy with your elephant shit coffee and trying to fuck the butler, but I *really* need this."

Vivienne's mouth opened and she gestured toward Aston. "Everyone, my son-in-law."

He looked left: ten ladies with wine and matching books in their hands.

He looked right: another ten ladies with wine and matching books in their hands, plus Noah. Lurch was there as well, frozen in the action of pouring Noah's wine.

Whoops.

"Ladies. Noah. Lurch," Aston nodded awkwardly, then gestured at Vivienne. "Kitchen?"

"Excuse me, ladies." Vivienne delivered her company a fake smile, then followed him.

"Okay, here's the thing…" Aston said as they entered the kitchen. "I need that chopper and I need it yesterday."

"No, *here's* the thing! You probably can't tell, but this is a very outraged frown." Vivienne pointed to her smooth forehead. "I've tried. God help me, I've tried to welcome you to the family, the community, despite October, your crassness, and obvious…" her hand motioned to the entirety of Aston, "You-ness. But I've had it!"

Aston stared at her. "I never *asked* you to be welcoming. I never *asked* to be a part of any of this shit."

Vivienne turned, if possible, even more stone-faced. "You think *I* asked to have a daughter *elope* and marry some rude… classless cop, when she was once engaged to a *Vanderpilt*?"

"A-ha, there it is!" Aston folded his arms across his chest and leaned forward. "Then why act so nice?! Why try so hard?!"

"Because of Sapphire!" she blurted out.

Aston's hands shot out in question.

"Because…I thought that if I got you to like me…maybe Sapphire would…too. I thought she might listen to you." She rolled her eyes. "God knows she has never listened to anybody else."

Aston regarded her as a heavy silence filled the kitchen.

"Because of how her father left us, I never…I never really moved on and I behaved horribly. I missed out on so much time with her…I don't want to miss any more. I want my daughter back."

The woman looked heartbroken—miles away from the shitty mother with the cold eyes from last year. Maybe Vivienne Dubois hadn't "changed." Maybe she'd *changed*.

"I'll call Petunia on one condition," Vivienne said, gathering herself. "You start hugging me and calling me *mom* in front of Sapphire."

The idea sent shivers down Aston's spine. "How about I *stop* calling you Tits McGee in front of her instead?"

Vivienne's mouth drew to a line. "*Mom* plus hugs, minimum of three times a week."

"No hug and one mom."

"One mom…on Christmas…in front of everyone." Vivienne held her hand out. "Deal?"

"Deal." Aston took it and shook.

Vivienne put her phone to her ear and looked at him as she waited. "And for your information, I'm not just trying to sleep with him. I actually really care for Radison. Like I said, he has that…*je ne sais quoi.*"

"Wow, that's big of you," Aston nodded. "I guess you'll just have to double wrap that sucker if the time comes."

Vivienne looked at him in bafflement, then beamed. "Petunia. Aunty Viv. Yeah. Darling, could I borrow the corporate chopper and the pilot for a tick?" She nodded. "Yes… Yes. Okay. You take care now, Hun." She hung up. "Yeah, not happening. She knew you were behind it."

"Fuck." Aston felt the stress return to his chest. With each passing minute, he could feel Sapphire slip further away from him.

"I'm sorry," Vivienne said, "but short of stealing it and flying it yourself, there's nothing you can do. Petunia's in charge."

Aston tilted his head. He did know which box held Sapphire's spare key fob to the office. He looked at the time. *And* DubCorp was about to shut down for the night. But…

"I can't fly a chopper," Aston mumbled.

"Obviously, darling. I was only joking." Vivienne grabbed a snack platter and held it out for him. "Nut pastry?"

"Barry?" The memory elbowed its way toward the forefront of his crowded mind.

"No, nut. Not berry."

Aston stared into the distance, watching his heist come together on an imaginary screen. He smiled as satisfaction set in. "Barry."

"I said *not* berr—oh, for Pete's sake." Vivienne turned back toward the living room with the platter. "My only child and she married a simpleton."

Heart racing, Aston pulled up his phone and dialed.

• • •

"Barry."

Barry stared out the window, his mind muddled. What was that feeling in his chest? Well, he knew what it was: doubt. But *why* was he feeling it?

"Barry?"

The feeling came moments after he stepped into the station this morning, and Chief Calloway stuck his head out.

"Officer Harry," he'd said. "My office."

He knows. Barry stopped, instantly drenched in cold sweat. His feet had become cemented to the ground. The chief knew Barry helped Aston and that he was involved with the takedown of the drug club. How? Who cared. Barry was about to be suspended, fired, executed.

"Now." The chief snapped his fingers, then disappeared into his office.

Barry closed his eyes, said a prayer, then pulled his legs out of the cement and moved with solemn steps. His heart pounded as he sat down opposite Chief Calloway.

"Officer Harry..." the chief took a breath, then raised a brow. "Are you hot?"

"No." Barry pulled on his collar and tried to swallow the lump in his throat. "Why?"

"You're sweating profusely."

"I have a...a gland problem."

"Sorry to hear that." Calloway looked down at his papers. "I'm going to cut to the chase here, Officer Harry. I know you helped Detective Ridder against my orders. You know, I've been keeping an eye on you for a while and…"

Barry felt like he was going hurl. In fact…

"Dear God, man!" Chief Calloway covered his mouth.

Barry set down the trashcan he'd puked in. "I'm so sorry, sir. I have a sensitive stomach."

"I'd say." The chief eyed him. "Anyway, I've been keeping an eye on you for a while and…"

This was it. He was suspended, fired, executed.

"I see a lot of potential in you."

Barry's surprised eyes met Calloway's. "Excuse me?"

The chief opened Barry's folder. "You're loyal. You take orders well, with only one exception. You don't complain. Your paperwork is *meticulous* and you always act professional. Honestly, I see a promotion in your near future."

Barry sat dumbfounded, then felt a smile crack on his face. "Really? Thank you. Thank you, sir."

He stood to shake the chief's hand, but the chief motioned him to sit back down.

"*However*…I do have one reservation about you." The chief walked over to the window overlooking the station's lush entrance path. "I feel there's one thing between you and an excelling career here at the BHPD."

"What's that?"

"Detective Aston Ridder."

"I'm sorry, sir." Barry shook his head. "I don't follow."

Calloway counted on his fingers. "He is unprofessional, rude, selfish. His work lives only in the gray zone, and he makes up his own laws. He will drag you down with him, Officer Harry, and not think twice about it."

Barry's mouth opened in shock.

"Watching the two of you interact, it's clear to me that Detective Ridder is using you as an errand boy for his personal vendettas without even considering what it could do to you and your career."

Barry felt a stone drop to his gut. Why? Why couldn't Aston just have said *yes, sir*? Then maybe he wouldn't be in this nightmare. Many people had called Aston Ridder rude since he walked in through the doors of the BHPD last year, but no one had ever argued his skills as a detective. Let's face it, the moment Aston strolled in, he became a God, and people, including Chief Anderson, went out of their way to please him. There was a reason for it.

Barry shook his head, trying to grasp what was going on. "What exactly are you asking of me, sir?"

"I'm not an unreasonable man, Officer. I don't transfer partnerships against people's will…but I'm asking you to start taking care of your *own* career, and turn your back on the haphazard personal rulebook of Detective Aston Ridder. Consider your options. Someone who's by the book, like Detective Rodriguez, might do you better."

Barry stared into space, trying not to hurl again as the chief got up. "Think about what I've said."

He was unable to focus on anything else for the rest of the day. He *couldn't* transfer partners. The chief was his boss, but Aston was…*Aston*, his mentor, his friend.

That's when he called.

"Barry," he had said after explaining everything. "Meet me at DubCorp, ASAP."

The chief was wrong. Because just like Barry knew Aston would always be there for him, Aston knew Barry would be there for him. He knew it so much that he didn't even have to *ask* Barry to come fly him. He knew he would do it, because that was the type of friendship they had…right?

"I'll be right there," Barry had said and hung up.

So, here they were, five thousand feet in the air, inside a stolen corporate chopper, about to rescue Sapphire Dubois …again.

"Barry?"

Barry squinted to the sky, holding onto the cycle stick. How many times did this make it now? Three…four? Ten?

"Oh, for fuck sake. *Barry!*"

"Yeah?" Barry turned to his partner.

"I said," Aston shouted into the headset, "let's land down there!"

"Oh…right." Barry veered, letting the chopper glide toward the snow-covered meadow.

"Okay," Aston threw off his headset after they landed. "Let's go."

Barry stared at his partner, unable to move. He couldn't get out, but why? "Um, I have…I have to…"

"Hey!" Aston clapped his hands. "Change your tampon later, Susan. Move it!"

Barry looked at his hand, still clenching the cycle stick, and the words just came out. "I haven't gotten my license yet."

"I know." Aston opened the door. "Fuck me, it's cold."

"I'm flying a stolen chopper, *unlicensed*," Barry continued, unable to stop himself. "Best case scenario, if I got caught, I'd get fined and wouldn't even be allowed to test for a license I've studied for, for *months*. *And* I'm supposed to be at work later. But did you even ask me if I could help you? No. And do you even care?"

"Barry." Aston glared at him. "My wife is missing, I haven't slept for almost a week, and if I don't find her by the 23rd, she'll die. *Of course* I don't fucking care."

The anger billowed in Barry. "I didn't want to believe it, but…I think he was right about you."

"Who?" Aston asked, then shook his head and jumped out. "Doesn't matter. Let's go!"

Barry looked at Aston, feeling his anger settle as the truth ascended. "I'm sorry, but…you're on your own with this one. I'm going to go return this before DubCorp knows it's missing."

Aston's gaze was somewhere between disbelief, hurt, and

anger as he backed away from the helicopter, and turned his back on Barry.

The moment Barry lifted and saw the small man on the ground work his way through the thick snow and toward the small town, he felt doubt again.

• • •

Sapphire awoke at the sound of squealing brakes.

Her body was weak, and her brain was *buzzing*, like there was a hive of bees trapped in her skull. She squinted into the dark, cramped space around her. She was in a car trunk. Her hands and legs were tied behind her back and she'd been gagged.

Muffled voices leaked in from outside. Ester and Jebediah, no doubt.

Sapphire twisted in the small space, feeling around for the flap. All cars manufactured after 2002 had an emergency release inside the trunk.

"Is he coming?" Ester yelled.

"I *just* said he's coming, goddamnit!"

Sapphire's tied hands blindly searched the material behind her back, until she felt the plastic anchor-shaped pull. *Yes!*

Sapphire yanked down and the trunk popped open behind her. She turned to see that it had only cracked slightly and pushed on it with her knees. It was stuck. Wire had been tied around it from the outside. *No!*

Sapphire swallowed a groan and scooted closer. She could see the street through the small gap. The bundled-up people of the small mountain town moved in and out of the Christmas decked-out shops, passing carolers and bell ringers on their way. The whole village was so yuletide-themed that it looked like it belonged inside of a snow globe.

Ester and Jebediah stood about three yards away from her, but hadn't noticed the trunk opening.

Sapphire was just about to look for a wrench or anything

hard below her where the spare tire was stashed, when her eyes latched onto the street. Sapphire shook her head. She must've lost her mind. Perhaps she was still high, or perhaps, her sanity had finally gone AWOL.

Then the man turned his head, and she knew she wasn't crazy. He was crossing the street and looking over his shoulder.

Aston! It was really him. The sight of his face was heaven. Tears of relief filled Sapphire's eyes and she opened her mouth.

"Aston!!!" The gag muffled her voice, turning his name into indistinct babble.

"Excuse me!" Aston abruptly changed his direction toward Jebediah and Ester.

Yes, Sapphire thought.

They walked up to Aston, leaving the car twenty feet behind.

"I'm here!" Sapphire's muffled voice tried to yell. "Aston!"

"I'm looking for an old friend of mine named Mer. It's kind of a surprise. Any chance you know where he lives."

"Bert?!" Ester yelled.

"*Mer*, you deaf cow!" Jebediah yelled.

"Who you calling a cow, you mouse!" Ester yelled.

They looked like they had suddenly become aware of Aston, because they both cleared their throats and smiled.

"Sorry," Jebediah said. "We've never heard of a Mer."

Sapphire screamed and banged her knee against the trunk flap. "Aston!!"

She watched his eyes move to the car briefly, then back to the couple. "Any town registry?"

"I dunno," Jebediah said, eyeing his wife. "Try the Mayor, Hedge. He knows everyone and everything that goes on around here."

Sapphire rolled back and forth in the car, making it rock.

Aston finally looked over at the car. "That car's rocking."

Ester turned to see the cracked trunk and her face broke out in panic.

"Teenagers!" Jebediah hurried. "Teenagers going at it."

"Pff," Aston nodded. "Been there. Am I right?"

The couple didn't answer him, but stared back at the car in fear. Jebediah grabbed Aston's shoulder and pointed as he turned him around. "You can find the mayor in Town Hall over there."

"No! Aston!" Sapphire screamed. Her heart dropped as she watched him walk farther and farther away from her.

Two seconds later, Ester's angry face blocked her view, and the trunk smacked down.

CHAPTER 13

"Merry Christmas!"

"Happy Holidays!"

"Good morning to you, sir."

Everyone Aston passed on the decked-out street on his way to Town Hall greeted him with a big smile, or a tilt of the hat. It wasn't just the way they greeted Aston, a newcomer, but each other as well.

"*Feliz Navidad...*" A Christmas song blared through the small speakers mounted throughout the street.

Aston gazed at the townspeople as they interacted, perfect smiles, laughs, and greetings as they passed one another. For someone from L.A., a city known for a population who spent 95 percent of their time inside a car, it was overwhelming.

He dove into Town Hall and hurried up to a secretary.

"Happy Holidays, sir!" she smiled, teeth bright white.

"Uh, right. I'm here to see the mayor."

"Oki-dokey." She kept her smile and grabbed a tray of cookies. "The mayor is unfortunately busy at the moment. He'll only be two shakes, but I can offer you a gingerbread cookie while you wait."

"I'm good. How long is he going to be?"

Her smile turned stiff as she blinked at him, cookie tray still up. "Two shakes."

"Yeah. That's not a real measurement of time." Aston peered at the door right of her desk. "Is that his office?"

"No, sir!" She flew out of her seat as Aston hurried to the door and reached for the handle, just as it opened.

A woman with a candy shop uniform stepped out. She flashed a quick, nervous glance at him, then slipped out and toward the exit.

Aston turned to face a forty-ish man with light hair, sitting at his desk, looking at him in surprise.

"Sorry to barge in like this Mr. Mayor, but it's an emergency."

The mayor sighed. "Alright. Sit, and call me Wilmer. Most do. Whether I like it or not."

Aston sat, though he was all nerves and would rather pace. "I was told you know everyone here."

"I'm the mayor," he smiled. "It's my job."

"I'm looking for an old friend of mine; man named Mer."

The mayor held his smile, but something in his eyes changed. "What did you say?"

"Mer. M-E-R, Mer."

The mayor's eyes pulled to his desk, then he leaned back and shook his head. "Nope. No Mer in Pleasant Pines."

Aston faked memory loss. "I haven't talked to him for years. Maybe it was his last name. You have a Thomas Mer? Tim Mer? Jim-Bob Mer?"

"Mr...?"

"Ridder."

"Mr. Ridder, I don't know how else to put it. We don't *have* a Mer. Maybe you're in the wrong town? Shadow Falls is bigger than Pleasant Pines. I could be wrong, but I believe they have a Mer."

Shadow Falls. It was the second town on the map, the one they'd dismissed. He was in the wrong fucking town. Aston shot out of his seat. "You have a car rental?"

"Yup. Go to Bill's. Third building to the left on Second Street. I'm going to give you a map of a shortcut to Shadow Falls."

The mayor picked up a piece of paper and Aston's gaze drew to the golden wedding band on his finger. "Married?"

"Um…yup," the mayor mumbled and his eyes flickered up at Aston before he finished drawing the map and handed it over. "Here. Should get you there in half the time."

"Thanks." Aston took it. "And where's Second Street?"

"It's the one that isn't First Street. There are only two roads."

Aston hurried out the door and through the small town, avoiding as many of the smiling greeters as he could. Bill's, as it were, was not a business but a man in suspenders named Bill, who owned three shitty cars and rented them out from his shitty garage for two whole dollars an hour.

Aston picked the least shitty car, a 1999 Toyota with a loose bumper and a rusty roof, and headed out of town with the mayor's map in his lap.

His eyes fell on the sign as he approached. *Hang on, Saph. I'm coming.*

Now Leaving Pleasant Pines.

• • •

Crack…

Crack…

Cold.

Ghost's eyes snapped open from the dream to face an even colder reality.

To her horror, she found herself outside, suspended in the air…the snow below her was so high it nearly reached her toes.

It took her a beat to remember how she'd ended up here. Mer had come back into the attic after a while—she wasn't sure how long. He'd mumbled something about a *hero's sacrifice*, and the *perfect setup*, before he grabbed Ghost and hauled her out into the biting cold. And then…fear filled Ghost as the memory fully emerged. *Sapphire.*

How could she warn her? She didn't want Sapphire to end up in the coffin. Dead people lay in coffins, like her mommy after the last day at home. Ghost had forgotten many days from her old life, but she remembered this one well.

"Ghost," her mommy had said and pointed at the floor of the empty living room. "Do you see them?"

Ghost shook her head.

"It's not real. It's not real. It's not real," her mommy mumbled.

Then the doorbell rang, and her eyes sprung wide open.

"Closet. Now." She'd pushed her toward the closet in her room. "And not a peep. You're a ghost, remember?"

The headphones were placed on her ears and the tablet was shoved in her hands, then the closet door slammed shut.

Ghost knew she shouldn't take her headphones off, but that was before she'd met Matthew White, before she knew he was her father. She put away the tablet and put her ear to the closer door.

"What on earth are you looking around for?" Ghost's mommy asked.

"Is she not here?" Matthew wondered.

"Who?"

"The little girl."

"Oh, for Pete's sake, Matthew, I told you. She's the neighbor's girl. Come here. I've missed you."

Kissing sounds followed.

Ghost sighed and put the headphones on again. She was happy Matthew had thought about her, but sad she wouldn't get to talk to him. Ghost watched her favorite princess movies until her battery died. Then she watched the black screen for a long time, imagining that the movie was still playing. Then she fell asleep, and when she woke up she could see the morning light penetrate through the bottom of the door.

She took the thick headphones off and stared at the white door. It had been a long time, longer than normal, and Ghost had to go to the bathroom. She waited and waited for her mommy, feeling the urge to go grow and grow, until she couldn't hold it in anymore.

Ghost pulled on the door.

After she used the bathroom, she found her mommy sleeping on the kitchen floor, next to a knife and a red puddle.

Ghost sat down and waited for her mommy to wake. She waited and waited until their neighbor came by. Susie screamed, then pulled Ghost away from her mommy, and away from their apartment, even though Ghost cried and wanted to stay.

The next time Ghost saw her mommy, she lay in a coffin, still sleeping. After the funeral, Ghost waited for the tall, bald man from her dream to come and take her to the home with the Christmas roses, but the woman from Social Services came instead. She explained that what had happened wasn't her mommy's fault even though she'd done it on purpose. She was very sick and couldn't help it. Then she asked Ghost if she knew her father.

Ghost said nothing, just like her mommy had asked. Then she was brought to Faith's, and the never-ending nightmare began.

Now, a different type of nightmare was going to come true. Ghost now knew the difference between purpose and accident, and between sleeping and dead, yet she could not stop it.

She could not stop Sapphire from walking straight into his trap.

...

Sapphire bumped into the back of the trunk as the car came to a sudden stop.

She'd never switched from the couple's car to Mer's truck. But she knew she'd been handed off. She'd heard them exchange a few words before they gave him the car.

Who was he, she wondered, to have such power over the

people in this place? He must've had power over the people at Club Scene back home, too. But how and why?

The trunk popped, letting in daylight, and a knife was thrown in through the crack. Sapphire pulled back, staring at the blade with hesitation.

What the hell? She grabbed it from behind her back and sawed at the rope. Once it snapped and she got the gag off, she sawed off the cords that held the trunk down on the outside.

The cord snapped and the trunk popped up. Sapphire saw nothing but snow and sky. No sight of Mer, Jebediah, or Ester.

Sapphire climbed out on shaky legs and planted her feet in the snow, feeling the chill of the wind blow through her. She held the knife up, and gazed at her surroundings.

Mer's house was twenty yards to her right and the cemetery lay in the opposite direction. Sapphire's eyes latched onto the car. It was still running, the driver's side door was open, keys still in the ignition.

This wasn't right, but she wasn't going to pass up a chance to escape.

Sapphire stumbled toward the open car door.

A small, sharp scream arose from her left. "Help! Help!"

Sapphire's head whipped toward the cemetery. It was the voice of a child. *Ghost.* Sapphire hurled herself through the thick snow and headed toward the gates.

"Help! Heeelp!"

The scream sounded strange, yet familiar.

"I'm coming!" Sapphire shouted, knife clenched in her hand. "Hold on!"

She pushed through the gates and her eyes landed on the girl. Ghost hung from a rope, tied around her waist, off the roof of the mausoleum, her legs kicking in the air.

"Help! Heeelp!" Again, the scream sounded familiar, but in strange way.

Sapphire scanned the graveyard for Mer as she ran, but it

was empty. The closer she came, the odder the scenario became. Ghost shook her head violently as her arms waved at her sides.

"Help! Heeelp!"

Sapphire realized that Ghost couldn't be screaming; she was gagged. The plea was recorded from a horror movie Aston had just made her watch. Mer was up to something, she just wasn't sure what. It didn't make sense for him to let her go just to snag her again, so Sapphire went for it.

She sprinted past a cawing crow on a stone, past a grave yet to be filled, and up to Ghost who was still shaking her head. Sapphire cut her down and out of the rope, then removed the gag.

"It's a trap!" Ghost shouted.

Snap! Sapphire looked down just in time to see it happen. A noose connected to a rope had been buried in the snow below Sapphire's feet. As the rope pulled up, the noose snapped in around her ankles and yanked her back.

She smacked into the ground and was pulled back toward the open grave. Sapphire screamed and dug her fingers into the snow in search of something to grab onto.

Ghost launched after her and grabbed her hand. But the girl was only dragged through the snow along with her. Ghost managed to clasp onto a small iron garden-edge fence, just as Sapphire's lower body dropped into the grave.

They came to an abrupt stop.

Sapphire felt a sharp tug at her legs as someone—Mer mostly likely—pulled back on the rope, trying to get her into the grave. Ghost shut her eyes and let out a piercing screamed as her small arms stretched to their fullest extent. She looked like she was about to snap in half.

When Ghost opened her eyes, they filled with panic. "I see him. He's coming!" she yelled through clenched teeth.

Sapphire cranked her head just enough to see Mer in the periphery, holding a bundle of rope in his arm.

Sapphire looked back at the little girl who was struggling to save her. "You have to run!"

"No!" Ghost screamed, horrified at her words.

"Get to town and find my husband!" Sapphire yelled, as Mer yanked at her legs again. "His name is Aston. He's wearing his dark green jacket with a gray hood, or maybe no hood. Don't trust *anybody*, but him. Now let go!"

"But…" Ghost struggled to hold on as tears of frustration tumbled down her cheeks. "You don't understand—"

"Ghost!" Sapphire screamed. "Let go!!!"

With a quivering lip and desperation in her eyes, Ghost let go of her hand and then ran.

Sapphire fell into the grave and smacked her head into something hard. She turned around, and grabbed her forehead as she opened her bleary eyes. She must've hit her head so badly it caused her to hallucinate, because the ground around her didn't feel cold and hard, but soft.

A blurry Mer appeared at the edge of the grave, with the roll of rope under his arm.

"Thank you," he said. "Thank you for making the right choice."

"What?" Sapphire gazed up at her hazy opponent as she tried, but failed, to sit up. "Why would you let me go, just to trap me again?"

Mer didn't answer.

"I don't know what sick game you have planned for tomorrow, but it's not going to happen!" Sapphire yelled. "My husband's here, and she's going to find him."

"She won't make it far." He squatted as he looked down at his prisoner. "And your husband's not here anymore. I'm sorry to tell you, he won't be returning."

A bolt of terror shot through Sapphire. "Where is he? What did you to do him?"

Mer's eyes were on her as he threw the rope down onto

her. Sapphire struggled to get the heavy rope off just as she saw Mer jump down in the pit.

Thud!

Everything turned dark. Sapphire stopped moving, stopped breathing. All noises, Mer, the wind, the cawing crow, had dulled. It was as if a muffler had been placed on top of her.

Sapphire pushed her hands against something plush. Nothing budged.

She closed her eyes trying to visualize what she was feeling. She hadn't been hallucinating. She was in a rectangle shaped box, lined with velvet. It was obvious and the unwanted realization crept over her skin before exploding in her chest.

She was in a *coffin*. Sapphire opened her eyes and screamed.

CHAPTER 14

The shortcut *sucked*. The road *sucked*. The forest *sucked*.

Aston peered at the dark bending path. He should've been there by now; he'd been driving for hours, just getting farther away from the highway.

After another look at the mayor's map, he grabbed his phone. His GPS wasn't working, but he had enough of a signal to get the 411 lady to patch him through to Shadow Falls Sheriff's Department. He didn't expect an answer—it was almost two o'clock in the morning—but he'd leave a message and hope they'd get back to him about their Mer.

"He-llo?" a sleep-filled voice answered. "Sheriff Morgan Freeman here."

"Oh," Aston said, then shook his head. "Morgan Freeman? Like the actor?"

A deep sigh. "Yeah."

"Any relati—"

"No."

"Bummer."

"I suppose. What can I do for you?"

"I'm a detective from California, looking for a man named Mer in your town."

"A Mer. Here? No, I don't thin…" His voice was replaced by static. "Mer what?"

"First name, last name, any Mer?" The road turned rough and Aston had to grab the wheel harder. He glanced at the mayor's map again to make sure he was on track.

"No…" Static. "…ure it's not a nickname?"

Nick name. Aston's mind's eye flashed to something. Could it be short for Mercer or...

Static. "...ere are you coming from?" the sheriff continued.

"Pleasant Pines," Aston said, squinting into the dark. His brights did little. The deeper into the forest he got, the worse the signal became.

"...ant Pines?" Static. "...careful...strange...keeping our eyes on...Two PIs...vanished...you can trust their law enforcement."

"What?" Aston yelled. "Vanished? The PIs vanished?"

More static followed by fragmented words. Aston's eyes drew to his headlights. Up ahead, the rocky ground appeared to disappear. There was nothing, but...

Nothing.

"Shit!" Aston dropped his phone and grabbed the wheel as he floored the brake.

The car skidded forward and swerved as the tires struggled to find traction. "Fuck-fuck-fuck-fuck!"

The hood entered the nothingness. The car came to a stop, and Aston stared out at the darkness, letting his mind catch up. He opened the door, took his phone, and got out carefully.

Away from the direct light of the brights, his eyes adjusted and he was able to see the whole picture.

His car sat at the edge of a deep gulch. The front tires teetered out over the massive plunge. His looked down at the 800-foot-drop as vertigo took a hold of him.

"Jesus..." That mayor and his fucking map. Then, Shadow Falls Sheriff's words finally registered. A nickname.

Wil*mer*. The *mayor* was the killer. He'd sat two feet from the man who had kidnapped Sapphire, and he'd believed him. Some cop Aston was.

When dawn broke, it would be December 23rd. He had to get back to Pleasant Pines ASAP.

The distinct sound of a shotgun being cocked came from behind him. "Get your hands up and throw me your gun!"

Aston's hands pulled up as he turned. A man, a hick, stepped into the glow offered by the headlights, shotgun aimed at him.

"I don't have a gun," Aston offered.

The hick under the camo cap raised his chin. "No gun? What kinda PI are you?"

"I don't need one." Aston nodded behind the hick. "My partner does all the shooting."

The hick swung around and aimed his gun at the partner who wasn't there.

Aston bolted toward him. Just as the hick turned back around, Aston pulled an elbow to the side of his head then grabbed the barrel of the shotgun. Groaning and struggling, they rumbled. The hick shoved Aston backward, using the shotgun as a bar. Aston fell and landed on his trunk. He could feel the car rolling toward the gulch behind him.

The hick used his leverage and pushed the shotgun to Aston's gullet, forcing him back with the car.

Aston's panicked eyes darted upward, knowing that when the car went over so would he.

"If I'm going…" Aston wheezed in a deep voice. "You're going with me."

He wrapped his legs around the hick's waist as the car tilted at the drop. The hick relinquished one hand from the shotgun in panic, and reached for Aston's leg.

Aston forced the shotgun up and smacked it into the hick's nose. The car dropped behind him and Aston dove to the ground. The hick tumbled forward and a scream rang out in the gulch. The echo lasted long after the man's death-yell ceased.

Aston lay on the ground, reaching out over the gulch. His car was gone. His phone had no reception. And he was probably a day's hike away from Pleasant Pines. He was fucked.

He got up and started walking, guided only by the moon's faint light. He stumbled right into a bush and smacked into something hard.

"Son of a bitch!" Aston cussed.

His hands fumbled down in front of him, feeling the hard plastic and skinny wheels.

"Son of a bitch," Aston grinned.

It was a dirt bike and the key, rather than being 800 feet down in the pocket of a smashed hick, was still in the ignition.

The hick must've hid it in the bush as he waited here for Aston. The mayor probably sent him to make sure the job got done in case plan A, the gulch, failed.

Aston mounted the dirt bike and turned the ignition. It roared to life.

An urgent fire burned in Aston as he drove into the dark forest, trying to find his way back. He had to get to the mayor before the mayor killed Sapphire.

• • •

Stay calm. Stay-calm. Stay-calm-staycalmstaycalmstaycalm.

Sapphire tried, but all she could think of was that she was buried alive, running out of air…

Her heart pounded, making her breathing speed up. The deeper she inhaled, the more oxygen she wasted. The faster the oxygen went, the more she panicked and the quicker she breathed. The four walls were hugging her and the dread felt like a million ants crawling and multiplying under her skin.

Stay calm! Think!

But there was no way out. She was already suffocating. The anxiety, heavy as lead, pulled her farther down. She could feel her lips turn blue, her lungs ache, and her eyes bulge.

But she didn't die. She hadn't run out of oxygen, for some reason, though she probably should have by now. It was a panic attack.

The psychic popped into Sapphire's mind. This was what she saw: a *coffin*. Didn't she say stuff about something big coming Sapphire's way? Something that would annihilate her world?

Was this it? The annihilation—the end?

But Sapphire didn't believe in psychics. For them to be real, life had to be predestined. And destiny, like her father had said, was a human invention. Life was chaos and science. William Dubois had proved it.

Yet, the psychic predicted a coffin, and here Sapphire was.

R.H. The psychic said R.H. knew Sapphire.

She hadn't thought of it at the time, but now, the image of the nurse from Halloween popped into her mind. Did she look like the woman from the picture? That nurse had stared at her like she knew her, like her only purpose was for Sapphire to see her. Or, perhaps, Sapphire's mind was only playing tricks on her. Aston never saw her after all.

Aston.

What if Mer had already gotten to him? The heavy regret filled her chest as warm tears swelled in her eyes. She never meant to end up here. How did it happen? Who was to blame for the mistake?

She'd left the studio that morning and headed south on the freeway toward Father O'Riley, her confidant of three years. He wasn't technically a "Father" anymore, since he'd quit the church, got married, and got a new job, but Sapphire was too used to calling him Father O'Riley, and really, not much had changed.

Sapphire stepped into the booth, closed the door, and spilled her guts through thin wall separating them.

"So…should I go?" Sapphire said after giving him the quick version.

Father O'Riley's voice boomed from the other side. "Couldn't you just leave an anonymous tip to the police?"

"Not enough evidence; they wouldn't take it seriously."

"You know what cop probably would take it seriously?" Father O'Riley said. "Your *husband*. Honesty is a vital part of marriage, you know. Interesting story: when my wife and I first met—"

"Oooh." Sapphire made jazz hands despite the fact that he couldn't see. "You've been married for what, three-whopping-months. Please tell me, what is the secret to such a long marriage?"

"I don't know what I dislike more, when you're being sarcastic or when you're being blasphemous." The distinct sound of unfurling toilet paper came from Father O'Riley's side.

"Oh my God," Sapphire winced. "Are you wiping? Gross."

"Well, maybe next time don't follow me into the *men's room*!" Father O'Riley roared, and flushed.

They stepped out of their bathroom stalls and Sapphire unlocked the main door to re-open it for the public, then leaned against the hand dryer. "What am I supposed to do then?"

"Well I do have an office, you know," Father O'Riley continued, washing his hands. "You're welcome there anytime."

"Pff." Sapphire followed him out into the college hallway. "So I can stand in line behind twelve bawling students waiting to see their counselor? No thanks."

"They don't always bawl."

Okay, *some* things had changed, Sapphire admitted. It had gotten a lot harder to get one-on-one time with him. Students were always in line for his office, and his new wife, Teresa, didn't appreciate Sapphire coming by their house every two weeks. People apparently thought it was weird that a twenty-three-year-old woman was friends with a man in his sixties. For this reason, she'd decided not to tell Aston about Father O'Riley either.

"I don't even understand what you're doing," he said as they moved down the hallway. "It's not like it was before, so ...why?"

Sapphire looked at him, feeling a bit thrown. "What do you mean, *why*?"

"You faced your demon, Sapphire. I can see it. You don't

have that obsessive gleam in your eye when you talk about this stuff, so why do it at all?"

Sapphire didn't know how to answer him, so she grabbed his arm. "Just tell me what you think."

"I *did*, Sapphire," Father O'Riley said. "NEXT!"

A bawling girl swooshed by them and into the office. Sapphire gave him a smug look.

"I said, they don't *always* bawl," Father O'Riley muttered. "We'll talk soon."

Sapphire had no plan of going to the institution, but as she hit the road, the Range Rover pulled in that direction. It was *basically* on her way home anyway. Twenty-five additional miles was nothing, if you compared it to say, Tokyo.

As always, she stopped to grab a box of donuts on the way.

"Oh my God," Shelly McCormick said the moment Sapphire entered with the pink box. "Raspberry filling?"

Sapphire handed the box to the security guard so he could check it. "Like I would dare come here without raspberry filling."

She sat down by the quaint table—as quaint as a table could be in a heavily securitized institution for the criminally insane. It actually wasn't a bad place. Mr. Goldstein, Sapphire's lawyer, had gotten Shelly into this little gem. Though Shelly knew nothing of her murderous second personality at the time, she'd tried to kill Sapphire, convinced only she could do the job as the Serial Catcher properly. But she was better now. The therapy and medications helped her control the True Serial Catcher at times.

"I love you," Shelly mumbled, cramming a raspberry-filled donut into her mouth.

"Aww, I love you too," Sapphire replied.

"I was talking to the donut. You, I'm okay with," Shelly said, then smiled and Sapphire joined in.

"How are you?"

Shelly shrugged, taking another donut. "They've got me on a new pill that turns my pee purple."

"Festive."

"Very. What's new?"

Sapphire glanced around the room, then lowered her voice and gave Shelly the basics.

"So," Sapphire finished, "what do you think?"

Shelly shook her head. "Are you asking me if you should do it? Or, if your plan is sufficient?"

Sapphire rubbed her forehead. "I don't know. Both."

Shelly shrugged helplessly. "The theory is weak. And… honestly, if you don't feel right about it, you probably shouldn't go."

Sapphire nodded. There was her answer. Two for two. She wasn't going. She reached for a donut, and watched Shelly's head lower and eyes close.

"Shelly? Are you alri—"

Shelly sprung across the table. Black-eyed and vicious, she grabbed Sapphire's collar.

"What the fuck are you doing?" Shelly hissed. "With me in here, there's nobody else out there protecting those girls."

"Long time no see," Sapphire groaned, trying to peel the True Serial Catcher off her.

"So, what? You're lying to your husband? Boo-freaking-hoo. Didn't he know who he was marrying? You have to catch that monster."

"But—"

"But what? You'll be happy if more girls die, while your skilled ass just wastes away at DubCorp?"

"But, Shelly said—"

"Oh, be honest, Sapphire!" The True Serial Catcher pulled her closer. "You didn't come here to see Shelly. You came here to see me, hoping I'd tell you to go."

Security swarmed in around them. They tackled Shelly to the ground as the orderlies rushed toward her with needles.

"So, go!" Shelly shouted, face squished to the floor. "Go!"

Sapphire left the institution, convinced. Clearly, she had to go, at least to check it out. She owed Mary Dunnigan that much. And, Shelly had been right too. The lead *was* weak. The probability of her actually finding the guy was so minute, it basically didn't even matter.

It all made sense then.

But now, here in this coffin, nothing made sense and Sapphire knew exactly whose fault it was.

It wasn't the man who'd kidnapped her. Or the manager, who may or may not have set her up. It wasn't Father O'Riley or Shelly. It wasn't even the True Serial Catcher's fault, though she had been right.

Deep down, Sapphire knew she had gone to see Shelly, hoping the split personality would come out and tell her to go. Truth was, it didn't really matter what she said. Sapphire was just looking for *anyone* to point her in a direction she already knew she was heading.

The fault was no one's but Sapphire's.

She opened her eyes slowly. Her breathing had calmed and the panic had eased. The velvet coffin didn't seem quite as tight and the lid above didn't feel as heavy. Her mind was busy elsewhere. It hadn't seemed as big when Father O'Riley asked the question, but it was.

Why?

Sapphire was happy with Aston. She truly had rid herself of the old obsession the moment she faced her father, so that wasn't it. Serial Catcher or businesswoman—she was neither, yet both. She knew exactly how risky it was to go back to her old life, and knew she couldn't trap killers like she had before. So why *did* she leave the studio that day?

She didn't have an answer. All Sapphire had was regret. She wished she could turn back time and choose to stay. Had she, she'd be with Aston right now, not here, suffocating.

Sapphire inhaled to keep the regret, self-anger, and panic

at bay. Aston was okay; Mer had probably lied. And Sapphire would be okay too. Yes, she was in a coffin. And, yes, R.H. could be Rita Hayes. But, life was molded by action not fate, and no psychic could tell her otherwise. She refused to die here because someone told her it was meant to be.

Ghost.

Ghost was action. She was out there somewhere, searching for Aston, and she was Sapphire's only hope.

• • •

Mer shuffled through the snow, pushing away the thoughts of the woman in the coffin.

It had been a few hours and she was likely in a panic. Being buried alive was something he wished on no one. Though, it seemed, this time he'd finally get everything right.

Moments after he said the word to Rosie, he'd realized it. Hero.

Only the heart of a soul willing to sacrifice himself, can harbor the soul of the buried in the blaze of the true moon and before the eyes of six.

He'd read the passage a thousand times, but he'd finally understood what it meant. Over the years, he'd tried every moon, every Alma look-a-like, every satanic dagger, every sign, but nothing had worked. He knew why now. Of all the things he'd done wrong, he'd never questioned the word *sacrifice*. He'd thought the women had to sacrifice themselves to become Alma, but the truth was much more obvious.

Every woman he'd ever captured had told him they were Alma, but they'd *only* done it to save their own lives. That wasn't really a sacrifice, was it? No. The soul who was supposed to harbor Alma's spirit had to be willing to truly sacrifice themselves for someone else. The soul to harbor Alma's spirit had to have the heart of a *hero*.

And she did just as he hoped she would. Instead of taking

the car with the ignition still on and driving off, Sapphire had gone for Rosie, making the sacrifice, proving herself as a hero.

He looked at his watch. She was now locked inside a coffin, emblazoned with a pentagram. He'd always been very meticulous with his schedule. Dinner, walk, then chants with the first and second shot. But that was before he truly understood the instructions. He revisited a passage he'd seen in the *Book of Resurrection: The True Death of a Hero*. The heart of a hero was different than the heart of a regular human. Death would not cause their resilient soul to leave their body. No, in order for Sapphire to vacate the vessel for Alma, she had to be buried while her heart was still beating, in a coffin emblazoned with a pentagram, a general staple when calling upon the dark lord's favors.

He'd had to get creative to get the timing of the coffin and the blood moon just right. If she suffocated too soon, the body would be no good. He'd drilled a hole that seeped in a small amount of oxygen to Sapphire. Exactly five and a half hours before the sacrifice would take place, he'd plug the hole and Sapphire would begin to suffocate to death.

He shivered, again pushing away the thoughts of her in the coffin, and visualized the reward instead. He watched the sun crack in the distance.

Ah.

It was finally December 23rd. Tonight, at eight o'clock, the blood moon would rise and by the time it vanished; at nine o'clock, he would finally have his wife back. Now he just had to find their daughter.

His eyes drew to a small footprint in the snow. Her trail. She was heading into town.

Perfect.

He picked up his phone with a smile.

• • •

Ghost came to a stop as she hit the edge of the frozen lake. She peered across it, beyond the giant Christmas tree, where the townspeople walked in and out of the stores decorated with lights, pine, and, ornaments. A song she knew well, both from now and before the attic, blared through the speakers: *Feliz Navidad.*

She looked at the men, moving through the streets. A few of them wore green jackets. Sapphire had told her not to trust anyone else, so she wouldn't, but how would she know which one was Aston?

She looked left, then right. The fastest way across was over the ice. She noticed a big red sign next to the lake, but Ghost didn't recognize most of the letters. The only one she knew was the upside-down horns: *W.*

She decided to hurry, and held her hands out for balance as she scurried across.

Crack...

Ghost stopped at the familiar sound and the dream came back to her. She watched in slow motion as the cobweb of cracks spread out from under her feet.

Crack...

Ghost looked up. *Cold.*

The ice floor cracked opened from under her, and she plummeted into to the dark water. The cold was mind-numbing, eating its way through her muscles and her insides. Ghost tried to get back up, but she didn't know how. She waved her arms, and kicked her legs, but she just went round and round. She opened her mouth to scream and her throat filled with the icy water.

Her hand reached for the light beyond the surface as the heavy, cold darkness pulled her down.

Then she saw a shadow of a man above her.

Soon, she felt something grab her wrist. She emerged out of the cold, and into the biting air as the man pulled her out.

She spat up water, and her squealing lungs pulled for air.

"Jesus! Are you okay?" He shouted as he put his jacket around her and picked her up.

Ghost's teeth clattered as he got them off the ice and onto land. He was a nice-looking man, with kind eyes. He looked a little older than Sapphire.

"What were you doing? Didn't you see the warning sign?" he asked.

Ghost shook her head then, remembering what Sapphire said, stumbled away from him.

He held his hand out. "I'm not going to hurt you."

Though her body ached with cold, Ghost kept moving backward, away from the man.

"Are you in trouble?" He looked at her clothes. "I can help you."

Ghost stopped, noticing the color of the jacket he'd placed around her shoulders. *Green.* She took a cautious step forward. "Are you...Aston?"

He gazed at her, a watchful look in his eyes. "Yes."

Ghost closed her eyes in relief, then took his hand as he reached it out again. He gently led her to the street.

"We have to save Sapphire," Ghost said, willing her voice stronger.

He tilted his head at her. "Sapphire?"

Ghost nodded eagerly.

He looked around at the townspeople with worry, then opened a car door. "Get in."

Ghost clambered into the car and relished in its warmth. Everything would be okay.

She'd found Aston, and now they would save Sapphire.

"Alright," he said, and turned the car on. "What do you know?"

A *wroooom* bellowed through the street. Ghost's eyes landed on a man driving a thin motorcycle. He drove fast, even faster than her mommy used to drive.

Ghost cranked her neck back to watch him pull in for a

stop. He brushed the dirt off his green jacket then removed his helmet. His piercing blue eyes landed on Ghost for just as second before they moved up to the buildings.

"Well," the man next to her smiled. "Go on. Tell me everything."

CHAPTER 15

Aston listened to the godforsaken *Feliz Navidad* repeat itself again as he lit a cigarette and dropped the pack back in his pocket.

"Hello," a woman smiled, passing him.

Aston nodded.

"Merry Christmas," a passing man greeted, fake smile plastered on his face.

Aston's eyes pulled from the goody two shoes townies to the town's big clock tower, and its bell, tolling for the new hour.

It was officially December 23rd, the day Sapphire had seen circled on the calendar. Was it too late? The sickening thought forced its way through his mind. Was she already dead?

He paced toward the building marked *Pleasant Pines Sheriff's Department* as he picked up his phone. The reception was better here than in the woods.

"Hi!" Barry answered.

"Hey, it's me, Listen—"

"You've reached Barry Harry. I'm unavailable at the moment…"

Aston tossed his cigarette and lingered outside of the sheriff's department as he listened to his partner's painfully long message. He watched the townspeople move about, laughing and chattering like they were extras in a freaking Hallmark Christmas movie. People were too pleasant, too friendly around here. Aston didn't buy it.

Beep.

"Barry," Aston said. "Listen, I'm sorry I risked your license, but…look. This town…there's something really off here. I'm pretty sure their mayor just tried to have me killed. I've spoken to the sheriff in Shadow Falls, and he has major concerns. If you could come back…I could really use a hand." He sighed. "Actually, truth is, I *really* need you, man. Please."

He hung up and was just about to step inside the sheriff's office when a woman with an oversized stormy kromer hat falling down over her face came out.

"They're not in there," she said in an air of frustration. She was the first person Aston had seen who looked like she had an actual emotion. "You'll have to come back."

"Oh…thanks," Aston nodded, letting go of the door. He waited until her giant hat had vanished among the big snowflakes, then stepped inside.

Their whole "department" was a cramped room, two empty desks, one tiny empty cell, and a sea of folders.

"Hello?" Aston yelled, just in case.

According to Morgan Freeman—the Shadow Falls Sheriff, not the actor—Aston could trust the Pleasant Pines Sheriff's Department, but a little snooping never hurt anyone. He moved deeper into the room and ran his fingers over the stacks upon stacks of folders on the sheriff's and deputy's desks. He frowned. A lot of paperwork meant a lot of crime. Unless every adult citizen in the small town of Pleasant Pines had a criminal past, it didn't make sense.

His fingers stopped on a thick folder with the name: Wilmer Hedge. Aston glanced around the room before opening it. Inside lay a picture of the mayor, coming out of a bar with a woman. The sheriff already had the mayor under surveillance.

"Just caught the Walden boy shoplifting," a voice said. "I let him slide, but we'll have to remember to make a folder and file it."

Aston shut the folder and turned to a man, the sheriff, who'd stepped inside.

His gaze was low as he took his hat off and brushed it clear of snow. The dude was old, ancient for a sheriff. His hair was chalk-white and his face was weighed down by wrinkles. He was in great shape, but they would've retired him ages ago in the city.

"Now what did you want—oh!" his eyes landed on Aston. "You're not my deputy."

"Observant. No wonder you're the sheriff."

The sheriff frowned, then smiled, taking off his jacket as he sat at his desk. "Sheriff Button is the name. How can I help you, Mr...?"

"Ridder. Detective Ridder from Los Angeles." Aston sat down opposite the sheriff and held up the picture of Sapphire. "My wife is missing, and I have reason to believe your mayor took her."

Sheriff Button ran his fingers through his white mane. "I've actually been keeping my eyes on him for a while. Two PIs came to town in the past few years, both interested in him. Then they vanished."

"Then why haven't you done anything about it yet?" Aston asked.

The sheriff laughed. "In a place like this you can't just go interrogate someone like the mayor. Should the evidence, which we don't have, not be sufficient, he could have me indicted and replaced. He owns this town. *Owns* it. If you think you've got hard evidence, I want in."

Aston exhaled. "My wife called me, and said she was held at a place with a big cedar tree out front?"

"Yup, that's the mayor's house alright." The ancient sheriff smacked his hands together. "Hot damn. I've been waiting years to nail that S-O-B."

Relief spread through Aston as the sheriff reached for his jacket again.

"I'll need a gun, because..." Aston said, about to make up some bullshit excuse of why he didn't have his own, or his badge if the sheriff wanted to see it.

"Here you go." The sheriff tossed Aston a nine-millimeter.

He took it in surprise. There was lenient, then there was crazy lenient. He followed the sheriff outside and toward the olive Jeep as he put the gun in his pant lining.

Please, he begged, *please let me find her still breathing.*

Aston opened his eyes to the tune of *Feliz Navidad* and shook his head. "You trying to lobotomize people with this song, or what's the deal?"

"It's the best one though, don't you think?" The sheriff smiled, then hummed along.

Aston glanced at the townspeople, all jollily singing along to the tune, on its millionth repeat.

"Sure. Not creepy at all," Aston mumbled, a chill running up the back of his neck. Though the townspeople's hands were on their shopping bags, and their ears were on the song, he could feel their eyes on him as he jumped into the Jeep.

...

Ghost clasped her hands as they drove.

She'd told Aston everything. Where Sapphire was and where Ghost had lived before she escaped, and about all the women who had come to the house but never left. Aston looked sick as he kept his eyes on the white, snaking road ahead of the car.

She looked out the window. She'd liked seeing all the lights and town decorations from inside the car. Maybe it meant Christmas was still coming.

They were far from the town now, and she still hadn't seen Mer's house. Her wishful thinking started to fade and turn into worry.

"Aston," Ghost said. "We have to save Sapphire now. We have to hurry."

"I know," he smiled, though it didn't reach his eyes. "I just have to make another quick stop and then we will go find

Sapphire." His first quick stop was to get gas, and after vanishing for a little bit, he'd come back looking solemn.

Ghost nodded, and soon he pulled into a snow-covered plane. "Stay in here. No matter what. Okay?"

"Okay," Ghost promised.

He stepped outside and Ghost squinted as he vanished into the white haze.

She looked at the dashboard clock. Though she couldn't tell time, she knew Sapphire had been by herself for a long time. Her eyes moved from the clock to the holder where his cell sat.

Ghost tilted her head at the photograph on the screen. It was of him, kissing a lady on a beach.

The lady was not Sapphire.

• • •

Snow had turned to slush in Aston's shoes and his socks squished at every step. He was a born and bred Angeleno; this real weather bullshit was not his cup of tea. Coincidentally, tea wasn't his cup of tea either; Aston was a coffee man.

He glanced over at the sheriff and his younger deputy, David Sanches, who'd joined them for backup a few minutes earlier. They certainly seemed cozy in their padded sheriff's hats and coats as they hiked up the snowy hill.

"So, detective…" the sheriff said, clearly one to be bothered by silence, unlike Aston. "How'd you meet your wife?"

Aston sighed. "She was a singer, a diva, and I was hired to protect her from a crazy stalker."

"Wow," the sheriff whistled.

The deputy frowned. "But…isn't that the plot of *The Bodyguard*?"

"Um…" Aston squinted through the thick snowflakes. "So how much farther is this house anyway?"

"Just over the hill there," the sheriff nodded, then beamed.

"Can't wait to get my hands on him. Heck, we'll probably make the *Pleasant Pines Gazette*, David."

The deputy glanced up. "Uh, sure."

Since the mayor's place was gated and rigged with cameras up front, the sheriff, Deputy Sanches, and Aston were taking the back route. They didn't want to risk the guy knowing they were coming so he could take off with Sapphire. Or worse.

Aston touched the nine-millimeter in his pant lining to make sure it was still there, still secure.

"This weather must be different from the holiday weather you have there in Los Angeles," the sheriff said.

"Yeah, you could say that," Aston said, reaching the top of the hill. "I don't know how you guys get anything done in this shit stor…"

Aston's words fell out as he took it all in. Below the hill was a steep ten-foot-wide, hundred-foot-deep crack in the mountain, mended by a small bridge. On the other side, at the bottom of the hill, lay a big house surrounded by vast land. Aston stared at the bridge as the pieces fell into place in his mind. *Shit.* How had he not seen it? It wasn't the mayor.

He grabbed the gun and swung around, already knowing where to point it. The sheriff and the deputy stood still, both guns up and aimed at Aston.

"Huh," the sheriff said, eyeing Aston's gun. "How'd you know?"

"The only person who can control that many people, is someone who can build files then blackmail them on their crimes and dirty secrets, like the mayor's affairs, like the shoplifter." Aston shifted his aim from one cop to another. "The only person who can access nationwide data on criminals with suspected business fronts like Club Scene, probably has the same vocation as a person who can wipe their own car registration." Aston stared at the sheriff. "Isn't that right, *Mer*."

"You know," the sheriff glared back at him, "I was concerned that David's poor acting skills would give it away, but your wife told me you'd find me, so I suppose I shouldn't blame him."

The deputy's solemn eyes were on the ground.

"Where is she?" Aston hissed through his teeth.

"I'm afraid it doesn't matter," the sheriff said. "You won't be alive to save her."

The sheriff moved closer and Aston pulled his trigger. He fired three shots at the sheriff's chest. To his horror, the man kept moving. *Impossible.* He was either a zombie, a vampire, or…

Aston looked at the nine-millimeter. Blanks. What better way to get your opponent to relax than to make him believe you'd armed him?

"I wish it didn't have to be this way," the sheriff said sullenly, and re-aimed his gun at Aston's head.

A gun cocked and was put to the sheriff's head.

Aston and the sheriff turned to Deputy Sanches.

"What on earth are you doing, David?" the sheriff asked perplexed, aim still on Aston.

The deputy's shaking hand held the gun to the sheriff's head. "It's gone too far. He's law enforcement for Christ's sake. We can't do it. Not this time."

"Don't take the Lord's name in vain, David."

"Sorry, sir." David's trembling finger was on the trigger. "But I'm going to ask you to put the gun down and put your hands behind your head."

"David." The sheriff eyed his deputy. "You know the moment I vanish those photos will go out. How's the good pastor going to feel when he sees his son in the arms of a prostitute in Thailand?"

Deputy Sanches's breath shook as he inhaled. "With all the things you've made me do, all the things I've pretended not to see, I'm going to hell anyways. I knew about the women. I knew. But children, sir. *Children.* I can't be—"

Bang! The sheriff shot the deputy point blank between the eyes.

The sheriff looked down at the deputy with regret, then turned to Aston and fired twice.

The first bullet hit Aston in the side of the neck, prompting his body to fall. The second bullet whizzed above his head as he tumbled into the hundred-foot drop.

Aston clawed at the ice, trying to get a grip.

He caught a small ice block, sticking out from the snowy wall. Despite the cold, warm beads of sweat formed on Aston's forehead as he looked down at the plummet, then squeezed his eyes shut.

He managed to pull himself up on it. Using it as a stand, he stretched and got his fingertips to the edge. Just then, the ice block crumbled under his weight. Aston groaned, squeezing his fingers into the icy edge as gravity yanked at his body.

The clear sound of someone shuffling through the snow came from above him.

The sheriff, most likely, returning to make sure Aston was dead.

To his surprise, a small hand grabbed onto the right sleeve of his jacket, then another small hand grabbed onto his left sleeve. A tiny grunt sounded from above him as the person pulled.

It wasn't much, but it was all the help Aston needed to get leverage and pull himself up. He heaved himself onto the ground and exhaled as he looked up. "Thanks..."

A little girl with dirty hands and long, unkempt hair hanging down over her face, stood in the snow, staring at his jacket. "You're Aston."

"Uh, yes I am," Aston said, then looked around and murmured, "creepy little forest girl who knows my name."

"Come on!" She grabbed his hand. "We don't have much time."

CHAPTER 16

The world was a shade darker as Sheriff Mervin Button made his way toward the car. David, his deputy, had parked it in the clearing with the girl inside.

Mer couldn't think clearly, and Alma's angry stare wasn't making it easier.

"What more do you want from me! Huh?" he yelled at her. "I'm trying, and after everything I've done, after all the sacrifices I've made, you're *still* angry with me. I'm *trying*!"

He came to a full stop as the car came into view. The door was open. "No…"

He ran up to it and looked inside. Empty. *Of course.* Mer screamed and slammed the door shut.

He turned to face her fury. "I killed *David* for you. He was like a son to me. Jeez…" Mer covered his mouth to scream as his legs folded under him. Tears pooled in his eyes.

Killing David was the worst thing he'd done. Using his job to find criminals running clubs and bars in the towns and cities that formed the pentagram had to be done. The women, the children, that detective he'd just laid two bullets into, all had to die. David didn't *have to* die.

Alma's cold eyes burrowed into him as he sat in the snow, wishing himself back to a time before his life changed.

Thirty years.

He wouldn't often allow himself to remember how much time had passed. His old age was nothing but a painful reminder of how long it had been since he'd lost them.

Every time he reenacted the dinner, it wasn't because he

wanted to relive it, but because the dark book said it had to be done. To put the events as they were on a loop was like tossing a rope out into the vast ocean of time, giving the dead something to grab onto. To freeze time was to help Alma pull herself back home when the dark lord called her name.

Mer had lived in the loop so long that when he looked at himself in the mirror he *still* saw the man, the husband, the father he had been in his forties. In his eyes, his whole being froze in time the moment he shot her. In reality, his skin was sagging and wrinkled. His blond curls had long turned white, and he was past seventy years old.

He closed his eyes to escape her anger. "I'll find her for you. I will have her there, waiting for you as you wake, I promise. Tonight, everything will finally be perfect."

Yes, he'd hand every hunter in town a tranquilizer and send them to search every inch of Pleasant Pines for her. *Everything* would be perfect tonight down to the entire town playing nothing but Alma's favorite Christmas song. She'd loved Christmas so much so that Mer had made the town move up the annual Christmas Eve parade to December 23rd to match the date and time of Alma's death, in hopes that it would help call her back.

Mer opened his eyes to find himself alone again.

He got up, and went back to his sheriff's jeep.

By the time the blood moon appeared tonight, he would have Rosie back. And soon, he'd get his blue truck and go fetch Sapphire's body from the grave. She had a little over three hours of oxygen left now.

Three hours and then her body would be Alma's.

• • •

"And to answer all your dire queries," the chief said. "Yes, we will now bring in donuts *twice* per shift."

A small cheer ran through the bullpen and everyone at the

Beverly Hills Police Department clapped. Everyone but Barry Harry, who was biting his nails.

If Aston heard that they'd all used the suggestion box to request donuts in the break room twice a shift he'd call them "fat fucks" and send them for a mandatory hour at the department's gym. That's why no one used the suggestion box when Aston took over the briefings. *Aston.* The same Aston Barry had abandoned in Idaho. The same Aston Barry saw a voicemail from moments before the briefing started. The chief had glared at Barry until he hung up, but he still heard Aston's last plea:

"*Truth is, I really need you, man. Please.*"

Barry's partner had never begged *anyone* for *anything*. For Aston to sound so desperate, things had to be bad.

"Officer Harry," the chief said, "I need someone at the Spelling residence. They had an attempted break-in last night."

"Me?" Barry touched his chest in surprise. "By myself?"

The chief laughed. "Sure."

As the chief finished up the meeting, Barry's breakfast bagel stirred in his stomach. He swallowed the vomit climbing his throat and walked up to the chief.

"I'm sorry to inconvenience you, sir, but..." Barry took a breath. "I won't be able to take on the Spelling case."

"Officer Harry," the chief chuckled, squaring his paper. "You'll be just fine on your own. How else are you going to grow?"

"No...I mean, I won't be able to take the case because I have to go home. I'm feeling very...under the weather," Barry said. He didn't even know if he could get his hands on a helicopter—couldn't very well steal DubCorp's bird in daylight—but Aston was in trouble; he had to find a way.

"Under the weather?" The chief looked up from his paperwork with steely eyes. "And did this feeling come before or after you got a call from, I'm assuming, Detective Ridder?"

Barry lowered his gaze. He hated lying, always had.

"I obviously can't prove you're not sick, and for legal reasons I can't keep you at work if you claim to be, but..." the chief grabbed Barry's eyes with his, "for your own sake, Officer, I urge you to *feel better* and go to the Spelling residence." The chief stared at him with expectancy, waiting.

Barry straightened his shoulders and looked his boss square in the eyes. "I'm sorry, sir, I can't."

Before he could see the disappointment in Calloway's face, he turned and marched out. Would it have been great to finally get a case of his own? Yes. But Aston needed him, and Barry refused to turn his back on his partner.

• • •

Boom. Boom. Boom.

This time, it wasn't a panic attack. This time, she was dying.

Something had happened to the coffin a few hours back. It had suddenly turned stuffy and the air felt as if it had started to thicken—along with Sapphire's head.

The red velvet looked like it moved above her, as if it were a river of blood. Like Styx, it carried a boat that had come to ferry her to the other side.

Sapphire had died and been brought back before. Death was easy then. It was easy to slip into the nothingness, and hard to want to fight her way back from it.

This time, she had something and someone she didn't want to let go of...

"*I do.*"

A Little White Chapel was busier than they'd expected, but once they got into the church it was only Sapphire, Aston, Elvis Presley, and a drunk homeless man named Jerry, whom they'd paid fifty bucks to be their witness.

Sapphire had found a white non-wedding dress when walking past a window at Caesars Palace's Forum Shops, and Aston had bought a bow tie from one of the pop-up boutiques on The Strip. It went great with his t-shirt.

Elvis himself, or rather the ordained impersonator named Kurt J. McGuffey, had walked Sapphire down the aisle while singing *Can't Help Falling in Love* as Aston waited at the altar, fighting to keep a straight face—which in turn caused a snorting laugh to escape Sapphire, which in turn caused Elvis's classically upturned lip to turn down in dismay. This wasn't their first choice, but the regular minister was booked up and neither Sapphire nor Aston wanted to wait any longer. It had already taken them ten months and several serial killers to get here.

When they reached the altar, Elvis finished his song, bowed to applause that didn't come, then nodded to Sapphire and Aston and greeted their wedding party. "Ladies. Gentlemen…"

Jerry, the drunk homeless man, turned to the empty pews behind him, taking a swig from his bottle.

"Thank you," Elvis continued, "thank you very much, for joining us on this very special day of Sapphire and Ashton's wedding."

"As-ton," Sapphire and Aston corrected.

"Right," Elvis winked and rolled his hips. "Now, love is a magical journey that can leave you *All Shook Up,* but if you're lucky—"

"Yeah, you know what?" Aston motioned his finger over his throat. "Let's kill the whole speech thing. Just the main stuff is fine."

"O-kay?" Elvis said, reluctantly flipping a page in his program. "Let's move on to the rings and the vow—"

"Well," Sapphire interjected, "we technically don't have rings yet, or anything to say, so…"

"So," Elvis squinted at them, "no speech, no rings, and no vows?"

"Right," Sapphire nodded, "just the one part."

"It's just, the speech, the rings, the vow, it's kind of why people do it," Elvis insisted. "Also, there's this part before you do your vows and place the rings on each other's fingers, where

I ask the guests 'if there's anyone with a *Suspicious Mind* who'd object to this union?'" He chuckled. "It's pretty funny."

"Nah, we're good," Aston assured then rolled his finger. "So maybe, a little less conversation, a little more action please."

"Ha!" Sapphire laughed. "Good one."

Elvis glared at Aston. "Okay, now you're just stealing my lines."

He gathered himself and got back in Elvis-mode by rolling his hips back and forth a few times. "Do you, As-ton Ridder take this hunk, a hunk of burning love, Sapphire Dubois, to be your lawful wedded wife and promise to love her tender?"

Aston's face, previously lit with humor, turned serious. "I do."

Elvis rolled his hips, then snapped his fingers and pointed at Sapphire. "And do you Sapphire Dubois, take this *Hound Dog*, Aston Ridder as your lawful wedded husband, and promise to love him sweet?"

Sapphire's smile turned soft as she looked at Aston. "I do."

"By the power vested in me by the state of Nevada and the spirit of Graceland, I now pronounce you husband and wife. You may now *Kiss Quick, While You Still*—"

Sapphire grabbed Aston by the neck and pulled him in for a hard kiss.

"Oh, come on!" Elvis threw his hands up. "It's my best line. You guys are the worst."

Aston grabbed Sapphire by the butt, picking her off the ground, and kept kissing her as they moved down the aisle, away from Elvis and past the snoring homeless man.

"Wake up, Jerry!" Sapphire pulled her lips away to shout. "Dinner's on us!"

They spent the rest of the week in their hotel room, only popping out every now and then for food, drinks, and the occasional show—one of which starred a familiar-looking showgirl named Ginger. Everything felt like it had finally fallen into place.

Boom-boom-boom-boom.

Sapphire's heart fought to keep her alive, beating faster to find more oxygen in her blood.

This was all wrong. Sapphire was dying and Aston…Mer may already have killed him. This was not the ending they were supposed to have. To Kurt J. McGuffey it had seemed like they were the worst couple, with no vows, proper attire, and a bribed homeless man as a witness, but the moment Aston and Sapphire's eyes met, they said it all. *I love you. I'll be there. I'll find you.*

They were finally *there*—that place they couldn't get to before. After all they'd been through, they'd made it and Sapphire fucked it all up.

Again, *why?* The weight of regret was crushing.

If she got out, if Aston was alive, she'd tell the truth about everything and anything. No more lying, no more hiding. It all seemed so asinine and redundant now. Like Shelly's alternate personality had said, Aston knew who he had married; the man had already seen the worst side of her and he still loved her. Yet, she'd lied.

Perhaps, Sapphire realized, she couldn't be honest with Aston because she couldn't be honest with herself. Perhaps there was another question, aside from *why*, that Sapphire had failed to ask herself when she burned her old life in the desert: if Sapphire wasn't the Serial Catcher, who was she?

The red river swirled above her like a bloody storm. Sapphire could feel the last of the oxygen vanish in the coffin. She pounded on the lid, feeling her muscles weaken. She had to get out and make everything right with Aston. She had to see her husband.

She was drowning in the river of the dead. She sank deeper, losing all thoughts that made Sapphire, Sapphire.

Just as she felt she may fade away forever, she heard a noise from outside.

"She's just up here!" Ghost yelled and pulled on Aston's arm. They sprinted through the cemetery, past the graves of children like Ghost. She had found him, Aston. And she could see the mausoleum now. Sapphire's grave was just behind it.

For a while, as they'd hurried through the forest, Ghost hadn't been sure where they were or if she could even find her way back to the cemetery, but then she recognized the path.

"Come on!" she yelled, running through the mausoleum and to the other side of the graveyard. No Mer in sight.

Ghost felt a flutter of joy in her stomach. She'd managed to stop it. She'd made it to Sapphire's coffin before the red moon from her dream appeared; she'd made Sapphire's death an almost dream.

She smiled back at Aston and pointed at the grave, then halted.

He stopped, too, and looked down at the pit. "Where is she?"

Ghost felt like a big, cold rock dropped to the bottom of her gut as she looked down at the empty grave. No coffin, no Sapphire.

"Where is she!?" Aston shouted, panicked eyes on her.

"I…I don't know…I don't understand," Ghost whispered, her bottom lip quivering. "I don't understand. She was right here."

"FUCK!" Aston roared.

Ghost jerked back.

"I'm sorry. I'm sorry. It's okay," Aston said in a softer tone and held his hand out to her. Then his fingers pulled to his hair and he squatted to rest his forehead on his palms. He took a deep breath, then looked up and his eyes moved to the aisle running between the middle of the graves.

"Look." Aston ran up and pointed at tire marks, leading to the big gate. "He must've just moved her somewhere."

A red dart whizzed over Ghost's head and vanished into the snow behind them.

Aston looked at her, eyes wide with realization, then scooped her up. He took off, out of the cemetery and into the trees. Night enclosed them as the dense pines above shut out the twilight.

Suddenly, Aston stumbled and let out a groan. His eyes were squeezed shut as he strained to set Ghost down. "I have a jacked-up leg. Can you run on your own?"

She nodded eagerly.

Snap. A twig cracked on their right.

A bush rustled on their left.

"Go…" Aston whispered. "Go."

A red dart whizzed over them. Another narrowly missed Ghost.

"Get behind me!" Aston yelled, trying to protect Ghost by reaching his arms back as he ran. "Stay as close as you can! If you can't keep up, you let me know, okay?"

"Okay."

Darts zoomed over, behind, and around them as they leaped through the woods. She stayed behind Aston, whose eyes were constantly searching the trees ahead of them.

Something bit Ghost in the back, like she'd gotten stung by a really, really big bee.

She tried to keep up with Aston, tried to keep running, but her legs felt wobbly and her body stopped listening to her.

Ghost fell to the ground and watched Aston disappear into the woods, arm still back, believing she was right behind him.

She opened her mouth to call for him, but she was so tired. So…so…tired…

CHAPTER 17

Aston's breath took body in the cold night as he gazed at the town of Pleasant Pines from a distance.

The clock tower showed it was 7:45 p.m. and some sort of Christmas parade seemed to be underway, moving to the music from a marching band.

Hundreds of people—likely the whole town—had gathered to greet their neighbors dressed as dancing ornaments, elves, and gingerbread men. Since the town was so small, the parade just circled around the giant Christmas tree over and over again. Each side of the main street had a roadblock and trucks guarding it. Men with rifles were gathered outside of the vehicles, on the lookout for Aston, no doubt. On the upside, this was the first time Aston had been here without hearing that godforsaken Christmas song.

He wasn't sure what do to from here. All he knew as he'd stood alone in the forest earlier was that Saph had been moved and Ghost had been taken. He'd been so busy scanning the trees, that he didn't notice them grabbing her. His best shot, he'd thought, was to get to town and find someone who knew where Mer could've taken them. He knew Sapphire was still alive, because…she had to be.

Now that he was here, it didn't seem like he'd be able to get past the blocks without being spotted by the men with the rifles. He needed his own weapon.

He spotted a man with a rifle, standing by himself, guarding the smaller, side-street entrance to the parade. Aston moved toward him, staying as close to the protective buildings as he could. He got up behind the man, whose eyes were on the parade, and knocked him on the shoulder.

Just as he turned, Aston clocked him in the jaw. He took his rifle, and pulled the unconscious man into the darkened side street. He peeked around the corner, counting adversaries and rifles, noting that he was severely fucking outnumbered.

"Stooop," a woman giggled, coming out of the mayor's office.

A man in a Santa suit looked around with paranoia then pulled her around the corner of Second Street and into a truck that had been made into a float, featuring a papier-mâché Santa in his sleigh, being pulled by reindeer.

It only took a second for Aston to decide to follow them, and by the time he got to the truck and knocked, the driver's side window had already fogged up.

"I told you, Phil," a dulled, familiar voice said through the window. "I'll be a couple minutes late. They can wait."

Aston knocked again and the window rolled down, revealing the mayor, beard pulled under his chin, hat pointing to the side, and a half-dressed young woman scrambling to cover up. They both stared at Aston and the barrel, aimed at the mayor.

"Where did he take them?" Aston asked.

"I…I don't know what you're talking about?" the mayor said, hands up.

"Alright," Aston changed the aim to the mayor's crotch. "I'll start with the pecker and see if that refreshes your memory. Probably doing your wife a favor, since you can't seem to keep it in your pants anyway." He cocked the rifle.

"Okay!" the mayor yelled, covering his crotch. "There's a glade on the other side of the lake. People say they've seen lights there."

"How do I get there?"

"Either through town or an hour hike up and around through the woods."

"Fuck." Aston shook his head as the idea came to him.

Between drinking elephant shit and dressing like John Vanderpilt, his ego had already taken a beating this week. "Scoot, then give me your costume."

Aston opened the door and forced the two to share a seat as he took the wheel. Getting the gear on while keeping an aim on the mayor wasn't easy, but Aston got the job done and turned the key. When the truck roared to life, so did the float.

"Feliz Navidad…"

"Are you kidding me?" Aston muttered, then pulled up the beard and nodded to the mayor. "Get down."

He found a tarp and threw it over them, then drove up to the roadblock. He pulled to a stop then one of the men knocked on his window and he rolled it down. "Thought you said you were going to be late. Done already?"

Aston nodded, trying to remember what the mayor sounded like. "Yup."

The man raised a brow at Aston. "You haven't spotted that cop Mer told us to look out for yet, have you?"

Aston's fist clenched around the steering wheel. "Nope."

"Alright," the man waved at his comrades and they moved the block. "Go on through, Mayor."

The young woman popped up from under the tarp. "Help! We've been kidnapped and he's going to shoot Wilmer in the pecker!"

The man raised his rifle and pulled the trigger, just as Aston floored the gas. The head of the seat behind him blew up as he took off. The remaining men dove out of the float's way.

Wilmer and the woman sat in horrified silence as Aston watched the men in the rearview mirror jump into their trucks to come after him, rifles high.

"Feliz Navidad…"

The moment Aston hit the parade, the marching band silenced and the crowd hollered with joy at the sight of Santa Claus.

Bang!

The truck swerved under him. His back tire was hit. People must've thought the gunshot was invisible fireworks because they just cheered louder and waved harder as Aston leaned on the horn, urging them out of the way. The only people who seemed to notice that something was wrong, were the men with rifles on the other side's roadblock. They, too, jumped into their trucks, rifles up.

"*Feliz Navidad...*"

"Move!" Aston screamed and motioned at the crowd. *Bang!* His side mirror was shot out.

"Dear God," Wilmer prayed, clasping his hands. "If you just get me out of this alive, I swear I will stop cheating on my wife and be a good man."

The woman gasped. "You said we were going to run away together."

"Oh come on!" the mayor yelled. "Like you actually believed it."

"Both of you, shut up!" Aston yelled as he skidded toward the thickest part of the parade where people had just now realized that the Santa truck had turned into a death truck. He saw it all change in slow motion. The children's faces turned in horror as they realized Santa had come to murder them. Christmas carolers stumbled over one another in their bulky dresses to get away. Mothers grabbed their tots. Wives grabbed their husbands. Shopaholics grabbed their 20 percent off Make-Your-Own-Candle kits. A fat boy opened his arms and smiled at the sleigh.

Aston swerved away from him and nearly crashed into the woman with the stormy kromer hat before pulling a sharp right. Wilmer and his lover screamed and hugged each other as the truck's side smashed into a roasted almond stand. The oil connected with the flame and set the whole stand on fire as the sleigh took down a cable. As it snapped off, it decapitated all the reindeer on the truck's roof, then grabbed a hold of the light set which, in turn, wrapped around Santa's neck and hoisted him.

The trucks coming at Aston had to swerve away from the crowd, then u-turned to go after him, joining the two other trucks in their pursuit.

"*I wanna wish you a merry Christmas…*" Shot after shot was fired at Aston as he saw his salvation up ahead. He pulled the emergency brake and floored the footbrake as he pulled left. The truck crashed into the giant Christmas tree.

"*I wanna wish you a merry Christmas…*"

The tree was knocked off its stand. Aston swerved away as it swayed. The screams rose in the night as fifty feet of pine and holiday cheer plummeted. It crashed down onto all the trucks behind him.

"*From the bottom of my heart!*"

Aston took it all in. Beheaded reindeer lay strewn about, Santa had been hanged, things were on fire, and children were crying. It wasn't far from Aston's childhood Christmases and it made him slightly nostalgic.

He turned the truck off and the song, that had just started over, finally silenced. No music was, ironically, music to Aston's ears. He staggered out and eyed the men that were knocked out cold between the branches. He shed the bulky Santa suit as he located a faint light, coming from the other side of the lake. He grabbed a firm hold of his rifle and headed for it just as the silver glow, shining down on them all, vanished.

Aston and the townies around him all froze and turned their gazes toward the moon and the full lunar eclipse.

The world had turned to blood.

• • •

"*Vos autem nuntius scientiae reditu furto et evigilare faciatis dormientis.*"

Ghost awoke to the choir of voices and the light of the red

moon. She had no idea where she was, only that someone was holding her.

She opened her eyes to see fiery torches that had been placed around a glade. In front of the torches stood scary creatures, wearing black cloaks and animal masks, chanting in a strange language. They all surrounded a table that was decorated with animal skulls. A sharp knife lay at the foot of the table and next to it stood Mer, chanting to himself.

Fear grabbed ahold of Ghost's chest as she realized that the "someone" holding her was one of the people in the animal masks.

She looked up at the rabbit mask, who looked back down at her with its hollow eyes. Ghost screamed and squirmed out of the cloak's arms. She smacked to the ground then ran for the trees.

"Grab her!" Mer yelled behind her.

Two cloaks grabbed her and yanked her back by the collar. She kicked and screamed, but to no avail.

"Quiet!" Mer yelled, then continued his chant and turned back to face the red moon—the one from Ghost's dream—that colored the snow below them a shade of maroon. Mer bent down to grab a needle, revealing the full table and the person laying on it.

Sapphire.

Her hair was cut short, jaggedly, and had been colored black. The liquid dripped from her strands, staining the snow gray below the table. Sapphire's chest, Ghost realized in horror, was still. Her face was as pale as paper. And her eyes…her eyes were open, but her stare was blank.

She was dead. Sapphire was *dead*.

"Nooo!" The shout came from outside the circle. The chants ceased and they all turned to the man, who'd just entered the glade.

It was Aston, and he stood with a rifle in his hand, staring at Sapphire's dead body as if the image had shattered him into a thousand pieces, a thousand times over.

Mer turned and his expression immediately filled with concern.

Aston's face distorted in pain and marched up to the table, rifle up, baring his teeth at Mer. "What did you do to her?!"

Tears streamed down Ghost's cheeks, her heart straining at the terrible pain—his and her own.

"What did you do to her!!!" Aston screamed, shoving the rifle into Mer's face as his other hand scrambled for the straps, holding Sapphire to the table.

Two of the cloaks took a step toward Mer, but he shook his head at them, eying Aston and the rifle.

"It's not what you think…" Mer said, hands up, keeping the needle pressed to his palm with his thumb.

His aim still on Mer, Aston got Sapphire's limbs out of the restraints and pulled her to him. Her dead eyes stared at the night sky and her limp arms dangled behind her as Aston hugged her to him. He let out a scream, one so full of pain Ghost felt as if something in her chest shattered.

Tears glossed Aston's angered eyes as he kissed her cheek and carefully lay her back down. He then stood so forcefully, Mer jerked back. His stare, vicious and without mercy, drilled into Mer as he shoved the rifle harder into his chin, forcing him back.

"You're going to suffer," Aston hissed, his face pressed to Mer's in disgust. "You think you know pain? You don't. Not yet."

"Look," Mer said, and showed him the needle. "I know this is going to sound crazy, but we both want the same thing. She can still live *if* we hurry. This is a shot of Epinephrine. Also known as—"

"Adrenaline," Aston interrupted, eyes on the needle.

"This shot, with mouth to mouth to get her lungs going again…" Mer started.

Aston's palm pulled down over his face, wiping his eyes. "You know how to use it?"

He nodded. "I've done it successfully, many times—"

"Do it." Aston stepped out of Mer's way and pushed him up to Sapphire. He noticed Ghost just then, and bobbed the rifle at the masks holding her. "Let her go."

They released Ghost and she ran up to Aston and grabbed a hold of the back of his jacket.

Mer glanced back at them, then looked up at the moon and held the needle up. "*Vos autem nuntius scientiae reditu furto et evigilare faciatis dormientis.*"

He stabbed Sapphire into the heart with the needle, then bent down to blow air into her mouth. Once…twice…then he waited and repeated.

Aston's hand anxiously flew from his hair to his face and to his rifle as they waited. Ghost closed her eyes and wished Sapphire to breathe. She'd do anything. She'd go back to the cold night in the attic, if only Sapphire could live again.

Mer suddenly pulled back, looking uneasy, maybe confused.

"What's wrong?" Aston yelled. "Why isn't it working?"

"I…I don't know," Mer mumbled. "It's always worked by now. Maybe…maybe…it's because I didn't do the first shot, but I thought…"

"Move!" Aston shoved Mer out of the way.

He lay the rifle down and pushed his lips to her. He blew, then waited, putting his ear to her mouth. He went for it again, this time with more urgency.

Sapphire opened her mouth wide and pulled for air. Her back arched and her eyes opened.

"Oh my God…" Aston put his hands to her cheeks, then closed his eyes and pulled her to him as she coughed. "I thought I lost you. I thought you were gone."

Behind Aston's back, Ghost saw Mer take the rifle. She

opened her mouth to warn Aston but one of the cloaks grabbed her from behind and covered her mouth.

Mer aimed the rifle at the back of Aston's head. "Thank you for the help, Detective, but I'll take it from here."

• • •

She coughed, struggling to fill her lungs with air.

She was mostly aware of what was happening around her, but she felt strange, like she'd been asleep for an eternity. She knew she'd been dead; she remembered the moment it happened. But she also felt a surge of energy run through her, like she could run a mile, tear a phone book in half, like she had an endless supply of adrenaline.

Mer looked down at her, his eyes alive with hope and fear. "Alma? Is it you, my love?"

She squinted at him. "What…what happened to you, Mer? You look so old…" She looked around anxiously. "What's going on?"

Mer gaped at her, seemingly in shock, as she sat up to take in long deep breaths, along with her surroundings. The bloody table she was on. The dagger by her feet. The people. Mer. His rifle.

"Alma…" Mer's voice turned to a whisper. "Is it really you?"

"Of course, it's me," she snapped, eyeing the circle of people in cloaks and animal masks. "Who are these people?" She touched her hair. "Why am I wet?"

"Uh, Saph?" It came from behind her. "What are you doing?"

Shock still dressing his face, Mer held out a trembling hand for her and helped her down. "I will explain everything later," he said. "I just…" he pulled her in and ran his raisin-like fingers over her cheek, pure happiness radiating from him, "I can't believe you're here."

"Saph!"

"Who is that?" She turned around. "And why are you aiming a rifle at him?"

"Are you fucking kidding me, Saph?" he yelled.

"Don't worry about him; he'll be gone soon," Mer hushed, gently guiding her face back and her mouth toward his.

"Mer," she whispered, and her lips froze an inch from his.

"Yes?"

"I…" she whispered, her voice unsure. "I've just…just… run out of things to say to distract you."

"What?" Mer's eyes widened and flew to Aston.

Sapphire ducked just as he threw the dagger at Mer. Mer managed to dodge the spinning knife, but Sapphire snatched the rifle out of his hand. She threw it back to Aston, who caught it and aimed it at Mer.

"Wow," Aston said, looking at Mer in amazement. "I can't believe you bought that. My wife is a terrible actress!"

Sapphire pointed at herself and gasped in offense, then turned toward the cloaked people—one of whom was holding Ghost. Sapphire stared at them and cracked her knuckles, still feeling like every atom in her body had been pumped full of electricity.

Five of them came at her with their torches up. She grabbed the first cloak's torch, spun it around to smack its owner in the head. As that one fell to the ground, she went for the next one. A kick here, a twist there, a kneecap there, then, suddenly, it was over. The five of them were all laying on the ground around her.

"Whoo!" Sapphire shouted and clapped her hands. After all that time in Mer's basement, after being drugged and weak for days, Sapphire finally felt strong again—like herself.

She looked up from the unconscious people on the ground and at the sixth cloak, still holding Ghost. The cloak stared back at her, then let go of Ghost and bolted.

Pushed by her energy surge, Sapphire took off after the masked person.

"What are you doing!" Aston shouted behind her. "Leave it!"

Too late, Sapphire through, tackling the cloak to the snowy ground, then ripping the boar mask off.

A boy, teenager, no more than fifteen, looking scared to death, stared up at Sapphire.

She wasn't sure what she'd expected from the cloaks, but this wasn't it. The boy saw her hesitation as his opportunity to take off again, and Sapphire let him.

She watched him go as her adrenaline seemed to settle, and felt more level-headed when she turned back to Aston, Mer, and Ghost who jumped up into her arms.

Sapphire laughed and hugged her back, then looked at Aston, still holding Mer at gunpoint.

You okay? Aston mouthed to her.

She nodded and they looked at each other, much like they had at their wedding, but this time, there was something more in Aston's eyes, something indecipherable.

"Come on," he said, breaking their gaze, "we'll bring him to town and hold him until we can get Shadow Falls Sheriff's Department over here."

As they moved, Sapphire thought she saw a smile flash across Mer's face.

• • •

Mer had never killed for pleasure.

He gazed at the blood moon—his final failure—as the detective forced him to enter town and toward the sheriff's station.

Some of the townspeople were still there, cleaning up a wrecked Christmas parade. They stopped to stare at this new parade of marchers with Mer at the front, hands over his head.

He watched the three behind him—the detective, Sapphire, and Rosie—in the reflection of a shop window. The couple was holding hands and exchanging glances of affection. That should've been him and Alma, not them.

Mer looked up at the clock tower, the time nearing nine o'clock, the end of the blood moon, the end of everything. He'd truly believed her, back in the glade. He'd wanted it so much that he couldn't tell his own wife's soul from a stranger's. When Sapphire revealed the truth, his heart had been crushed. He didn't know what had gone wrong, but he was certain it had to do with the two of them, the couple behind him. They ruined it somehow. It was as if they'd taken Alma from him all over again, and they had the audacity to laugh about it. Never before had Mer felt such animosity, such rage as he felt in the woods. He wanted to crush them the way they'd crushed him.

No, Mer had never killed for pleasure, but he would tonight.

More and more people noticed them, and he leered to himself, watching Rosie bounce by Sapphire's side. He hated her too, he hated them all.

Any minute now he'd get his revenge, because...

"Drop it," Jebediah said.

Ester cocked her rifle at them. So did Janet, Peter, Jim, Bobby, and Daniel.

"Seriously?" the detective said and dropped the rifle. "God, I *hate* this place,"

Because this was Mer's town.

He wasn't sure what delusion the detective had been under. Perhaps he thought the folk of Pleasant Pines wouldn't interfere once he had their leader under "control." *Fool.*

Mer dropped his hands as Sapphire, the detective, and the girl huddled together. He turned to the citizens of his town. Some watched in silence. Others left, pretending not to see. A few helped by taking the rifle from the detective and prepared to get their hands dirty.

It had started decades ago. One of the Almas had escaped and was found by Jebediah and Ester. Mer had been on the verge of arresting them, knowing they cooked meth in their cabin. Jebediah made a suggestion. *Look the other way, and I'll look the other way too.* Soon, Mer needed another favor, and agreed to tear up parking tickets to get it. It rolled on from there. He eventually went out of his way to catch the townies breaking the law. Sometimes for big things, like with Jebediah and Ester, but more often it was just lies, deceit, or minor infractions that Mer threatened to expose or put them in jail for. He told them their secrets would go out automatically if something happened to him. A small, but very beneficial lie.

As the years passed, people started acting differently, putting up a front in town. They seemed to think Mer would be blinded by their perfect smiles, greetings, and friendly gestures. He didn't mind it. Because of it, Mer now lived in the politest town in Idaho and he learned the rule fast: the wider the smile, the bigger the secret.

He smiled, feeling the rage overtake him as his helpers separated the three screaming out-of-towners. He accepted the rifle that was handed to him as Jim and Paul, the lumberjacks, slammed the detective down and forced his face into the snow.

"Now, let's see," Mer mumbled, moving the rifle between Sapphire and the detective. "Who to start with? Who should have to watch who die?" He stopped on the detective and sent Sapphire his most vicious of smiles. "It's only fair, after all."

"Noo0!" Sapphire screamed, trying to fight off the men holding her down.

Mer passed Rosie, who was crying her eyes out, and stepped up to the detective with the weapon ready.

"What is wrong with you people?!" Sapphire yelled at the town and the men holding her husband. She pushed up on her knees while they held her arms back. "How can you just stand there and watch him kill an innocent man?! There's one of him and hundreds of you!"

The Pleasant Piners looked at her mutely.

Mer's eyes slid over his town, giving them a warning, just

in case. Among them, she stood, scowling at him. Her pale skin and jacket, dripping in red.

I know I've failed you for the last time, honey, he thought. *But at least I can make them pay for what they cost you.*

"I know you're not killers. You're just normal people who are scared!" Sapphire continued. "But you can do this! Together you can stop him!"

Jebediah, who was standing by the detective, laughed at Sapphire. "This isn't Fresno or whatever fancy city you folks are from. This is Pleasant Pines, we got our own way of handling our business."

"I don't know what's more disturbing," Sapphire said. "The fact that you refer to murdering as business, or that you think Fresno is fancy."

"Ha!" the detective laughed, face still in the snow.

"Shut up," Jebediah said, and kicked him in the abdomen.

Feeling the hate burn his insides, Mer glared down at the detective and placed the barrel on the back of his head. Sapphire screamed again, this time in utter panic. "Nooo!"

"Dad?"

Mer stood still, finger resting on the trigger.

"Dad!"

He turned slowly, his mind racing, his heart beating out of his chest. His eyes landed on a woman in a big stormy kromer hat. The moment she removed the hat and revealed her face, Mer's world smashed into pieces. She was three decades older, but he knew his own child.

"Rosie...my Rose." He stared at her as she stepped out from the crowd. She wasn't a mirage; she was real. "You're alive...you're...here."

"I got your letter. I've been looking for you all day." She pulled his stationery out of her pocket, looking from his rifle to the man under it. "What are you *doing*?!"

Mer looked around and took it all in. The detective, a fellow policeman. The woman pinned down, frantic eyes on her husband. The little child, crying in fear. What *was* he doing? What *had he* been doing?

Ding. Ding. Ding.

The tower's clock struck nine and as the bell tolled, the blood moon came to its end. The moon's silver light washed away the red-tinted world. The rose-colored veil over Mer's life lifted along with it. For the first time in thirty years, Mer could see clearly.

He saw his delusion for what it really was. He saw his cemetery and its endless graves of women and children. *Oh God.* The guilt hit him so forcefully, he felt as if it would tear him in half. Alma was gone; she'd passed thirty years ago and she was never coming back. Not through God, Satan, or a new body. Everything he'd done, every life he'd taken, never had to happen.

He looked at his daughter, *his* Rosie, feeling the thick lump build in his throat. He walked up to her and pulled her in long and hard, feeling a release as he embraced her. He pushed down the sorrow as he pulled away and smiled. "Let Mrs. Hemming take you into the station and make you a cup of tea. I'll explain everything later."

"Okay," Rosie said, her voice unsure as Mrs. Hemming hurried to escort her.

"And, Rosie," he called. She turned expectantly and he smiled at her through tears. "I'm so glad you came home."

She nodded, still looking confused, and then followed Mrs. Hemming into the station.

Mer turned back to the townspeople, the detective, Sapphire, and the little girl whose real name he couldn't recall anymore. "I'm so sorry…for everything. Please, put down your weapons. Let them go. They're innocent."

His people half-lowered their rifles, looking at each other in bewilderment as Mer laid the rifle in the snow, then stepped back and grabbed the cuffs from his belt. "Detective…"

The detective pushed Mer's men off of him and moved cautiously.

Mer kneeled, then lay his cuffs in front of him and put his hands on his head. "You can radio Shadow Falls from my office. Tell Sheriff Freeman they have my full cooperation. I'll tell them everything."

As the detective hurried toward him, Mer looked up to see his wife. She was no longer bleeding, no longer pale, but full of color and life.

After all these years of haunting him, Alma finally smiled.

• • •

Sapphire exhaled. It was over.

She hurried to grab Ghost from the baffled townies as she watched Aston take Mer's wrists, one by one, and place them in the cuffs.

BANG!

Aston's face sprayed with blood.

Ghost screamed and everyone gasped in shock as Mer fell face first to the snow. The back of his skull was missing and all that was left was a gory mess of bloody brains.

Jebediah emerged, rifle still up and smoking. All six cloaks had made their way back to town, even the runner. With no animal masks in sight, they stepped out from the crowd, too.

"Jebediah," a librarian-looking woman said, removing the hood of her cloak, "what did you do that for?"

The rest of the cloaks removed their hoods, allowing their robes to open. Sapphire eyed Mer's collection. A librarian, a doctor, a candy shop girl, a lawyer-like woman in a suit, a pharmacist, and the teenager in a Peter's Peppered Pickles & Pies uniform.

"Think about it, Mabel!" Jebediah tapped his head. "He was going to tell them everything! We're *all* accomplices. We'd *all* be going to jail."

"But Rosie just came back!" Mabel argued.

Aston and Sapphire's eyes drew to each other. She discreetly signaled toward the *Now Leaving Pleasant Pines* sign, and her husband responded with a subtle nod. She grabbed Ghost's shoulders and moved, ever so slightly, watching Aston do the same.

The doctor took the woman's hand. "He's right, Mabel. What happens in Pleasant Pines has to stay in Pleasant Pines."

The other cloaks and the crowd of townies nodded at each other. Then, as if their minds had melded to one, their heads simultaneously turned toward Aston, Sapphire, and Ghost, trying to sneak away.

Oh shit! They froze as all rifles pulled back up and aimed at them.

"Sorry. We can't let you leave," Jebediah said.

"Leave!" Ester yelled. "Are you crazy? We can't let them leave!"

Jebediah turned to his wife. "I *just* said that goddamnit!"

Knowing what was to come, Sapphire rotated Ghost's face away from the rifles and in toward her body, then stepped closer to Aston and took his hand.

Her chest filled with guilt, old and new. "We would've never been here if it wasn't for me. You're the one person I should've been honest with and I went to everybody but you. What I did, how I acted, is *not* how I want us to be. It was a mistake and I'm sorry, Aston."

Aston studied her earnest expression, and released a breath, one it looked like he'd been holding forever. "Okay."

They stood together, hand in hand, and turned back to face the firing squad who were positioning their rifles and placing their fingers on the triggers.

"Now what?" Sapphire asked.

"Now," Aston said with confidence, "we're fucked."

There was no way out. This was it. Judgment Day. The

end. *Something that will annihilate your world* the psychic had said. Sapphire squeezed her eyes shut. *Lucky guess.*

The thunder of helicopters filled the air. The whole town and its prisoners looked up to see two choppers hovering over them. One read: *Shadow Falls Sheriff's Department*. The other: *Kraft, Inc.*

"People of Pleasant Pines, place your weapons on the ground, then put your hands on your head, and lay down!" Barry's voice boomed through the speakers.

Sapphire exhaled and Aston cussed in relief next to her.

One by one, the townies began lowering their weapons and dropping to the ground.

There was a quick rustle of air, then Chrissy's voice sounded. "And freeze, suckers!"

Everyone stopped moving, rifles and bodies halfway to the ground.

"Give me that!" Barry's voice faintly barked before it boomed again. "Please proceed with the first instructions. Thank you."

All around them, rifles and Pleasant Pines residents dropped to the ground. Aston pulled Sapphire in for a hug. "I'll be back. Gotta go talk to Morgan Freeman."

"The actor?"

"The sheriff."

"Oh," Sapphire said, disappointed.

She watched him rush off toward the sheriff chopper, then looked down to see Ghost gazing up at her with sorrowful eyes.

"Hey." Sapphire knelt and grabbed her shoulders. "We're safe now."

The little girl spoke so softly, Sapphire had to strain her ears. "When I saw you in my dream before, I was scared you were too good to be true and that you wouldn't come."

Ghost launched in and hugged her hard as the helicopters landed.

"But you did," she whispered into Sapphire's hair. "You did come and you saved me. Thank you."

The truth hit Sapphire hard.

Though she only semi-grasped what Ghost was talking about, her words had flipped a switch. Sapphire's questions had been answered. Who was Sapphire Dubois after the Great Desert Fire, and why did she leave that day? Because of *this*.

When she started catching serial killers years ago, it was subconsciously to find her father. But that obsession was gone, and it had *nothing* to do with why she left for the club.

It wasn't about Sapphire, serial killers, or the thrill she used to feel anymore. It was about *them*, the Marys and Ghosts of the world. She was meant to use her odd skills to help people; she could feel it. That's why she was here. Sapphire had done the right thing, she'd just gone about it the wrong way.

She looked at Aston, speaking to the Shadow Falls Sheriff, and knew. She had run away from him, when she should've embraced him. *Aston* was the answer.

It was all so clear now. She knew in the depth of her soul that it was right.

For the first time in her life, Sapphire knew *exactly* who she wanted to be.

. . .

"I don't get it," Aston said, "you told me I could trust their law enforcement?"

"No." Sheriff Morgan Freeman shook his head. "I said, I'm *not* sure you can trust their law enforcement. We've been suspecting foul play in this town for years, but we've had no evidence until now."

People all around them were being interrogated and arrested by the Shadow Falls Sheriff's Department. Their deputy and Barry were talking to Rosie Button—or Rosie

Sanders as she'd gone by for the last three decades. She cried and shook her head, looking distraught.

Aston's eyes landed on the Kraft chopper where Chrissy sat, pale face leaning against the glass. She'd hopped out when it first landed, looking like she was heading for après-ski.

"Here I am," she'd yelled, arms out. "Ready to save the day!" She took one look at Mer's half-skull and bloody brains splattered in the snow, and turned back around. She jumped into the chopper, and refused to come back out.

Aston told Morgan Freeman—the sheriff, not the actor—what he could and fibbed where he had to, to protect himself and Sapphire. When the sheriff saw Sapphire and Ghost standing close together, he'd assumed she was their daughter and Aston didn't deny it. After everything the girl had been through, he wanted to make sure he got her back to her parents personally.

After hours upon hours of sorting out reports and wrapping things up, the sheriff and Aston exchanged information and said their goodbyes. The first thing Aston did was walk up to his partner. "Barry, you sly son of a fucker, c'mere."

Barry's face lit up as Aston pulled him in for a man-hug.

"Thanks for getting the Shadow Falls Sheriff, and for coming back. I owe you."

Barry grinned. "How about *you* have coffee ready for *me* every day from here on out?'

"Yeah. No." Aston moved toward the Kraft chopper.

"On Fridays?" Barry followed.

"Not a chance."

"Once a leap year?"

"I'll think about it."

"Sweet." Barry balled his fist in victory, then put his headgear on and jumped into the helicopter.

The propellers wound up above them and Aston froze halfway in, staring at Sapphire. She and Ghost were sound asleep in the back, cuddled up under a blanket. He looked at the gray-ish hair that was pasted against her cheeks and a strange, elusive feeling scratched at his insides again. He shook it off. Everything was okay now, wasn't it? The thing that had bothered him since she went missing had worked itself out, hadn't it? Sapphire knew what she'd done was a mistake, and she'd never do it again. They were finally on the same page. They would go home and everything was going to be alright.

"Oh. My. Gawd!" Chrissy yelled at him from the front. "Either get in or get out. I've got to get to my therapist, like yesterday."

He got inside and Barry lifted the bird into the sky as the sun rose. They hovered over the snow-covered mountains as Aston settled next to Sapphire and leaned in to give her a kiss.

Her eyes were still closed, but she inhaled and mumbled, "You smell like smoke."

Aston pulled back. "Wha-no...*really*? Pff, weird."

"And *I'm* a bad actress?" Sapphire opened her eyes and stretched tentatively, careful not to wake up Ghost, whose head rested on her arm. "Everything go okay?"

"Yes," he said, nodding to himself. "Everything's all right. I just want to get out of here and go home and be us again."

"I know what you mean." Sapphire turned her eyes to the miles of pines below, glowing orange in the morning light. "And I know who we are now. What we can be."

Aston let out a puzzled laugh. "What do you mean 'what we can be?'"

When his wife turned to him, her eyes sparkled with excitement. "I realized it. It all just fell into place. We're *them*."

"Who?"

"Nick and Nora Charles."

"What do you..." Aston stopped as the image of the old, black and white detective and his heiress wife came to him. He understood *exactly* what she meant.

"Think about it; think about us, back in the woods." Sapphire motioned back toward the town. "We're the answer. We do it together. We find them and catch them together and then you bring them in, totally legal. It's so obvious now. It's been there the whole time, just staring us in the face."

Aston's heart went from peaceful taps to furious thumps. In one second, she'd unveiled the awful truth. The truth Aston had *really* feared. The truth that was so much worse now, after what he'd seen.

She leaned her head on his shoulder again and closed her eyes, a satisfied smile resting on her lips. "I can't wait to get home."

"Right." Aston stared at the burning sky, feeling sick to his core. There was no more lying to himself, no more denying the obvious. "Right."

CHAPTER 18

"You're back!" Vivienne Dubois opened her arms for a hug, then stopped and grimaced. "What happened to your *hair*? It's all jagged."

"Oh…" Sapphire entered the mansion. "It's a new trend. The…er, lawn mower cut. Have you seen Aston?"

"No. Now let me look at you." She grabbed Sapphire's shoulders, eyes on her boobs. "Oh…they're not very big, are they?"

"Uh, no?" Sapphire watched in horror as her mother disappointedly stuck a finger out and poked her boob. "What are you *doing*?"

She swatted her off, then covered her chest and moved into the kitchen to grab her phone from the basket Aston said he'd dropped it in. "Do we still have my old clothes in the closet?"

Vivienne followed her. "Sure. Why?"

"I'll explain it later." Sapphire sprinted toward the stairs, going through her phone. He hadn't called or texted.

"Are you feeling okay?" Vivienne shouted after her. "You look sick!"

"I'm fine!" Sapphire yelled, heading for her walk-in. She was fine…besides the fact that her husband seemed to have vanished into thin air.

Moments after they landed on the hospital's roof, Aston mumbled something about work he had to do. That was hours ago. Even Barry had hung out longer before going to the station to check Ghost's background—a hard feat considering Ghost didn't know her own name or her mother's, and clammed up when asked about her father.

Sapphire had used the hospital's phone to call Aston several times as she sat on the bed next to Ghost who was being examined by Doctor Wells. Ghost apparently wasn't the only one being observed, because the doctor's gaze hopped between the girl and Sapphire.

"What?" Sapphire asked as she hung up.

"Nothing. You just…nothing." The doctor looked down at his chart. "I want to keep, uh, *Ghost* here for more tests, just in case, and…I'd like to look at you as well, Sapphire."

"Me?" she said, surprised at his troubled face. "I'm fine. Worry about her."

She was a bit light headed, sure, but she'd had a hell of a week. Sapphire got up and Ghost grabbed her hand. "Don't leave."

"I'm just going to go home, see if Aston's there and…" She took in Ghost's dirty, out-grown, and hole-riddled clothes, "get some other stuff, then I'll be back. You're safe here; I promise."

Right as Sapphire reached for the door, Barry returned, paperwork in hand.

"I found a match." He held up a photo of a younger Ghost, then lowered his voice. "Unfortunately, her mother is no longer…she, you know, died before the girl went missing."

Sapphire turned back to Ghost. "I thought you said you had a mother."

Ghost shrugged. "Everyone has a mother."

"And," Barry said. "Ghost's real name is Ruby. She went missing nearly four years ago on the way from school to her foster home in Brooklyn, New York."

Sapphire gazed at Ghost…or Ruby, staring down at her hands with big, sad eyes.

"Anything about her father?" Sapphire wiped away the sweat that had accumulated on her forehead.

"Father unknown."

Sapphire exhaled into her hands. Ruby, the girl who'd been chained in an attic for years and had witnessed atrocities, *deserved* a happy ending with her actual family.

"I'm not supposed to say it." The small voice was nearly inaudible, but they both turned to Ruby.

"What are you not supposed to say?" Sapphire asked softly.

Ruby looked up at them with unsure eyes. "My father's name."

Sapphire sat down next to her. "You have to tell us, so we can find him for you."

The girl looked unsure, but her eyes glittered with hope. "It's…Matthew White."

"Thank you. I'll be back soon." She smiled at Ruby, then nodded to Barry to follow her out. "Call me with updates, and if you hear from Aston."

Barry nodded and Sapphire headed for the mansion. Her phone didn't ring until she was in the walk-in of her old room, halfway through her saved childhood clothes.

She pulled up the phone. "Did you find Aston?"

"No, sorry," Barry said, contrite. "And I wasn't able to find anything on her father."

"Oh," Sapphire said, disappointed for the girl.

"Sorry. I found a few Matthew Whites in the Tri-State area, but none with any connection to Rita and Ruby Hayes."

"What?" Sapphire dropped the sparkly shirt she was holding. "What were the names?"

"Daughter: Ruby Hayes. Mother: Rita Hayes."

Several things hit Sapphire at once. One: the girl somehow knew of Sapphire before Sapphire knew her. Ruby Hayes was *R.H.*

She got out of the closet, and let her mind work the puzzle as she climbed up to the attic. Her face was covered in sweat as she removed the loose floorboard and took his wallet. She pulled out the circled picture of Rita Hayes, then flipped through dozens of driver's licenses before it appeared. Sapphire slumped to the floor.

Matthew White. New York. One of William Dubois's many identities. Sapphire didn't need the evidence. She knew.

Ruby Hayes, Ghost, was her half-sister.

She went downstairs, her head foggy with shock, and her eyes still on the wallet's contents. This was why Doctor Wells had kept staring at the two of them at the hospital and it why she had overheard the Shadow Falls Sheriff assume they were related. Sapphire could see it now that she knew. They both had William's hair, eyes, and prominent features.

Sapphire had been wrong. Her father had been wrong. This wasn't chance. *Something* had taken Ruby away from New York. *Something* had led Sapphire to Pleasant Pines and to the horrid house where a little girl was held captive. A girl who "happened" to be her sister. There *was* such a thing as destiny; Sapphire was staring at it.

"Darling?" Vivienne stood close by, but her voice sounded distant.

Everything swayed as Sapphire looked up at Vivienne's face, warping until it was unrecognizable.

"Sapphire!"

The floor moved on its own. It came closer and closer until…

• • •

When Sapphire opened her eyes, Aston was back. He stood by a dark window, his arms crossed and his expression morose.

"Oh, good. You're okay," she mumbled, drowsy, then realized she was in the hospital. "Why am I back here?"

Aston kept his eyes on the window. "You have a slight concussion and some pretty bad scratches on your back. But Doctor Wells said you passed out due to dehydration. They hooked you up to an IV. You'll be okay."

Sapphire sat up. "Where's Ghost, or Ruby…her real name is Ruby, by the way."

"I heard," Aston said, eyes still averted. "She fell asleep, so they put her in a bed in pediatrics for now."

"There's something I have to tell you about her…" Sapphire said, then her eyes fell on the stack of papers in his hand. "What's that?"

Aston ignored her and moved to the chair next to her bed. He sat and inhaled into his balled fist as if he was about to puke. When he finally spoke, his voice came from somewhere low. "I can't do this anymore."

Sapphire nodded and sat up. "I know, me too. I'm done with hospitals. But it's Christmas Eve so I'm sure Doctor Wells will let me out in a couple of hours."

"No, Saph…" Aston's eyes were fixed on the papers in his hand. "I can't do *us* anymore."

Sapphire let out a small laugh. "What do you mean *us*?"

Aston finally looked at her, and his expression was one she'd never seen. His eyes, normally bright blue, were somehow dark and accompanied by under shades.

"When you vanished," he said, "and I stood there in our empty apartment, I've never felt so helpless, so powerless in my life."

Sapphire looked at her husband, knowing he was just worried. He wasn't really serious. "Look, I know I lied, but this is different. *I'm* different, and it'll be better now with you and me. We can do this together! No more lies."

"I'm not angry because you lied, Saph. I'm not…angry at all." Aston gazed at her. "But when you keep doing this, you know who's going to end up hurt?"

Sapphire rolled her eyes. "Me."

"No, you're going to end up gone again. *I'm* the one who's going to be left behind."

"It's *not* going to happen. I know what I'm doing, Ast—"

"No, you don't! You're *not* a cop and you're *not* trained

for things like that!" Aston got up. "With or without me, you don't have a fucking idea what you're doing to yourself or anyone around you. The moment you left to go to that club you chose to hunt them over us. Your father was right; I just refused to fucking believe it."

"My *father*?" Sapphire stared at him, waiting for him to snap out of his temporary insanity. "How does he relate to anything?"

"It all relates." Aston lay the papers next to her. "And it's why I have to do this."

The word *divorce* at the top of the document stared back at her.

"What is this," Sapphire said, suddenly angry, "an ultimatum?"

"It's not an ultimatum." Aston stared at her with disbelief. "Jesus…you were *dead*, Sapphire! I had to sit there and hold your dead body! I thought you were gone, and someday soon, you will be because you *won't* give it up! Don't you get it?" He pointed at the papers. "This is me choosing my own sanity over your insanity."

"Oh, come on! It's not like it's the first time I've died," Sapphire said. "This isn't new."

"It's not the same now. We're not the same." Aston gave her a last look, then turned his back to her and headed for the door. "All my stuff will be gone from the mansion by the time you get home."

Sapphire stared at the open door as he vanished. He'd be back any minute; he always came back. It was their thing.

Before he could, Barry appeared in the doorway. "Hey. Came to talk to Aston, but…I couldn't help overhearing. Sorry."

"It's fine." She waved it off. "He's not serious, Barry. He's just being Aston."

"Uh, no, Sapphire. I'm pretty sure he's serious. When you were missing…" Barry shook his head. "You didn't see him."

"Please." Sapphire shook her head. "It's not like he's actually going to sign the papers. It's just a ruse."

Barry held his hands up and shrugged. "You didn't see him."

He left and Sapphire flipped through the papers, shaking her head. Her eyes fell on the last page, and she knew. The pain started in her abdomen and moved its way up. A malicious hole appeared in her chest and spread through her body, leaving a sear in its wake.

Aston had already signed them.

. . .

A hospital was a great place to be because Barry felt sick.

He jogged down the hallway and reached the glass doors just as Aston Ridder got to his car. His partner had rushed out so fast, he didn't even see Barry in the hallway. This was not a good time, but if Aston found out from one of the boys, instead of Barry, it'd be much worse.

"Hey!" Barry called, stepping out. He wished it could be different, but in the end, it wasn't about Aston. It was about Barry.

"Hey." Aston, about to step into his car, turned.

Barry was taken aback by the darkness in his eyes. The man somehow looked worse now than he did when Barry showed up to Pleasant Pines.

"I'm glad you're here." Aston ran a hand down his face. "I really need a fucking drink. Let's meet at Noir."

"Um…" Barry squirmed awkwardly.

"Oh, sorry," Aston sighed. "Would you like to meet me at Noir for a fucking drink?"

"Well, I…um…I can't." Barry couldn't meet his eyes. "Because I work tonight."

Aston looked at him tiredly. "We don't work nights, Bar."

"Well, actually…I do."

Aston cocked his head as if he was unable to grasp the words.

Barry tried to smile, but it came out wrong. "When I went back to the station to run another background check, Calloway called me into his office. He offered me something. He said, if I switched partners, he'd promote me to detective and I'd be learning under Rodriguez. And I...I took it."

Aston's face, already weary, fell to a worn-out shock.

Barry shook his head. "I appreciate everything you've taught me, but I need to do this, for me."

When the chief offered Barry the position, he realized something. His new boss was right, not about Aston's character, but Aston *did* make up his own rules and, as long as they were partners, Barry would never turn his back on him. In order to grow and have a career of his own, Barry had to do this. He had to leave Aston...no matter how much it hurt him.

"I see." Aston's eyes turned to the ground. He neither yelled, cussed, nor punched. This wasn't the man Barry was used to, and he felt a crisp sting in his chest, watching his ex-partner. "I'm sorry. I overheard everything with Sapphire and..."

Aston held his hand up to stop him, then gave Barry a forced smile. "Don't be sorry. You're getting your shield, that's huge. Congrats."

Aston stepped into his car.

Barry knocked on the window and Aston rolled it down. "Are we...okay?"

"Yeah, Barry." Aston started the engine. "We're okay."

As soon-to-be Detective Barry Harry watched Aston Ridder drive off, he knew. They may be okay, but things between them were never going to be the same.

...

The blue SUV smashed into Aston's car at the intersection of Wilshire and Beverly Drive.

Aston's car propelled into another car and soon, the intersection was clogged by a cluster-fuck of cars. People all around him honked and screamed, but Aston stayed behind the wheel and stared into space.

He felt no anger toward the blue SUV, just like he felt no joy at the star-filled sky, or the stores around him decorated with lights. He felt no regret when he thought of what he had done, because he felt nothing at all.

When Aston left the hospital, the pain had been excruciating, but then, some sort of numbing agent kicked in and the pain dulled to nothing. *Nothing.*

His phone buzzed on the dash. Probably Calloway again. He'd already left two voicemails about Aston dropping by the station to have a talk about his "future" at the BHPD.

He glanced at it. *000-000-0000.*

"Hey, moron!" The guy from the blue SUV banged a fist to Aston's window. "This was your fault, so maybe you should get out of your car, you dick!"

Aston stared at the phone until it stopped ringing. Whatever this Marla chick was selling, she clearly wouldn't give up. A voicemail popped up on the screen. Aston sighed, then grabbed it and pressed play.

"Hi, Mr. Ridder. This is Marla, *again*. I'm calling about…"

As he listened to her speech, his brows burrowed, then rose, then burrowed again.

It was great news. Probably the most longed-for news he'd ever gotten, but he felt nothing thanks to the numbing agent.

"Dude, what's the matter with you?!" The SUV owner yelled.

Aston eyed the screaming man tiredly through the windshield. It wasn't Aston's fault. The SUV had turned illegally, but who gave a shit anyway?

Honk! Hooooooonk!

Emptiness was better than what Aston felt when she was dead. He couldn't go through that again. He couldn't lose her in the future so he had to get rid of her in the present.

He listened to the woman telling him what time she would call him back, and stared at the gridlock, instinctively knowing how to un-jam it.

Honk-hooooooonk!

"Get out of your fucking car, man!" The SUV driver had been joined by other drivers who also would prefer it if he got out of his fucking car.

Aston glanced at the rearview mirror once, then twice. Someone was running in the distance and sliding over the hoods of jammed cars. Aston took a moment, then opened the door.

"Dude!" the SUV guy yelled and spread his arms. "What's your problem? It's Christmas!"

Aston pushed past the crowd gathered around him and stared at her.

It was 40 degrees outside, and she was running through the standstill traffic, barefoot and in nothing but her hospital gown. She leaped over a sideways car in the intersection and slid over its hood.

She landed on her feet and kept her eyes on Aston as she stood straight.

"What are you doing?" Aston said, feeling tired. So. Fucking. Tired.

"Oh, *now* you talk!" The SUV owner shouted.

Sapphire stood still, out of breath, white feet on the black asphalt. "I'm done."

Aston scoffed and turned around. "Considering the last time you said those very words was one kidnapping and one killer ago, pardon my ass if I don't believe you."

Sapphire grabbed his arm and turned him around. She looked at him, her eyes big with desperation and fear. "I'm done."

Aston gazed at her. "This is not something you can take back. It's not done for just today, or this month. This means you're done forever."

"I know *exactly* what it means," Sapphire said with conviction. "I choose you."

He believed her. Not because it was what he wished for, or because it was the easy way out, but because he saw it in her eyes. The smell of bullshit did not taint the smoggy air around them. She was telling the truth.

Aston looked at her and felt the numbing agent leave his body. He opened his mouth to speak as all the emotions, painful or not, washed over him.

"Dude!!" The SUV guy cupped his hands an inch from Aston's ear and yelled. "Are you fucking deaf?!"

All the emotion.

"One sec." Aston turned and clocked the SUV guy in the face.

The crowd, that had now gathered around to yell at Aston, gasped. He didn't care; he turned back around to look at Sapphire with grave intent. "There's something else I need from you…"

"What?" Sapphire asked anxiously.

"I need you to never…ever…*ever*," Aston proclaimed, "do my laundry again."

Sapphire closed her eyes, letting out a quick laugh, then looked up at him with fake exasperation. "So, no serial killers, and no laundry. What else is there, couponing?"

He smiled. As angry shouts, honks and fights broke out around them, Aston pulled her freezing body into his coat and kissed her.

After an appropriately timed make-out session, Aston calmed everyone down, took care of the gridlock, then exchanged information with the blue SUV owner, who seemed scared of him for some reason. Soon, they were on their way back to her hospital to get Ruby.

"About Ruby," Sapphire said. "There's something you need to know."

Aston drove in silence as Sapphire explained it to him.

What she was telling him was big; and the question she asked him, even bigger. Still, Aston couldn't help but glance down at his phone, knowing who'd called him.

CHAPTER 19

Ruby stirred from her strange dream.

Ruby. She remembered the name that Faith and the other kids had called her. Sometimes they'd yell it when they made fun of her clothes, her hair, or lunch. They yelled that her mommy was crazy, and that Ruby's clothes came from a garbage can. They said it to be mean but, sometimes, it was true. Despite this, the name felt familiar and warm, as if she wasn't a ghost after all.

She opened her eyes to find herself in the backseat of a car. Streetlights flashed by in the night outside, as Aston and Sapphire talked about how to tell Ruby that her father had died. They didn't know she was awake and they sounded concerned. They didn't have to worry; Ruby already knew.

She'd just dreamed of Matthew White. It was a new kind of dream, in which he showed her things *after* they'd already happened. He showed her he wasn't always a good man, but also that he sometimes was—when he could control the beast inside him. Years ago, he'd noticed Ruby's mother in the streets of Brooklyn and stalked her with the intent of killing her. Instead, he grew fascinated with her enigmatic mind and started a relationship with her. Though he wouldn't admit the true motivations to himself at the time, he'd worried Ruby was unsafe with Rita, so he killed her in the kitchen and made it look like a suicide.

Then Matthew, whose name wasn't really Matthew, smiled at Ruby the way he had at the fair and said goodbye.

As Aston and Sapphire continued talking with low voices,

sleep took her away again and she dreamed another dream, a special one. It was the future, near rather than far, and Ruby wasn't in it at all; Sapphire was. She was scared and unable to move. She cried out for help, but nobody could hear her. She was all alone.

When Sapphire screamed in the dream, Ruby screamed too.

Ruby sat up, covered in sweat. Her thoughts and dreams were all jumbled and everything was confusing. She looked around, eyes still bleary with sleep.

She wasn't shivering like she always did in the attic; she was wrapped in warmth. She didn't smell dog kibble, but fragrant food. She didn't hear Mer's footsteps on the stairs, but the sound of talk and laughter from below.

Ruby's eyes slowly adjusted. She was sitting in the biggest, softest, and pinkest bed she'd ever seen. Above her rested a canopy, like the kind the princesses in her movies slept under. Plush, friendly-faced stuffed animals surrounded her. A woman with charcoal hair stepped up to the foot of the bed.

"Merry Christmas, Ruby," she smiled and held her hand out. "Come on. Lez get you dressed."

Ruby looked at the woman with the strong accent and felt anxious.

"Es okay." The woman led her toward a door. "My name es Julia. Sapphire asked me to help you pick a dress for Christmas."

Julia opened the doors and Ruby's eyes widened.

It was a room, but like a closet. Shoes of all colors sat lined on lit shelves. Hundreds of dresses, pants, and shirts hung in color-coordinated sections. A plush island sat in front of three conjoined mirrors.

Julia gestured toward a section. "These are all Sapphire's old dresses. Which one do you like?"

The colorful princess dresses were the most beautiful things Ruby had ever seen. She smiled shyly and pointed at the prettiest one.

"Excellent choice," Julia said, then took Ruby to a giant tub filled with warm water and bubbles.

Ruby bathed, feeling her long, cold winters in the attic fall off her and into the bubbles. When she was done, Julia helped her into the dress and did her hair up in a bun that she decorated with pearls. She took her hand and brought her down a curved staircase and into a house so big and elegant the sight of it awed Ruby into wide-eyed silence.

"Come on," Julia said and looked at the time. "I think he just arrived."

Who? Ruby wondered as Julia led her into a living room. Every nook and cranny of the room was decorated to the max, and dozens of colorful packages lay below the lush Christmas tree next to the fireplace. Music, faintly familiar to Ruby's memories, streamed out of a small cylinder box on top of the mantel. Beautiful people held small glasses of white liquid or big colorful mugs in their hands, and greeted Ruby with warmth as they passed. An enticing scent lured Ruby to an extravagant spread.

"We'll get you some of that later," Julia winked.

"Oh my God!" A beautiful woman with very large breasts looked at Ruby. Her perfect hand drew to cover her mouth as it opened. "She looks *just like* Sapphire at that age."

"Sí," Julia said.

"I'm Vivienne," the woman said, and took Ruby's hand with a look of awe.

Julia glanced out the window. "Oh, they're still outside. Come on." She threw a big, warm scarf over Ruby's shoulders and opened the door.

Sapphire and Aston stood in the big driveway with someone else. Ruby was so excited to see them that she hopped down the steps.

Then he turned, and her feet stopped dead.

"Hello Ruby," he said.

The tall, bald man from her dream, the Social Services

man who would take her to the house with the Christmas roses. He was here. It was happening after all.

Ruby had wished to see this man so many times before, knowing he would bring her to her new home and new family. Why then, did her heart feel so heavy now that he was here?

"Come on." Julia tugged gently on her hand.

"Ruby! Look at you." Sapphire's face broke out in a smile. "I knew they'd fit."

A baby's cry sounded from inside.

"Oh," Julia said. "That's me."

She vanished inside, and Ruby looked up at them, trying to push back the sadness. The dress, the bath, the tree, the people were all very nice, but Ghost's heart *ached* when she realized she'd never see Sapphire again. Maybe, if she asked, she could stay just for a little longer.

"Ruby," Sapphire smiled, "This is Sal."

Ruby tried to be polite, tried to say hello, but her throat was clogged with grief.

"He's here because we were wondering," Sapphire said, "Aston and I, if you would like to stay with us."

Ruby looked at her wide-eyed, feeling hopeful. "For the *whole* day?"

"Uh, no," Sapphire said. "We were thinking more like, forever…or until you get sick of us, whichever comes first. Sal, or Mr. Goldstein here, is my lawyer. He came for the party and to help us start the legal process."

Ruby couldn't believe her ears. "Stay with *you*…forever?"

"If you want," Sapphire said, and Aston nodded.

Ruby's throat grew thick with tears and her chest tensed as her eyes watered. "Yes."

"Alright." Mr. Goldstein folded the papers and the three moved toward the door. "With the DNA result and what-not we shouldn't have a problem."

Ruby had no idea what they were talking about, but had a feeling she'd find out soon.

She stood still, watching them in shock, unable to fathom what happened and *how* it had happened. Her eyes landed on the big white flowers planted beside the entrance. Christmas roses.

"Come on, Ruby!" Sapphire called, waiting by the open door.

Ruby ran toward her with a new warmth in her chest, knowing she was finally home.

...

"Sir," Lurch said. "There's a homeless man in the foyer, asking for you."

Aston moved toward the door to find the homeless man sitting on the Dubois's French bench. How the Duboises knew the bench was French and not say, German, he had no idea.

"Pops," Aston said in surprise, the un-delighted kind. "What are you doing here?"

"You invited me. You think I'd be in this snobby fucking neighborhood if you didn't force me?"

Aston put the cold beer to his forehead. "That makes no sense. We both know I never invite you to anything."

"Well," Joe Ridder held up an invitation card, "that blonde with the big tits did, then."

"Hey," Aston snagged the card, "you're talking about my mother-in-law."

"Fine," his father sighed. "Your mother-in-law with the big tits did, then."

Aston stared at the old man. "Okay, you can come in. Just don't sit on anything, and don't pee on anything or…anyone."

Sadly, it had to be said.

Aston held up his finger as he moved toward the living room. "And *don't* tell the fucking story."

"Cold-hearted whore," Joe muttered. "Good thing you never got married, son."

"I *did*. I just *did*. Remember?" Aston said. "*You* told me: 'life's too short, marry someone you love.'"

"I did?" Joe said, then shrugged. "Huh. Well, fuck me. What happened to the stripper? I liked that one."

"Same girl, pops. Also, not really a stripper."

"Well that's disappointing." Joe's eyes wandered over the Christmas party. "Bah. Rich people. They're all the same."

"No," Aston said, surprising himself. "They're not."

He looked around the room. Ever since he got to Beverly Hills, Aston had judged every person he came across, and put them in the rich-asshole category. It had been easy to stand there on stage in October and point, reducing an entire person and their history into one word. However, Chrissy Kraft wasn't only spoiled, but also loyal, generous, and surprisingly clever. Mrs. Dubois wasn't just a sex-crazed trophy wife, but someone desperately trying to make amends for her past. John Vanderpilt wasn't just a rich dumb douche, but also a...um... alright, he was just a rich dumb douche. But almost everybody else was more than what Aston had once believed.

He watched Joe Ridder move through the party, scaring people with his appearance. He should go make sure his old man didn't pee on anything or anyone, but it was Christmas, and not giving a fuck was Aston's present to himself.

"Ridder," John Vanderpilt said, and put a hand on his chest. "Chrissy explained that you guys were just in a play." He laughed. "Lucky I didn't kick your ass back at Club Scene, right?"

Aston took a moment. "So...she told you we were in a play, inside the office of a club, without an audience."

John thought about it, then nodded. "Yes."

"Alright, man." Aston patted his shoulder and walked. "Hey, make sure you try the coffee."

"I will."

Aston moved over to the fireplace and the home-hub where Sapphire, Chrissy, and Ruby stood. He gazed at the kid, unsure if he'd even be capable of co-raising a child. He'd said yes when she asked him because it felt right, but the last person Aston had raised was himself and, honestly, he didn't turn out that great.

"There he is," Chrissy said. "Tell your wife how cool I was at Club Scene. She doesn't believe me."

Aston put his hands out, as if weighing a scale. "If by cool you mean, almost-crapped-your-pants, then yeah, you were *really* cool."

A giggle sounded from below him. It was Ruby, looking up at him. "You're funny."

Aston looked down at her in amazement. "I *am* funny."

He felt better. Parenting was clearly going to be a fucking cake walk.

"*Feliz Navidad...*"

Ruby, Sapphire, and Aston slowly turned their heads to glare at Chrissy, who'd changed the song.

"What?" Chrissy touched her nose. "Booger?"

Buzz. Aston looked down at his phone. *000-000-0000.*

"I gotta take this." He gave Sapphire a kiss on the temple and moved toward the deck, passing his father who was standing with Noah and O'Riley, doing exactly what he wasn't supposed to do: telling the fucking story.

"So, I come home from the bar to see my young one, all on his own. And I found this on the fridge..." The sound of Velcro, then he pulled it up: the old, faded Post-it.

Noah took it and read. "I'm leaving you. You take Aston. Roast's in the fridge. Heat at 375."

"She left us," Joe spat. "Took my heart with her, my *heart*. Cold-hearted whore."

Aston slid the deck's door closed, then took a deep breath and answered. "Hello."

"Oh finally, Mr. Ridder!" she said. "This is Marla from the Federal Bureau of Investigation. I know it's Christmas, but we're running out of time for processing now. We received a *very* persuasive recommendation a couple weeks ago that urged us to relook at your applications. You've applied three times, correct?"

"Uh, right." Aston scratched the nicotine patch on his arm. He'd forgotten about the third application. It was right before Sapphire's verdict came in. A time when he couldn't look her in the eyes, much less imagine a future with her. He suddenly realized he had no idea who would've recommended him. Chief Wendell or Chief Anderson? Must've been one of them.

"Anyway," Marla continued. "Third time must be the charm because you've been accepted for training, Mr. Ridder. Congratulations. Can we expect you at HQ on January first?"

Aston had already heard this in the voicemail. He knew all the facts.

He knew them yesterday. He knew when he carried Ruby into Sapphire's old bedroom, and he knew when he went to the station for the chat his new boss had demanded.

After a quick altercation outside the station involving a pretzel, a Chihuahua, and Morgan Freeman—the actor, not the sheriff—Aston had plopped into the chair and glared at the chief, who sat behind his desk in a full-on Santa Claus outfit.

"Detective Ridder."

"Santa."

"Funny." Calloway looked annoyed.

"I'd say so." For Aston to put the Santa suit on in Pleasant Pines, it literally had to be a matter of life and death. Calloway, on the other hand, looked a little too snug in the costume.

"It's a thing I do every year," Calloway said, stroking his white beard. "I dress up as Santa on Christmas Eve and hand out small things, coffee cups, pencil holders…it keeps the spirit up for those who have to work the holidays."

"I already have a coffee cup, so if that's why I'm here—"

"It's not. The gifts are for working employees and you still have a few days left of your suspension."

Aston meant to ask why he was there, but it didn't come out that way. "Why did you do it?"

"Excuse me?"

"Barry's promotion," Aston said. "He's not ready to be a detective. The kid still pukes when the pressure gets too high. You're throwing him to the wolves and you know it. So, it was what, just to mess with me?"

The chief gave a sly fucking smile, then shrugged. "I didn't call you to discuss Detective Harry. I called to discuss your future. Throughout your suspension, I spent a lot of time weighing my pros and cons with you. I even made a list."

"And tell me," Aston said. "Did you check it twice?"

"I'd stop making jokes right about now, if I were you," Calloway said soberly and removed his hat. "In the end, I realized, I could keep you, or I could let you go. And I decided…I'm going to leave it up to you. You choose if you want to work here or not."

"What?"

"There will be one regulation, should you choose to accept a position at BHPD." Calloway held up a finger. "You will be stripped of your shield and retrain under Detective Furlong until I feel you've learned your lesson and can be trusted on your own. If that day comes, you'll regain your current position."

If. Aston couldn't believe his ears. "You're demoting me to officer? You're putting me back in blue after giving Barry his shield? Wow." He laughed angrily, rubbing his jaw raw. "And if I opt out?"

Calloway nodded in satisfaction. "The door is right there."

Aston had an offer to start training for the F.B.-fucking-I. And, man, did he want it now. His whole essence was screaming: *Go! Take the job you've dreamed of your whole life!*

The problem? Quantico was in Virginia and Sapphire's corporation was here. Should he pass training, he would spend years either in Virginia or traveling. It wouldn't work. Sapphire and him, and now Ruby…it wouldn't work.

"You're awfully quiet, Detective," Calloway said with a little too much merriment.

Tension swirled in the air around them, the fight of the two alphas. If Aston wanted to stay, he'd have to lay down and bare his throat.

He could quit. His wife was a billionaire. He *could* quit. But what would he become then, if not one of Beverly Hills's sad trophy husbands. The thought was repulsive. That wasn't Aston. Without his job, he'd lose himself.

He drew a breath. "I'll stay."

A grin grew on Calloway's face. "I'll stay, *what*?"

Aston inhaled, then exposed his throat further. "I'll stay …sir."

Calloway leaned back in his chair, satisfied to his core, and exhaled like he'd just had an orgasm. "That'll be all, *Officer* Ridder."

Aston felt the sting as he left the office and stepped into the elevator where Seal stood, holding Princess Sofia, the hamster, to his cheek.

"Oh, good," Aston said in an attempt to ignore his regret. "They found your daughter's hamster."

"Uh…right," Seal murmured, lowering the hamster as the doors closed. "My daughter's."

Even now, Aston wanted to change his mind. He wanted to scream *yes* to Marla on the phone, but his eyes locked onto Sapphire.

He watched her move behind the glass door, a big smile on her face. He couldn't do it to her, the woman *he* had just asked to give up her poisonous hobby, and he couldn't do it to them.

"Sorry," Aston said into the phone. "I'm going to have to pass."

The woman huffed. "There won't be another opportunity like this, Mr. Ridder. Think about what you're doing or you'll end up regretting it."

"I won't," Aston said and hung up, eyes on his wife. He knew what he'd done, and what he'd sacrificed for her. He said it again, this time to convince himself.

"I won't."

• • •

Sapphire smiled.

Sapphire *smiled*.

"Why don't you open up your presents?" Vivienne strolled up to Ruby. "I think Santa left all the ones with purple wrapping for you."

Ruby's eyes widened with surprise before she sprinted toward the tree. Sapphire smiled as the girl tore through the mountain of presents that Vivienne somehow managed to get her at three o'clock in the morning. Earlier, Sapphire tried to explain that they had the same father, but Ruby seemed too overwhelmed to grasp it.

"God, she looks so much like him. Like *you*," her mother gushed.

They hadn't told Vivienne where they found Ruby, only that she was her ex-husband's daughter. She'd acted excited to meet Ruby. And perhaps, she actually was.

"Yeah." Sapphire ran her fingers through her new hairstyle. Her mother's hairdresser had magically appeared outside the door this morning, asking if anyone needed a haircut. It only took him ten minutes to reshape the "lawn mower cut," but an hour to get all the ink out. It felt fitting. New hair, new Sapphire.

Her eyes landed on Aston as he came in from the deck, phone clenched in his hand.

She watched him move through the room in amazement. He no longer walked as though the mansion's walls and people confined him. She'd even seen him and Chrissy crack jokes earlier. She was even more surprised when he veered away from Sapphire, and walked up to her mother instead.

"Merry Christmas, M…" Aston brought his fist to his mouth as he was about to hurl, then took a breath. "Mmm …om."

"Oh," Vivienne hollered. "Merry Christmas, son."

"So…" Aston nodded to the butler. "Still nothing, huh?"

Vivienne shook her head. "And I know he likes me, because…well, you've seen me naked. You get it."

Sapphire choked on her beer and coughed.

"You know, Lurch is a professional." Aston's finger tapped to his chin. "Maybe he doesn't want to shit where he eats."

"And I'm the poo in this scenario?"

"Uh…point is," Aston continued, "he's a professional."

"I see…" Vivienne said then left, looking deep in thought.

Sapphire stared at Aston as he scooted closer to her. "You've seen my mom naked?"

Aston grimaced awkwardly. "Just the one time."

"You should've told me," Sapphire shook her head, then cracked a grin. "I would've hooked you up with the support group. They meet Tuesdays and Thursdays."

Aston chuckled and took a drink of his beer as they watched Vivienne walk up to the butler. "Radison, you're fired."

A rumble came when Radison dropped a tray of mini quiches and pulled Vivienne in. The two entwined for a deep kiss.

"Why are you helping the man-eater anyway?" Sapphire asked. "What did poor Radison ever do to you?"

"No. I think she really likes him," Aston said. "I mean, he has junousekwat, and she doesn't even care."

Sapphire gave him a puzzled look. "Are you trying to say *je ne sais quoi*?"

Giggles sounded from the new lovers as they continued the excessive PDA.

"Noah!" Sapphire called, eyes closed. "How long for the house?"

"Four weeks tops," Noah said, swooshing by. "Six months at the most."

Sapphire tilted her head back and groaned.

Aston laughed and pulled her in. "We'll live."

"Who *are* you?"

He let out a cunning smile, then kissed her. "I'm going to go grab another beer. Want one more?"

Sapphire shook her head and he vanished. She turned to the window and her eyes landed on the street as she took a sip. Right below their driveway stood a familiar woman. One Sapphire had seen before.

The nurse. She was looking up, *right at* Sapphire. As if she knew her, as if she were waiting for her.

"Saph."

Sapphire turned to face Aston. The second he saw her expression, his eyes flittered to find the danger. "What's wrong?"

"Look." Sapphire turned and pointed out the window.

Once again, she was gone.

"It was that nurse again, from the Halloween party. She was here. In the driveway."

"Okay." Aston looked out at the empty street, then snatched her bottle. "No more beer for you."

"I saw her," Sapphire insisted, agitated. "She was there."

"Sure, she was." Aston kissed her cheek, then went to toss her beer in the trash.

"She was!" Sapphire shouted after him. "She *was!*"

She sighed, looking after Aston. As she had lain there in the hospital bed yesterday, staring at the signed document, Aston's words about her father had been spinning in her head. How had she not seen it? In spite of her father's warning, Sapphire had abandoned Aston, her family, and chosen the hunt, just like William Dubois once did.

She didn't feel differently about her revelation; she still

wanted the life she'd envisioned, the life that felt so right, but she could not be William Dubois. And she would not, not now, not *ever*, knowingly choose anything that would cause her to lose Aston. He meant everything to her.

She looked down to see Ruby, holding a big doll. And, Sapphire smiled, she had Ruby to think about now.

"It's not real," Ruby said, looking up at her with big, alien-like eyes.

"What's not real, Ruby?"

Ruby blinked several times then shrugged, and skipped back to the Christmas tree as Aston returned. Sapphire looked toward the empty street. No nurse in sight. She must have imagined her. She must have.

She took her husband's hand and joined her friends and family at the Christmas party.

Sapphire exhaled and *smiled*. She smiled to make the chill on her neck vanish. She smiled to help mend the loss of the future she'd sacrificed. She smiled to mute the psychic's voice, whispering in her ear.

Something big is coming your way. Something that will annihilate your world as you know it.

EPILOGUE

The nurse opened the door and smiled. "She's ready for you."

"Great, thanks." He got up, hearing the Superman theme in his mind. He was exactly like a superhero after all…except for his physique, looks, and the fact that he killed people instead of saved them. Other than that, he was *just* like a superhero.

He moved through the yet-to-be-opened waiting area, still reeking of fresh paint. The old cracked floor and the ceiling, however, they'd done nothing about.

He stepped into the office, noting the scattered white boxes. A doctor stood behind a desk with her back to him, letting her nimble fingers flip through a filing cabinet.

"Hello," she said, shooting him a quick glance. "Sorry things are so unorganized, but we're still in the process of moving in."

"No problem, doctor." He smiled at her, trying to avoid looking at the three pigs by the barred window. They wore white coats and shook hoofs with each other, saying: "*Doctor, doctor, doctor.*"

"Now, your merits are extensive and very impressive." She picked up his resume, then let her cold eyes latch onto his. "But you're a jumper."

"Excuse me?"

"A job jumper. You jump jobs often."

He held his sigh in. He'd hoped this one wouldn't care. It used to not be so hard, but the more jobs he switched, the tougher it was to get hired. He *really* needed this job. He smiled. "I was under the impression that this position may be temporary anyway."

"True," she said, eying him. "But I'd still prefer someone who I know won't bail until the position has expired, if it expires. And based on your frequent jumping, I'd say, you're not it."

He cleared his throat. "Well, to be honest with you…"

I job jump to keep the mysterious death count from piling up at each location.

"My mother was sick. I sometimes had to quit without much notice to take care of her. But it won't be a problem anymore."

"She's better?"

"She's dead."

"I see," she said, folding her eyes away from his. He knew she pitied him, but he could also tell she didn't like him. "Well, I'm sure you've been informed about the discretion of this particular ward. You'll need to sign an NDA, pass an extensive—some would say invasive—background check, as well as a psychological evaluation before we can employ you. What happens at Saint Charles Psych Ward, stays at Saint Charles Psych Ward."

Two words that had always tickled his pickle were *psychological evaluation*. When he was a child, his mother caught him speaking to Mr. Mortimer, the giant panda. She sent him to a psychologist to evaluate him. It was so easy to pass, despite the fact that Mr. Mortimer talked to him the whole time. All he had to do was lie about everything he saw that no one else did. By the time he was done, the psychologist apologized for having inconvenienced him, and his mother begged for his forgiveness, which of course he gave to her momentarily. He waited until just the right moment, years later, to get his revenge.

As for the other "extensive" *psychological evaluations*, all he did was pretend he was like everyone else, and they believed him. Their system was fool-proof after all, no crazies could get past them. *Ba-HA!* They never found his weakness, the one crazy he could not control.

Not that he *was* crazy. *Crazy* was just how the rest of the world decided to label people like him; those who saw things that weren't "real" and experienced things "normal" people didn't. Those poor *normals*, stuck in their boring, concrete world.

"I assume that's okay?" her voice turned cold as her eyes burrowed into his.

She seemed suspicious of him. Maybe he'd looked at the doctor pigs too long, maybe her trained eye spotted a "crazy" person from a mile away, maybe he shouldn't have eaten tuna for lunch—his breath stunk.

He smiled big. "No problem at all."

She did not smile back. "Moving on. How would you describe your everyday relationship with the patients?"

She was making him nervous. He wasn't going to get the job. Everyone else refused to hire him due to his unstable job history and he really, really, really wanted this job, because it would make it really, really, really easy to kill at least a handful of them before he moved on.

"Hmm…" His finger tapped his chin as he looked up at the decaying ceiling. Really, he was just looking away because Mr. Mortimer was pretending to slit the doctor's throat. Hilarious.

"I try to be a friend as much as I can, but when the situation calls for it, I'm no longer their pal, but the person who'll keep them safe and healthy…"

Until I drag them to a secluded spot and kill them.

"Okay. Most of our patients are being transported from the old facility and arriving here in the next few days. *If* hired…" Her emphasis told him his chance was zero. "When would you be able to begin work?"

Oh no. Not the B word. Not now.

"*Where it began,*" Mr. Mortimer's smooth voice sounded through the microphone in his paw. "*I can't begin to knowing…*"

His fingers clenched around the seat cushion. He could ignore a lot. He could lie and cheat many things, but this, oh…no.

"*It was in the spring…*"

His eyes widened as the doctor pigs showed up behind Mr. Mortimer with drums, a guitar, and a trumpet.

The doctor stared at him. "Are you alright?"

He clenched his teeth, trying to hold it, trying to get words out, verbal ones. Words…*any* words.

"*Touching me…*" Mr. Mortimer reached his furry paw to the doctor. "*Touching yooou!*"

The doctor leaned forward in question. "Sir?"

He balled his fist to his mouth and squeezed his eyelids shut. He really *needed* this job, but he couldn't…hold it…in.

"*Sweet Caroline!*"

His mouth opened and belched it out. "Bam-bam-baaa!"

The room silenced. Mr. Mortimer and the pigs vanished; the music died. All that was left was the doctor interviewing him, staring as if he was…well, crazy.

"Did you…" she said, mystified. "Did you just sing that in-between bit from *Sweet Caroline*?"

He exhaled, letting his shoulders sink. "Yes. Yes, I did."

She stared at him somberly, then broke out in a smile. "Oh my God, I *love* Neil Diamond!"

He gaped at her as she pulled out a necklace from under her coat, then dangled it for him. It had a picture of Neil Diamond and read: *Neil 4-ever.*

"Don't you just *love* Neil?!" she talk-yelled in excitement.

He broke out in a smile. "Yes! Forever!"

"Oh my God!" she yelled back, then smiled at him. "You know what. I feel like we can cut this interview short."

"You mean…"

"You're hired!" she smiled and stood. "Wait here. I'll go

get the paperwork for your background check so we can get you started."

"Great!" he smiled, ecstatic.

"It'll take me a couple of minutes so feel free to have some coffee." She moved to open the door, then turned to him and shot him with a finger gun. "Bam-bam-baa."

He shot her back. "Bam-bam-baa."

She giggled and vanished.

He went over to the coffee pot and poured himself half a Styrofoam cup. He took a victorious drink and inhaled. *Finally.*

Mr. Mortimer leaned against the filing cabinet, holding his paw out, as if evaluating a manicure. The panda's eyes rolled pointedly to the side, toward the files.

"Oh!" he said. "Good thinking."

He hurried up to the filing cabinet, and kept an eye on the door as he rifled through the folders, picking some up, then putting them back.

"Who-to-kill-who-to-kill-who-to-kill," he mumbled, then opened a new file. "Oh. Me like-y."

She was both pretty and pretty disturbed. Based on the evaluation she lived in a world of her own, much like he did.

Patient 13. Sapphire Dubois.

MIA THOMPSON is a Swedish-born author living in California with her husband, daughter, and dog, Oreo. She is known for her internationally bestselling series, featuring heiress and vigilante: Sapphire Dubois. Prior to her life as a novelist, Mia studied Filmmaking in Europe, and Screenwriting in Los Angeles.

authormiathompson.com
@mia_thomp
facebook.com/authormiathompson/

Lightning Source UK Ltd.
Milton Keynes UK
UKOW04f2057041217
313878UK00001B/63/P